About the Author

Maddie Please was born in Dorset, brought up in Worcestershire and went to university in Cardiff.

Following a career as a dentist, Maddie now writes full-time, and lives in Devon with her exceptionally handsome and supportive husband.

Also by Maddie Please

The Summer of Second Chances
A Year of New Adventures
Come Away With Me

THE MINI-BREAK

Maddie Please

avon.

Published by AVON
A division of HarperCollins*Publishers* Ltd
1 London Bridge Street
London SE1 9GF

www.harpercollins.co.uk

This paperback edition 2019

First published in Great Britain by HarperCollins*Publishers* 2019

A catalogue copy of this book is available from
the British Library.

ISBN: 978-0-00-830523-9

Typeset in Birka by Palimpsest Book Production Limited,
Falkirk, Stirlingshire
Printed and bound in UK by CPI Group (UK) Ltd,
Croydon CR0 4YY

This book is produced from independently certified FSC™ paper
to ensure responsible forest management.

For more information visit: www.harpercollins.co.uk/green

For Brian.
Unfailingly supportive and encouraging.
Thank you.
LYL
M xx

Chapter One

Five years ago, my sister and I were skiing together (Val d'Isère, a chalet full of our friends and a case of Grey Goose vodka to get the party going) and Jassy took a tumble and dislocated her knee. Apart from the pain – which must have been awful – she was furious. She'd made us get new salopettes for the holiday too, really attractive, and matching fur-bobble hats. There were paparazzi all over the place photographing some Swedish princess and her family, but instead we attracted all the publicity, the sort Jassy wasn't used to.

After several weeks of medical attention and physio we thought her knee was healed, but then in January she was on the ice rink at Somerset House, fell over and as a result needed an operation. Leg in plaster, the works.

The trouble was, with Jassy's knee and with me going through a bad patch with Benedict after a rather disappointing Valentine's Day, both of us had lost focus. We needed a break. Jassy came up with a plan and as usual she was very persuasive; she had a first draft of her latest book to finish while her husband was away in the West Indies, commentating on some mind-numbing cricket matches, and from all the media evidence, enjoying himself a bit too much *out* of the commentary box.

I had some structural edits to do on *Choose Yes* (okay, more of a rewrite if I'm honest) and a partner who was starting to get on my nerves. I know Benedict was stressed at work and I did sympathise, but all he ever seemed to do was complain loudly and at length about colleagues who were being more annoying and incompetent than usual. I really needed some peace and quiet, no arguments about whose turn it is to put the recycling out or when the water filter was last changed. Benedict is very particular about the water filter, you'd think what came out of the tap was poisonous.

And so, there were lots of reasons why we had borrowed our literary agent's holiday house near Dartmoor. Jassy thought it was a good idea and it sounded fun. We would take some time out to get our writing wagons into a circle, do some proper work and recover after the alcohol-fuelled madness that had been our Christmas and New Year.

Sally had described in mouth-watering detail the glorious view across pretty fields and opening the diamond-paned windows to breathe in great lungfuls of clean air. Which is a joke as she smokes like a chimney.

We pictured ourselves sitting in comfortable armchairs next to a gorgeous fire. Jassy would be wrapped up in her pink cashmere robe, with her laptop open on her good knee. I'd be flicking through my proofs, ticking things off with the silver propelling pencil Jassy gave me for Christmas. Occasionally we would look up and grin at each other, pleased with the way things had worked out.

Peace, quiet, rest, lovely meals, large glasses of Merlot glowing like rubies in the firelight. I imagined a bird feeder in the window with all sorts of little birds fluttering around it.

Well it wasn't a bit like that.

*

For a start the weather was rubbish. But then it was February in Devon. I suppose we should have expected horizontal rain and red mud everywhere.

One week in and I wanted to go back to London with just about every atom in my body. Back then my idea of a breath-taking view was the glass canyons of Knightsbridge. I'd been invited to a really brilliant birthday party at the V&A and turned it down to come here. What was I doing there with only sheep and my sister for company?

You might well ask.

I write romances – the sort where ditzy girls take over cafés or inherit cottages from their godmothers and find a wonderful and passionate love with the local surfer dude. I've written a whole series of medical romances too where the handsome surgeon falls in love with the feisty little nurse. Don't sneer, you've read them, you've heard of me: Lulu Darling. I've sold millions of books; I know what I'm doing.

I look like one of my sweet-faced heroines too. Blonde and cute, and almost tiny enough to tuck in your pocket.

Just try it, Buster – all those years of writing about something that didn't exist had knocked my corners off a bit. And the last few years had reinforced my rather jaundiced view of men, relationships, love and all that sort of thing.

My sister is pretty. She looks clever too, in a dark-haired, high-cheekboned sort of way that makes people assume she's pondering deep thoughts when in fact she's probably wondering if it's possible to drown someone in a kitchen sink or poison a husband with household products without leaving evidence. That's the sort of book Jassy writes you see, and she's very successful too. But by the end of last year she was seriously behind with her latest book and her publisher was starting to nag. In a polite way, of course, because Jassy sells almost as many books as I do.

We were the Darling sisters after all: a brand, a sparkling little oasis of success in the middle of the dark scramble for sales. We were photographed at glossy events. We went to glamorous parties. Designers lent us stuff.

Jassy was asked to go into the last *Big Brother* House. Of course she refused; we do have some standards. I've been on *Have I Got News For You* because apparently my ample chest made them think I'd be an easy target for mild sexist banter. They were so wrong. They won't try that again.

*

Very quickly I realised coming to Devon had been a mistake and while she didn't say much I could tell Jassy thought the same. I think she felt more responsible because she had talked me into it. Not that she would ever admit it.

The house was lovely though. Sally had spent a fair bit of money doing it up – you know the sort of thing, Crucial Trading floor tiles, a pink Aga in the huge kitchen, and in the beamed sitting room, velvet sofas that were really comfortable. But it felt literally bloody miles from anywhere.

I wasn't used to that; I was used to corner shops that were open all hours of the day and night, takeaway cafés and patisseries, wine merchants who deliver, Ubers at the touch of a phone. Barracane House was stuck on a sloping field in the middle of nowhere. As for the magnificent views, we couldn't see them through the rain and the low cloud. The road to the house was an unmetalled track that had turned into a mudslide and the wind (which never seemed to slacken) howled up the hill straight towards the front door. Benedict would have been horrified.

We didn't sit and work next to a glorious log fire because the wind kept blowing down the chimney the wrong way, puffing smoke into the room. There was intermittent mobile phone signal, pathetic or no broadband, and Jassy had forgotten her laptop cable so it ran out of charge after three days.

As far as the delicious meals went, we'd forgotten that we would have to prepare them and neither of us knew 1) how to cook the sort of meals we had imagined or 2) use an Aga. So the whole experience had been an unqualified disaster.

On top of that it was getting colder by the day.

And then I got a puncture.

*

I'd been looking out of the window, sick to death with my latest work in progress, not even able to email Benedict because of the rubbish Wi-Fi, wondering if I knew enough about vicars to work one into the story, when I noticed my car was on a slant. I tried to persuade myself I had parked on an uneven bit of ground, but closer inspection showed a flat rear tyre.

'Phone the AA,' Jassy said, looking panic-stricken.

By this point she was certainly not lying on the sofa being creative and taking inspiration from the glorious countryside outside our windows. And she had been forcibly reminded that while I am a fun companion and have a certain amount of superficial medical knowledge gleaned from my foray into hospital romances, I'm a rubbish nurse. The idea that we might go home was beginning to appeal to both of us.

I pulled out my mobile and waved it at her.

'The house phone doesn't work and there's no phone signal, remember?' I said.

Jassy whimpered under her blanket. 'Are you sure?'

'Positive. I even went to the top of the mountain yesterday to check, not even one bar of reception at the moment.'

Thinking more clearly, it wasn't a mountain, more of a hill. But you see I wasn't used to that either. Where I lived was all lifts, escalators and flat pavements.

'What are we going to do?'

'I could go for help?' I said doubtfully.

I looked out of the window at the dark afternoon and the rain lashing against the windows. There was a sudden ghostly howling noise in the hallway and Jassy hid her face in her hands.

'What the hell was that?' she whimpered at last. 'Go and look. Quick!'

Great. So now not only was I driver, cook, nurse and bottle washer but also Security apparently. I didn't want to go out onto the cold, flagstoned hall any more than Jassy did, but as I hesitated she rubbed her injured knee and gave me a pitiful look.

I wrapped my throw more tightly around my shoulders, picked up the nearest solid object for protection and peered out into the hallway.

'I've got a gun,' I shouted bravely and waved my weapon above my head. I swiftly realised the wind must have changed direction and it was now wailing through the letterbox. Which was just as well because I wouldn't do much damage to an intruder with a Limoges ceramic banana.

After Jassy stopped howling with laughter we had a quick

discussion about what would be the best thing to do and I stuffed the letterbox with a tea towel. It wasn't as though we were going to be receiving any post, was it?

'While you're out there, can you bring another bottle of wine?' Jassy shouted from her cosy nest on the sofa. Somehow she managed to sound imperious and feeble at the same time.

*

Two days later I was progressing quite well with my latest novel, but Jassy was moaning that working with a pen and paper was akin to medieval torture and we were down to our last six bottles of wine. Okay, we still had some gin and some weird green liqueur. We'd bought it in France years ago because it had a rather suggestive-shaped bottle, but we'd never opened it. At this rate we would have to. I bet it was horrible too; one of those really sweet, yucky drinks that needs to be camouflaged with five other ingredients to make a cocktail with a stupid name that is embarrassing to order. Like *Big Dick* or *A Bonk Please.*

I was looking out of the window at the rain, wondering if my latest heroine would be better off a tragic widow rather than a dumped bride. I kept changing my mind. I wondered what Benedict was doing and how he was coping without me. I bet he hadn't remembered to put the recycling out.

It was so incredibly quiet that I think we could have heard our hair growing if Jassy had turned the radio off.

I heard his tractor coming up the lane a long time before I saw him. I sat up in my chair, like a dog hearing the rattle of a biscuit tin and, realising what it was, I made a dash for the door.

I stood in the middle of the lane, waving my arms above my head, almost weeping with relief at the thought of speaking to someone other than Jassy.

He slowed to a muddy halt, opened the tractor door and shouted down from the height of his seat.

'Are you okay?'

'Yes, yes, no actually,' I gabbled. It was still raining and in seconds my newly washed hair was plastered to my head, not an attractive look and he – the tractor person – was rather eye-catching.

'Do you need help?' he said, and he climbed down from his cab. My first close-up view was of his Hunter wellington boots, which were reassuringly large.

Did I need help? Well yes I did. He looked a capable sort too, and very tall, at least six feet four I would guess, and wrapped up in a big waxed jacket. He was rather broad, with bright blue eyes in a tanned face, actually quite yummy under different circumstances.

'Yes,' I shouted, 'yes I do!' By now I was so excited I was hopping from foot to foot.

'Well?' He raised his eyebrows, waiting for me to go on.

'Have you got a charging cable for a MacBook Air?'

He looked puzzled.

'A what?'

'It's my sister. Jassy. Her laptop has run out of charge and she's forgotten ...'

My voice tailed off as I realised the idiocy of my question. Of course he didn't have a bloody charging cable for my sister's laptop. I'd be surprised if he'd ever heard of a MacBook Air or broadband or electricity for that matter.

He grinned at me, a big sort of Olympic-standard grin that would have been lovely if it hadn't been directed towards my daftness.

'Have you tried putting a new elastic band in it?' he said.

I stopped to process this idea with my mouth open and then realised he was almost laughing at me.

'No, but thank you for the suggestion,' I said with more than a touch of acidity, wiping the rain out of my eyes. This was perhaps a mistake as I had been messing about with flicky eyeliner that morning; anything to postpone the evil hour when I would have to get on with some writing.

'Well, have you considered putting some shoes on?' he said.

We both looked down at my feet, which were encased in blue cashmere socks and mud. I'd been so keen to dash out and stop him I'd forgotten about putting on wellingtons.

'I came over because my mother said she saw lights on the other day. Wanted to make sure there weren't squatters or burglars. You're not from round here are you?' he said, and now he really was laughing.

'No, I'm not,' I said, almost tearful. 'I'm from a place with proper roads and shops and phone reception. I need to somehow get in touch with a garage or the AA so they can fix my flat tyre and my sister and I can get back home!'

'Got a puncture, have you?' he said.

No, I just let the air out of my tyre for the fun of it.

I took a deep breath. 'Yes, I have.'

It's the only thing keeping me here in this bloody place.

'Well, perhaps I could help?' he said.

'What? What? Really?' I spluttered, my heart lifting.

'Have you got a spare tyre?'

I had no idea. How should I know?

Surely they had to give you a spare tyre when you bought a car? Wasn't it the law? But if he wanted to know where it was I was scuppered. I'd only had the car for three months. I didn't actually know how to open the bonnet either.

'Of course,' I said at last, in a confident voice.

The rain was now lashing down and my feet were frozen. It was getting dark too, which made the whole thing even more depressing.

'I'll pop back then,' he said and he climbed back into his tractor.

He started up the engine with a throaty roar, turned round in a nearby gateway and drove back the way he had come, leaving me sopping wet and muddy.

'When?' I yelled after him as he passed me. 'When will you pop back?' but all I got was a jaunty wave.

I went back into the house and stood peeling off my muddy socks.

'God, shut the bloody door!' Jassy shouted.

I did so with feeling and went to get a towel to dry my hair.

'Who was that?' she said. 'And why are you so wet? You've got black splodges all over your face.'

'I don't know and because it's pissing down,' I replied, glancing in a mirror and realising I looked like a sad clown. I scrubbed at the black streaks with a tissue. 'He was passing because someone had noticed there were lights on and he was checking we weren't squatters.'

'Who in their right mind would squat here?' Jassy grumbled.

'He's offered to do the spare tyre.'

Jassy brightened up. 'Oh my godfathers! When?'

'Don't know, he says he's going to pop back.'

'Pop? *Pop back?* Oh FFS! It took ages for him to notice we were here in the first place so I won't hold my breath!' Jassy said. 'Why didn't you grab him, Lulu? Make him do it now?'

'Because it's getting dark and it's bloody raining!' I said, furious with myself for not doing exactly that.

'Jeez,' Jassy said, sending me a dirty look, 'we could have been out of here in the morning. We could have made it to Kirsten's book launch. Now I expect we'll be stuck here for another fortnight. We're going to die here, starve to death. Sally will eventually realise I still haven't delivered *Evil Has a*

Price and then she'll come looking for me with a bread knife. By then it will be too late and all because you didn't ask some filthy old farmer to change a tyre.'

'Actually he wasn't filthy or old. He was rather attractive,' I said, but Jassy wasn't listening, she was too busy refilling her wine glass.

Chapter Two

We waited with scarcely concealed impatience for another two days. Okay, the first day we concealed our impatience; the second day we weren't concealing it at all. Jassy and I were at each other's throats; snapping and snarling like a couple of barely house-trained puppies.

'I mean what did he mean by *pop back*?' Jassy moaned for the billionth time.

'I have no idea, Jassy. Stop asking me. I would mean I'd be back in five minutes but this is the country, isn't it? He might mean next week or next year – who knows?' I said unhelpfully. 'He might never come back.'

Jassy threw back her blanket and stomped unevenly to the window to look out at the rain. It was still raining.

'Come back, you sod,' she shouted and then turned back to me. 'Are you sure you don't know how to change a tyre?'

'No, I don't know how to change a tyre,' I snapped back. 'I wouldn't know where to start.'

Jassy slumped back down onto the sofa, her mouth drooping with misery. 'Nor would I. Surely there's an instruction book? We're never going to see London again. We're going to die in this bloody place, just die.'

She sounded so mournful I went to give her a hug.

'No we're not,' I said. 'Don't be silly. People don't die just because it's raining and they have a puncture. There's plenty of food in the freezer and we have four bottles of wine left. And the green stuff if we get desperate.'

She shrugged me off.

'Stop being so bloody cheerful,' Jassy said, huddling down into the cushions.

'Well you're being miserable enough for both of us.'

'Oh, just shut up!'

'You shut up, Jassy! We could have gone to Vanessa's flat-warming party. This was your idea remember – your big drama about Ralphie and that woman, the draft that needed finishing. I could have done my editing anywhere—'

'Don't give me that! You wanted some time away from Benedict in the hope that he would stop taking you for granted!'

'—I was expecting to have a lovely time with roaring fires and a restful few days before we went back to London.'

'Well so was I! You agreed! I didn't force you to drive here!' Jassy shouted.

I could feel my temperature rising.

'Yes, but I didn't expect to be still stuck here, listening to you moaning twenty-four seven!' I yelled back.

'I'm an invalid!'

'You're not a bloody invalid.'

'I am!'

'You've got a bandage on one knee. This apparently means you can't cook a meal, wash up, tidy your stuff away, or do anything except sit on the sofa drinking wine and complaining.'

'You'd be the same in my place. And the one time we have a chance of someone getting us out of this place, you let him run off with the vague promise he might "pop back". Why didn't you offer to pay him? He'd have popped back a damn sight quicker if you'd waved a tenner at him.'

This thought had crossed my mind on several occasions but I didn't need my sister reminding me.

I made a mature and considered response.

'Oh shut up!'

'You shut up!'

Jassy gave a furious scream and bit the edge of her blanket.

'Hello? Anyone at home?'

Jassy yelped and we swung round to see the dark silhouette of a man standing in the doorway leading out to the hall.

'Sorry to interrupt, ladies, but you didn't seem to hear me when I knocked.'

It was him.

The man with the bright blue eyes and the tractor.

There is a God after all. I was beginning to wonder.

'Sorry, I didn't hear you,' I said, trying to sound calm and measured and not as though I had been in the middle of a heated screaming match with my sister.

He pulled off gloves, which looked as though they had been constructed from old wet suits and held out a hand towards me. I shook it. His fingers were cold but his palm was warm and I felt an odd shiver of something. He reached over to say hello to Jassy who was busy being tiny and fragile and thoroughly irritating under her blanket.

'Joe Field. I'm guessing you haven't managed to fix the puncture?' he said.

Trust me, if I had I wouldn't be here talking to you, I thought, but that would have been rude and Joe Field might have been offended and left us to it. I wasn't going to risk losing him again. I moved round a bit so I actually blocked his exit route.

'I'm Louisa Darling, and this is my sister Jassy Sutton.'

I waited a beat to see if he realised who we were. He didn't so much as flicker. Oh well. Perhaps he didn't look at the gossip columns or read much chick lit or psychological drama?

'No,' I said, 'I'm afraid we haven't managed to fix it. Jassy has a very fragile knee and of course I have to look after her full time.'

I made it sound as though she couldn't be left for even a second, which was far from the case. In fact I'd gone to bed leaving her asleep on the sofa twice and yesterday I'd refused to bring her lunch on a tray and made her come to the table. I don't think Jassy had been out of her pyjamas for three days and she was beginning to fall into the helpless, dependent patient state of mind.

'I see,' he said, rubbing the warmth back into his fingers.

'So can you fix it?' Jassy said.

'I expect so, if you have a spare tyre. Or some tyre sealant.'

Tyre sealant? What the hell was that? Something like massive Sellotape?

'I'm sure we do,' I said. 'Would you like some coffee?'

'That would be lovely,' he said. 'Just give me the car keys and I'll go and have a look and see what I can find. I've brought my compressor in case you don't have one.'

What's a compressor?

We watched him go outside. I had a sudden leap of optimism.

'You don't think he's going to steal your car do you?' Jassy said.

For a moment I gnawed at a thumbnail and thought about the possibility and then gave an exasperated sigh.

'It's got a flat tyre, Jassy, remember? This isn't London.'

'Well watch him – that's all I'm saying.'

I went out into the kitchen and switched the coffee machine on and got some mugs out of the dishwasher. Then I tweaked the kitchen curtains back a bit more and watched him. He was rather watchable too, if I was honest.

He was very tall and broad in a muscly way and he had an ideal profile of strong straight nose, lovely cheekbones and a full lower lip that is supposed to mean a passionate nature. Well, it does in my books anyway.

The rain had stopped at last and the morning was the best since we had arrived. There was a bright blue sky and even some sunshine, which was burning off the early morning mist that had been hovering over the river down in the valley.

It was cold though, and a brisk wind was ruffling his dark hair. He made me think of Cormack McDonald, hero of my third book *The Life I Always Wanted*. Tall and big and rather – oh, for heaven's sake.

Joe opened the boot and rummaged around for something and then pulled out a weedy-looking tyre like a toy with a red middle. He looked up, saw me watching him and gave a big grin and a thumbs-up. I shrank back and began making coffee.

'Can I have some?' Jassy yelled from the next room. 'And I think there are some KitKats in the cupboard over the sink. If they aren't there they'll be in the stone jar in the larder.'

'How do you know? I thought you couldn't move off the sofa?' I yelled back.

Bloody hell.

Meanwhile Joe was messing about with the flat tyre and constructing something that looked like a giant tin opener whilst jacking the car up off the ground. In a matter of minutes he had replaced the real tyre with the toy one and put the damaged one in the boot. Then he attached some engine sort of thing and pumped the spare tyre up a bit. It was very impressive.

He came back in the back door, bringing a cold swirl of air with him and the faint scent of wood smoke.

'Okay, should be fine,' he said, 'but get a proper one fitted as soon as possible and don't go over thirty miles an hour until you do. Could I just—'

He went over to the sink to wash his hands and I waited with the kitchen towel like some sort of theatre nurse by his side.

'Thanks,' he said, drying his hands.

The kitchen towel had little embroidered vegetables along one edge and he had hands like shovels so the two weren't exactly compatible. It looked like he was using a handkerchief.

'So, I can drive? I mean I do understand I need to get a new tyre. Where can I get one from?'

'Depends where you're heading,' Joe said, handing me the towel.

I gave him a mug of coffee.

'London!' Jassy shouted from the other room.

Joe went into the sitting room where she was still bundled up on the sofa in her nest of blankets and cushions.

'Then your best bet is Okehampton,' he said. 'You know how to get there?'

'We'll find it!' Jassy said with feeling. 'We've been in this ghastly place for long enough. We'll find it!'

It struck me that this desperate haste to leave could be seen as rather insulting.

'I mean we've had a lovely break,' I said, 'but we have appointments in London we really should keep. So thank you so much.'

'Lovely break? Are you insane?' Jassy grumbled. 'It's been the longest ten days of my life.'

Joe sipped his coffee and looked thoughtful. 'Well, you haven't exactly had good weather, I'll give you that. I don't suppose you've had a chance to get out and about either?'

'We were supposed to be working,' Jassy said, calming down a little. 'We're both writers. We have deadlines to keep, with our publishers. We wanted to recover after Christmas and get back in the groove. But it didn't quite work out like that. Technology failure I'm afraid, amongst other things.'

'Ah, the MacBook Air cable. I see the relevance now.'

Jassy smiled up at him through her lashes. I could see a familiar pattern here. Now the car was mended and our escape route was established, Jassy could relax and stop being a stroppy cow and start flirting.

Jassy flirts with everyone; it's what she does and being married doesn't stop her. She's been known to flirt with policemen, car park attendants and even our accountant. Trust me, our accountant is not the sort of man anyone flirts with – he might have the financial skills of a sorcerer on speed, but he also has halitosis, dandruff and a comb-over. She would find a man as good-looking as Joe Field irresistible.

Suddenly I didn't want my sister to flirt with Joe Field. I stepped briskly between them and gave him a warm smile of my own.

'We're very grateful, Mr Field.' I looked at my watch; it was half past ten. If we set off soon we could get a new tyre, be back in Notting Hill by early evening and even have time for a comfort stop somewhere too.

'Right then, here are the keys. I've put everything back as best I can,' Joe said.

He dropped my car keys into my palm; they were still warm from his hand and it was rather thrilling. My fingers curled round them.

'Thanks.'

'You're welcome. And thanks for the coffee.'

He tipped his head back to finish his drink and Jassy watched him with narrowed and speculative eyes.

'Would you like a KitKat?' she said.

'Um, no thanks, I don't think so,' he said.

'Tunnock's Tea Cake? Orange Club? I think we've eaten all the mint ones.'

'Jassy!' I muttered.

Joe pulled on his gloves and gave a grin.

'I'm fine thanks. I'll be off and let you get all packed up and back to the bright lights.'

I followed him to the front door. I felt a bit reluctant to let him go. I mean we're all liberated, independent women aren't we, but it doesn't mean we don't appreciate it when a handsome man wanders through our lives.

'Thanks again, Joe,' I said.

He turned in the doorway and shrugged his shoulders under his big, waxed coat.

'You're welcome,' he said. 'I'm always willing to help a damsel in distress.'

'What do you do?' I said. 'I'm guessing you're a farmer.'

'Right first go. I'd better go and get on with it. My farm manager is away for a couple of days. I have sheep up on the moor.'

'Gosh, sheep!' I said as though it was something really unusual, although I knew from occasionally watching *Countryfile* that sheep were about the only thing that suited this part of Devon.

'Anyway, I must get on. Don't forget about that tyre,' he said.

'I won't, absolutely not!'

I watched him walk back down the track to where he had left his mud-splattered Land Rover and then I went back into the house.

Jassy was already upstairs in her bedroom, gathering together all the discarded clothes and carnage that routinely surrounds her.

'He was rather nice,' I said.

Jassy wasn't listening. 'We're off!' she carolled happily as I stood watching her. She stuffed a handful of scarves into her case. 'We'll be back in London tonight. Proper central heating and takeaways and Wi-Fi and actual phone signal.'

'You've perked up then,' I said.

'I have. Haven't you? And let's make a sacred pact never to come back here. Ever.'

I looked out of the window, watching as the sun rose over the valley. It was a beautiful day, and something inside me appreciated for the first time how lovely it could be.

'I think it might be okay if the weather was halfway decent.'

'You have to be bloody joking!' Jassy said, widening her eyes at me. 'I'm never going to set foot out of the Greater London area again unless there's a frigging good reason and a five-star spa at the end of the journey.'

From being unable to walk further than from her bed to the sofa, Jassy now seemed to have miraculously recovered her mobility and was packed and fidgeting by the front door in no time.

'Hurry up!' she said. 'Otherwise it's going to rain, or there will be a landslip, or some criminals will escape from the prison or something.'

'All right, calm down!'

We bundled everything into the back seat and boot of the car, left the front door key under the upturned bucket by the kitchen door where we had found it and were off down the road at a jaunty thirty miles an hour heading for a new tyre in the metropolis of delight that was Okehampton.

Chapter Three

Equipped with a splendid new tyre and filled with joie de vivre, we were back in London in time to dump our bags (no sign of Benedict at mine) and meet up with the usual suspects for an early supper. After a few shrieking and excitable phone calls Jassy decided we would try the new tapas bar that had opened in our absence. It's like that where we live: someone opens a great new fusion restaurant in a fanfare of publicity and fire-eaters on the pavement and five minutes later it closes and reopens as a French patisserie.

The Gang were all there and they welcomed us back as though we had been off finding the source of the Nile. I scanned the room but Benedict didn't seem to be around which was disappointing.

'Darlings, so pleased to have you safely home where you belong!'

It was Jassy's sister-in-law Maudie who had done something strange to her hair so that the roots were still dark brown, but the ends were now frazzled pink.

'Maudie!'

Jassy embraced her and we all sat down with the others

with a great deal of fuss and noise while a waiter hovered in the background with menus liberally sprinkled with pictures of bulls and matadors. I wasn't actually sure I approved of that if I'm honest. I mean bull fighting is so horrible.

'Ralphie was on the phone last night, complaining about the heat in Antigua. I said don't give me that, you bastard; try London in the pissing rain. He's missing you and can't understand why he hasn't been able to get through when he's called,' Maudie said. At this point she spotted a latecomer and waved a languid hand. 'Keira, come and sit here! I want to know how the wedding plans are going.'

'I haven't decided if I'm going to forgive him yet,' Jassy said, pouting. 'Those pictures of him in that nightclub were pretty annoying. And he'd better not give me all that "what goes on tour stays on tour" rubbish.'

'I told him you were still in Devon but I don't think he believed me. Anyway—' she waved a hand '—first I want Keira to tell you about Mark and Buzz. You will *not* believe what you are about to hear.'

Keira, a friend for several years, was engaged to Fergus, a computer nerd who whilst monosyllabic and mildly weird probably had more money than the lot of us put together. I was going to be one of her bridesmaids and the wedding was much on her mind these days.

I sat letting the noise wash over me while she recounted a tale of road rage and forged parking permits that had resulted in several arrests and a cracked windscreen. At the same time

I tried to decipher a menu that promised various selections of tiny dishes but didn't seem to have got the pricing right. I mean four dishes for twenty-five quid or five for twenty quid. How does that work then?

As the evening wore on I began to feel strangely out of it. I watched Jassy across the table, laughing and happy. She seemed to have forgotten her aches and pains. Perhaps it was the alcohol?

I nudged my neighbour Tanny, an ex-flatmate and friend since school days in Gloucestershire who now organised extravagant parties for American companies.

'Have you seen Benedict at all?'

'Well I haven't for a few days, but the last time I saw him he was complaining about his workload for the tax evaders in Dubai or something.' Tanny's face screwed up into disapproval. 'I think you are being an absolute saint, putting up with that.'

'Putting up with what?'

'Putting up with him moaning all the time. I thought you said you were fed up with him?'

'Oh I didn't mean that. I was just cross and tired. Has anyone else mentioned seeing him?'

'Ask Toby – he lives in your building. Toby, have you seen Benedict recently?' Tanny yelled across the table to where Toby Sedgemoor, a limp-looking but very successful financial whizz was draped across his latest girlfriend.

'Benedict? Toby? Where is he?'

Toby blinked a bit. 'Well his bike was chained up on the landing last night. I've told him he's not supposed to leave it there and he says he's going to sort it but he never does.'

'But have you seen him?' I said.

Toby's eyes slid away from mine. 'Isn't he here? Oh I don't know. You know. I mean – oh bugger, look anyone want another drink?'

I bit my lip and took a deep breath. Toby might be a bright spark when it came to financial matters and fund management – he wasn't called Sedge the Hedge for nothing – but he was notoriously unreliable when it came to everyday life. Eventually, several bowls of tapas later and topped up with the best part of a carafe of red wine, I got a taxi back to my flat.

*

I felt quite excited as I got home. I was genuinely looking forward to seeing Benedict again. Maybe being away from each other had done the trick and it would help rekindle the spark we seemed to have lost. But the very first thing I noticed when I reached my door was Benedict's blasted bike chained to a radiator. Yes I do understand it is far too valuable to be left outside overnight, though why he had to spend seven grand on a bike just to pedal less than two miles I'll never know. It shouldn't have been there at all. It should have been in the basement garage in the bike rack. The sight of it and its stupid anorexic tyres immediately ruined my good mood.

I could so clearly visualise him in his equally irritating bike helmet and his monumentally unattractive bike gear as he steamed through Hyde Park, roundly cursing every pedestrian who got in his way.

With new and uncharacteristic reserve, I closed the front door quietly behind me and went to put my keys in the brass bowl, only to find it wasn't there and a particularly vile ceramic dish had replaced it.

I went through into the kitchen and found Benedict sitting on one of my new Calligaris gas-lift bar stools watching a blonde chopping onions. She was wearing my Statue of Liberty apron over a dress that was falling off her shoulders at the top end and hardly covered her assets at the other.

'What the hell is going on here?' I said, in a voice that had somehow raised itself by several octaves.

Benedict looked startled. 'Oh hi, Lu, this is Tess. I'm not sure if you've met?'

The blonde waved at me with *my* eight-inch chef's knife and carried on chopping.

'I said what are you doing? Who is she?'

Benedict looked a bit wild-eyed. 'You're supposed to be in Devon. I didn't expect you back for a few days. Tess offered to show me how to make French onion soup.'

'I bet she did,' I muttered.

'She's just a friend, Lulu,' Benedict said patiently, getting the situation under control as though I was in the slow learners group. 'I don't know why you're making such a fuss.'

'Because I'm home now,' I said. I was starting to feel a bit foolish, wondering whether I really had over-reacted. Benedict has that effect on me.

'And it's simply wonderful to see you, petal,' he said, coming over to kiss me. 'Have you had a lovely time?'

This is my flat, I wanted to shout. After all, Benedict had never paid a penny towards the mortgage. We'd had discussions about that before now and he had recently taken over paying the electricity bill. Why that should make a difference, I don't know.

'Percy was going to come round later for a quick drink,' Benedict added, 'to celebrate the Winston versus Hardman win.'

Percy was a particularly odious friend of his who seemed to do nothing but oil his way around the chambers of the Old Bailey pretending to be more important than he was.

'To be honest I'm tired. I'd rather he didn't.'

Benedict opened his mouth to argue and then, seeing my expression, did a bit of back-pedalling. 'Okay. I'll text him. Look, don't be sulky, sweetie. I've missed you; I just didn't know you'd be back today.'

'Didn't you notice my bags in the bedroom?'

Benedict looked vague. 'No.'

The blonde pouted and looked at Benedict. 'Perhaps I'd better go?'

'Good idea,' I said, pulling my coat off, '*Tess*.'

Benedict sighed. 'Better find your things, sweetie, thanks anyway.'

She flounced off into the hallway, her pert bottom wiggling, and Benedict had the nerve to watch it go for a few seconds before I cleared my throat rather loudly and brought his attention back to me.

'So what's going on?' I hissed.

'God, nothing is going on. Look, Lu, you've got to stop being so neurotic.'

'I'm not neurotic,' I said.

'You came back before I expected you.'

'So this is my fault?'

'No – well, partly—'

'Okay, I'm sorry—'

As the words left my mouth I was furious with the way I was backing down yet again. I should stand my ground and sling him and the bottom wiggler out into the street.

At that moment the blonde returned looking petulant.

'I've called an Uber; have you got some cash, Benny?'

Benedict gave her a fifty-pound note and they exchanged three, slow air kisses in a rather infuriating fashion. Then she gave me a little wave and a white, gleaming smile.

'*Lovely* to meet you,' she said.

'So?' I said as the front door closed behind her.

'So?' Benedict repeated, stabbing at his phone.

'So what was she doing here? Why was she in my flat, in my kitchen?'

'What on earth is the matter? Look, I've put Percy off – now come here, you're getting hysterical,' he said, holding out his arms and looking at me with the expression I know he thought was sexy and irresistible. I took a deep breath.

'I'm entitled to be annoyed when I come home unexpectedly and find you entertaining another woman. How would you feel if you came back and found me with another bloke here?'

'I wouldn't mind a jot, sweetie. I wasn't *entertaining* as you put it. Aren't we above all that sort of silly insecurity?'

'Well I'm not,' I said angrily, 'and if you're so keen to see Percy all the time why don't you go and live with him?'

Benedict looked a bit panicky for a moment. 'What are you saying, darling? You don't mean that. I don't want to go and live with Percy. I love you, I like living here. With you. Come on, I've said I'm sorry. I was thoughtless.'

'Yes, you were.'

'Well let's forget all about it. I promise I'll be good.'

He looked at me with sad puppy dog eyes and a little pout and despite myself I laughed.

'Oh stop it, you fool.'

'Right, well let me pour you a glass of wine but first of all, come here and give me a kiss. You're looking superb. The country air must suit you. Fancy a fuck?'

*

I woke up the following morning after a restless night avoiding Benedict's hands. I had a shower and then, wrapped in a towel, sat on the side of the bath to consider my options. I'd definitely let Benedict off far too easily. Anyone else would have had a hissy fit and slung him out on his ear. Why hadn't I? Don't think I wasn't tempted. I knew he needed to *think about what he'd done*. And show a lot more consideration on a regular basis. I needed more time away from him before doing anything rash. I would focus on my work and when it was finished I would decide what to do next.

I know I'm my own worst enemy and I should have brought some of my muscular, attractive men friends round to make Benedict sit up and rethink his attitude. It crossed my mind that Joe Field would have made short shrift of Benedict and his over-groomed, metropolitan body. He would have swept him, his hair products, anti-allergy nose drops and Xbox out in record time, but of course Joe Field was several hours away and I didn't know anyone else like him.

My parents were somewhere in America touring around the national parks in a Winnebago large enough for a scout troop. I suppose I could have gone to stay in their house, but they live near Inverness and they have a lot of rules about smoking and wine consumption and knowing my luck the fridge would be empty and the freezer full of vegan, gluten-free, preservative-free meals. At my age I need all the preservatives I can get.

I mentally ran through my address book and couldn't think of anyone who would have me in their house for an indeterminate time while I got some much-needed distance from Benedict or with whom I could bear to share a bathroom.

Property prices being what they were in London, hardly anyone I knew could afford to buy a two-bedroom flat and most of the people I socialised with these days were child-free like me and didn't need to consider a flatmate, so that automatically meant a sofa bed. Perhaps I was getting soft in my old age? Or perhaps I was just too fussy. I suppose the same constraints applied to Benedict. And let's be honest he'd have to be desperate to move in with Percy. I couldn't do that to him no matter how cross I felt.

I could have gone to stay with Jassy but the following day Ralphie came back from Antigua.

I mean I quite like Ralphie; he's handsome in a floppy, public schoolboy, blond Hugh Grant sort of way. He's reasonably tidy and clean and well behaved – well he has to be after all the bad behaviour on cricket tours of years past, otherwise he'd lose his job. But for all that he has to be one of the most boring people on the planet, unless you happen to like cricket of course. There can't be many people who can hold forth on the Bodyline tour of 1932 with knowledge and enthusiasm for as long as Ralphie can. If there are I hope I'm never in the same room as them.

Added to this I once slept on their sofa bed and discovered that he and my sister are very enthusiastic in the bedroom and incredibly noisy. Lying awake at half past three in the morning listening to them giggling and whooping I thought about complaining or getting some ear plugs and then I realised I should be a bit more considerate. After all in her position I'd have been the same. I don't mean with Ralphie of course but you know what I mean. And perhaps I should have said in her *situation*, not position.

*

How had it come to this? I mean I don't seem to get it right when it comes to men and personally I think I have something to offer. I'm well educated thanks to nine years spent at vast expense in Cheltenham and three years at Oxford. I'd had two years of visits to the orthodontist and I have my own flat and a comfortable bank balance following years of hard work churning out book after book for my devoted readers. I'd once had high expectations for my relationship with Benedict, but two years on, deep down I knew I wasn't happy with the way things were going. I had hoped we could work through our differences like grown-ups and commit properly. Perhaps even buy a place together. But at that point I wasn't sure.

I never seemed to meet a decent man. What do I mean by decent? A man like the heroes of my books, I suppose. A man who doesn't gawp at other women when he's out with me, tidies up after himself, doesn't eat with his mouth open, and while we are what Benedict playfully describes as 'an item', only has carnal knowledge of me and no one else. Is that too much to ask? When things go pear-shaped, as they inevitably do, I'm always useless at getting rid of them.

Why, when I can control every tiny aspect of my fictional characters' lives was I unable to sort out my own?

I needed to think fast. At the back of my mind an idea was doing some shrieking of its own and it began to look more and more appealing as the minutes passed. I dressed quickly and found my mobile. I couldn't explain why but something was drawing me back to Devon.

'Sally? I need to ask a favour.'

Chapter Four

A few days later I packed a bag and went via Waitrose and stocked up on all the essential things I might need: gin, Fevertree tonic, chocolate biscuits, that sort of thing. And I left a short, pithy note for Benedict to think about. As I drove past his chambers I was tempted to open the car window and shout a few farewell reminders, but then I saw a PCSO and thought better of it. Five and a half hours later I was back in Devon walking through the front door of Barracane House.

Funnily enough, this time it seemed okay. Well, more than okay. Everything that had been depressing and muddy and dull on my previous visit with Jassy was now fresh and clean. The air as I got out of the car was as cold and clear as crystal, bringing with it the promise of spring. The wind that last time had swept down the chimney with howling rage was now helpfully blowing the clouds away to the distant coastline, leaving behind a blue, washed sky. I felt as though a weight had been lifted off my shoulders and I felt an unexpected little leap of optimism.

I unloaded my bags, looked at the gin and then put the kettle on. It was going to be different this time. I didn't have to worry about Jassy; I would focus on myself and *Choose Yes* and get hours of productive and satisfactory rewriting done. I'd get back into the plotting groove too, a place I hadn't actually been for several months. I have no idea why – there always seemed to be something more attention-grabbing to distract me from a morning at the laptop, banging out words. Sometimes I even did the ironing and that's not a thing I do out of choice.

I'd have the damned book ready in no time, and meanwhile I would forget about Benedict and London. I would be rejuvenated and invigorated. I might even start to plot my next book. I'd been thinking about it for ages. I just needed to put stuff down. I'd found a fab notebook in Paperchase and that's always a good start.

*

That night I slept better than I had for months, if not years. The bed was warm and soft and snuggly. I certainly didn't remember that from my last visit. It had just seemed unfamiliar and irritating. Perhaps I was tired from the drive and the stress of Benedict and my own lack of focus? But I'd rather enjoyed driving away from everything I was familiar with. It felt exciting and daring. As though I was having a mini-break. Actually, thinking about it, it seemed like an adventure. I'd been on long stretches of motorway where there wasn't any lighting at all. And once I had left the M5 near Tiverton and got off the dual carriageway there were even roads where I hardly saw any other traffic. Once, I had to pull into a gateway and let a tractor pass and instead of feeling exasperated, I gave the driver a carefree toot on my horn and received a cheerful wave in return. This was the life.

I showered and dressed and went downstairs to have breakfast. Barracane House was Sally's investment and occasionally a holiday destination for her family and friends, so it was well equipped and beautifully furnished and decorated. Not like some rental properties I've been in which are full of cast-offs and none of the china matches.

I sat and ate my breakfast croissants and apricot jam, looking out of the kitchen window and admiring the sweeping view down the valley and feeling quite affectionate about the place. I even had a little wander around the utility room, reminding myself how to use the washing machine and tumble dryer.

And then, unable to stop myself, I thought about Joe Field.

Not with the aim of establishing any sort of *romantic* thingy. I mean, I was still in a relationship with Benedict. Just because we were having a bit of a wobble, it didn't mean I'd looking for something or someone else. Obviously I wasn't looking for ... Well, I mean Joe was very attractive and I've always had a thing about broad shoulders ... and there is something about a man who is both strong and competent, isn't there? And he really had got us out of a hole when he sorted out that flat tyre, so it would only be neighbourly to make an effort to thank him properly, wouldn't it?

Hmmm. But he was probably married. Men who are that age and look like that always are. Probably to someone who looked like whatshername on *Countryfile*. You know the one I mean. Smiley and outdoorsy with a figure that looked good in jeans and Barbour jackets and fleece hats and clear, glowing skin from all the fresh air and clean living. A woman who says she loves animals and doesn't just mean kittens. The sort of woman who could bake bread and drive a Land Rover through a stream and gut a fish without screaming. Not like me, who couldn't do any of those things.

I was overthinking this situation. Joe might live with a disreputable family in a massive old farmhouse like you see on episodes of Miss Marple, where there is a mad aunt weeding the borders in a floppy sunhat and a grandfather who looks like Ranulph Fiennes but without the frostbitten fingers.

I saw an article about him in *The Times* the other day; he's very rugged.

I decided to put on my new, white, oversized cashmere sweater so I was warm and comfortable and also so I looked chic in case Joe Field should come calling and then I settled down to work on *Choose Yes*.

The morning really did fly past and I got some good words down for the first time in ages. After a bit I rewarded myself with some coffee and opened the packet of Wagon Wheels I'd chucked into my trolley. I don't know why because I'd never had a particular liking for them. But then I started looking out of the window again and thinking about Joe Field some more. I mean, what a waste of time. I was guessing he was about my age and how often do you find a decent man without attachments?

He might be engaged or of course he could be gay.

I've actually been 'in a relationship' with men who were both those things. For example I met Charlie at some awards thing. I was getting an engraved silver salver for book sales and he came over to my table with a couple of pissed friends to ask me to sign a book. How dumb was I? Did I really believe 'little Anjelika' was his much younger sister? We went out for months, with me never questioning why he hardly ever came over at weekends, why he wasn't around at Christmas and why he had three phones but I only had the number of one of them.

I eventually met 'little Anjelika' when she saw us having dinner in the German Gymnasium to celebrate our six-month anniversary. She came over, all spiky legs and gnashing teeth to tip his langoustines into his lap and chuck his engagement ring into my salad. They of course had then gone off to have a first-class row, leaving me to pay the bloody bill. When we heard her shrieking what she intended to do to his nether regions once she got her hands on some house bricks, every eye in the place turned enquiringly to look at me and see how I was taking it. I crept away wishing I could pull my coat over my head.

And then there was Luke who was a fitness fanatic, built like a bookcase and strangely hands-off. Eventually when we got to date number twelve and he still hadn't made a move on my virtue, such as it was, he admitted he was only dating me to keep his ailing grandfather happy. Shortly afterwards the old chap died, the will was read, I was unceremoniously dumped and Luke went off to Peru with Piers. To be honest I had wondered why Piers was always hanging around, and why he and Luke seemed to share a wardrobe. I don't think my gaydar is particularly good.

Perhaps Joe Field was off women because his wife went off with the ... who would it be? Who would call at these farms with any regularity? A seed merchant? No he did sheep, didn't he? A man selling bales of hay then? Or sheep food? Or a *sheep shearer*. A shearer called Alan!

Of course. It was almost like a ready-made plot! An Australian sheep shearer who looked like Hugh Jackman. Perhaps Joe's wife had been left on her own once too often while Joe went out across the moor on his tractor doing farmerly things. I wasn't actually sure what. Perhaps he would have a couple of faithful sheepdogs with him who would look at him with actual dogged devotion and sit under the table with their paws on his feet when he had his meals.

I wasn't convinced that was right actually. Didn't farm dogs live outside in all weathers in kennels? They were working animals after all, not pets.

I came to and realised I had wasted half an hour staring out of the window and thinking about what Joe Field did.

So, back to work.

It was already getting a bit dusky outside as the clouds rolled in across the valley and it was only early afternoon. In London it never gets really dark. There are streetlights and shops and cars. Still, I didn't want to be wandering around the house in the gloom, did I? So I put on some of the upstairs lights. And then I stood looking out of the bedroom window, watching a big bird wheeling about over the darkening moor. I wished I had some binoculars.

I didn't actually know where Joe lived but he had mentioned seeing my house lights last time so this was as good a way as any of attracting his attention. And if he could see this house maybe I could see his? I started rummaging in my make-up bag for a lipstick and then stopped.

Pathetic. What the hell was I thinking?

I turned all the lights off again and went downstairs, stamping on each step, annoyed with myself. I was here to work, not think about some unsuspecting farmer I didn't know.

*

To be fair once I got into some sort of routine I began to enjoy myself. It was a curious liberation not having decent Wi-Fi or much mobile signal. I didn't have to reply to emails; I didn't spend time online looking at handbags or clips of raccoons. I adore raccoons. It was only then that I realised how much time I wasted on social media pretending I was doing research. Back in London I would have been googling pictures of Hugh Jackman by now.

After a couple of days I actually did need to go out to get milk so I made my way to the nearest sizeable town. First of all I spent an hour in a café with free, reasonable Wi-Fi to check on my emails. But there wasn't anything much of interest apart from three emails from Benedict asking why I had gone off in a strop for no good reason, when was I coming back and where was the toothpaste?

I sent a brief reply saying I was working, I wasn't sure when I would be back and the toothpaste was in my bathroom cabinet where it always was. Then, feeling a bit guilty I sent a second, slightly kinder email saying I was okay, we could have a proper chat to iron things out when I got back and I hoped the latest case was going well.

A couple of miles down the road I found a Superfine Supermarket and stocked up on a few basic provisions.

Then I carried on shopping and found some stuff I didn't need, like cake, more Wagon Wheels (I seemed to have developed a taste for them) and – as a gesture to my emotional turmoil – some *cigarettes.*

I hadn't smoked for a while because of course Benedict didn't approve. He was always banging on about clean eating and exercise and used to make swamp-like smoothies for breakfast, leaving me to clean the stringy bits out of the blender. He had tried to persuade me to buy a bike too, presumably so we could both look like complete prats as we scythed our way through Notting Hill on our way to the organic, wholefood, vegan market he liked. Actually, I think the only reason he wanted me to get a bike was so I could take pictures of him on my head-cam and then he could post them on Twitter and admire himself. The distance between us seemed to sharpen up my focus. He really could be Smug on a Bike.

I drove home liking the way the weak, winter light scattered across the dark moorland spread out around me. The road was almost straight, like something the Romans would have built, and it was deserted and pitted with the sort of frost damage that would have attracted TV camera crews in London and outrage about what the GLC was spending our council tax on.

I was in a mood. I wanted a man who wore tweed, waxed jackets and chunky sweaters and could do useful things like clear gutters and put the recycling out without doing rock, paper scissors first. A man who liked fried bread and double cream and beer. Preferably at the same meal. A man who used fewer products on his skin than I did. A man who didn't believe every health scare he read. A man who nicked himself shaving and didn't make a three-act drama about it, not a metrosexual twat with sensitive skin.

I was being irritable and disloyal. Benedict loved me; he'd said so. And he'd ended his message with a sad face emoji and a GIF of two kittens hugging.

We'd been together for two years. We had shared Christmas

and holidays and thrown each other surprise birthday parties. We had fun. He could be kind and unexpectedly generous. Why wasn't it enough? Why was I feeling like this?

*

When I got back to Barracane House I put the shopping away and, feeling quite daring, took a cup of tea and a cigarette outside.

It wasn't quite as marvellous as I remembered, and I did quite a bit of coughing and inhaled a bit of tea, which caused me to start spluttering and choking, and just as I made the most unattractive hawking noise and spat my tea out, someone came round the side of the house and started laughing.

'Are you quite all right?'

I looked round, my eyes streaming with the effort to stop, and of course it was Joe Field standing watching me, and close on his heels were two black and white sheepdogs.

'I'm fine,' I croaked, fishing in my pocket for a tissue. 'Just having a breath of fresh air.'

'Doesn't sound like it,' he said with a grin.

One of the sheepdogs stepped forward on hesitant paws and then stopped at a brisk hand signal from Joe.

I got myself under control and tried to look vaguely sane. 'Can I help? Were you just passing?'

'I saw there were lights on again. I just thought I'd come over and see if it was you.'

He'd remembered me? How marvellous.

'Yes I left my sister in London. Her husband is back from the West Indies and then – well, for various reasons I came back. I have a book to finish after all.'

'Keen reader are you?' he said. 'The woman who bought this place is something to do with books.'

'She's my literary agent,' I said.

'Ah.'

'I'm a writer.'

'Oh yes, of course, you told me. Well as long as you're getting on okay,' he said. 'I like to keep an eye on things. Not that there's much crime around here but you never know.'

'No I suppose you don't.'

We stood silently for a moment while the two dogs sat at his feet, watching him and trembling slightly.

'I'll leave you to it then,' he said at last.

He was on the point of going and I felt the need to say something.

'I wanted to thank you for sorting out my puncture,' I said.

'You did thank me.' He tightened the blue woollen scarf at his neck. It looked hand-knitted and I hoped it was one his aged aunt had made for him, not his adoring wife. He was bareheaded, and the breeze ruffled his dark curls. He didn't seem to notice. If Benedict had been here he would undoubtedly have been wearing some foolish tweed cap in a pointless nod to rural life.

'Well I wanted to thank you *properly*,' I said.

God I'm such an idiot; that sounded as though I wanted

to have sex with him or something. I could feel myself blushing and puffed at my cigarette again, not noticing that it now had an inch of ash on the end, which fell onto my boobs and lay for a moment like a tiny slug before I brushed it off.

'Really there's no need,' he said, 'but what did you have in mind?'

I think he was laughing at me again and I nearly lost my nerve. For a second I couldn't even look at him. But if it was okay for Benedict to spend time with *friends of the opposite sex* then it was okay for me. He'd said so.

'A drink?' I said, my voice squeaking with tension.

He thought about it for a moment. 'Yes that sounds like a nice idea. Thank you.'

'When would be good for you?' I said, taking another puff and hoping I looked sophisticated. I had the awful feeling I looked like a complete idiot. Probably with mascara running down my face from my coughing fit to add to the glamour.

'I'll pop back,' he said, 'meanwhile, I must get on.'

He clicked his fingers at his dogs and they followed him, their synchronised noses close on his heels.

Like an idiot I let him go and watched as he disappeared up the hill, around the bend in the lane and presumably into the fields where his sheep were.

It was only later that the nebulous nature of the phrase 'pop back' dawned on me. Buggeration. What did that mean this time? Tomorrow? Next week?

*

I went back in and carried on writing and then I decided to make some soup to sustain me through the evening. That was a rural, rustic thing to do, wasn't it? That morning I'd loaded up my supermarket trolley with loads of vegetables. None of them were organic so Benedict wouldn't have touched them but they were an absolute bargain. A bag of carrots from an actual farm for less than a pound! A massive bag of potatoes from the same farm for two quid! It must be an enormous farm because they sold onions, leeks, swedes and pineapples too. And kiwi fruit and bananas. I had vast quantities of stuff for under a tenner. Considering Benedict had once bought six muddy purple carrots for nine quid I could hardly believe my eyes. There was no doubt about it, living in the country was much cheaper than in town.

I started peeling vegetables and in no time I had a vat of soup bubbling away like something out of Harry Potter. It didn't taste of much so I slung in some curry powder and some other stuff I found in a drawer. I felt quite Nigella-ish too; perhaps I should have tried cooking before?

When I got back to London perhaps I would have the kitchen remodelled? I could have a KitchenAid, a really cool retro one in shiny chrome. And one of those racks that hang over the cooker to keep all my tools handy. Perhaps I would diversify into writing cookery books? *Recipes for Hungry Writers*? Or *Say Goodbye to that Writer's Arse*? Brilliant idea!

I left the vat simmering on the Aga and went back to my writing with a glass of wine and another Wagon Wheel. Well it was nearly five o'clock and everyone knows red wine is full of something or other, almost a health food. I worked on for a while, rather enjoying my new role as a countrywoman who made her own meals. I would spend the evening sitting by the fire with some fortifying soup, more red wine and one of the books I'd been sent on my Kindle and not got round to reading. I would not spend the evening watching rubbish on TV and picking the last of my nail varnish off.

*

I turned the TV on at six o'clock and listened to the latest ghastly headlines before turning over to a quiz programme and shouting the answers at the screen when I knew them. After a while I was aware of an unusual smell. Hmm, perhaps there was something on the last piece of wood I had jammed in the wood burner? Moss or something?

I topped up my wine glass and flicked through a few channels. There were only a few, no cable or satellite TV here. Well everyone knows there is nothing worth watching half the time unless there's a David Attenborough on or *Strictly*. I got mildly absorbed in a programme about a couple buying a house in Orlando. Jolly cheap there too. So if you moved to Florida and made your own soup ...

I shot out to the kitchen where the air was starting to thicken with fumes from my soup cauldron. Miraculously I caught it just in time before it actually burned, although the bottom of the pan was thick and claggy.

I added a load of cold water and put some of it into the blender rather carelessly.

Big mistake.

The lid of the blender shot off and in seconds the front of my gorgeous new white cashmere sweater was splattered with vegetable gloop.

I stood rooted to the spot with shock for a moment and then let out a despairing wail. Bloody hell! This wasn't supposed to happen.

Of course at that precise second someone rang the doorbell.

And yes, it was Joe, *popping back* with a bottle of wine in his hand.

He bit his lower lip and looked at me for a moment.

'I can see this isn't a good time, sorry.'

'No, it isn't,' I said, wiping a glob of soup off my forehead.

'It's just I never quite know when I'm going to get an hour to myself.'

'I absolutely understand,' I said calmly, dabbing at my sleeve with the tea towel. 'I need to just y'know? Go and—'

I was going to say have a shower, but I was suddenly reluctant to share that sort of imagery with him.

'—tidy up.'

'Of course. Can I help?'

He was wearing an Aran sort of sweater under his waxed jacket. That would look nice with some of my pond-slime soup all over it.

'Absolutely not. I have it under control here.'

'Perhaps another time?' he said.

'Of course.'

'What exactly are you doing?' he said at last.

'Me? Making soup,' I said and closed the door.

I could hear him laughing as he walked away. Bloody hell.

I spent the next couple of hours cleaning up the mess. I don't know what power that blender had but it had splattered soup all over the ceiling, worktops, cabinets and floor. And I seemed to have developed a new sort of industrial-strength adhesive in the process. Left to its own devices, the soup began to solidify into immovable blobs. I could have wept.

Fortified by a couple more glasses of wine I flopped into bed exhausted and then realised I still had soup in my hair. So I dragged myself out again and went and had a shower. Picking up a towel from the floor I managed to whack my cheek on the sink. Stunned and rather wobbly I then dropped my hair dryer and fused it.

This was not good news on any level; if I went to bed with damp hair I would look like I'd stuck my finger in the light socket by the morning. And I was going to accessorise that with the beginnings of a black eye.

It hadn't been a great day after all. In fact it had been an Olympic-standard bastard of a day with knobs on. What was I doing here again?

Chapter Five

I camouflaged my developing black eye with several layers of Touche Éclat and went out again the following day as I had decided I was low on something. It might have been loo cleaner or olives. I can't remember and really I was just looking for an excuse to get out and about. To see people and talk to them. Which was odd because in London no one talks to anyone unless they absolutely have to and it never bothers me. And if you do they look at you as though you're some sort of maniac rather than just someone who is asking about delays on the tube.

In Superfine Supermarkets I was unreasonably thrilled to see my latest paperback was on the shelves at number four. I looked around furtively and then moved my book to take over the top space, which should have been filled with Dan Brown's new one but it had sold out. Yes, I know it was very childish but I was sufficiently pleased with myself to take a shelfie, which I then posted onto Twitter with 'Oooh look, I'm doing well in Devon!'

You would think after all the books I've written and all the bestsellers I'd be immune to it but I'm not. I bet even

J.K. Rowling is pleased to see her books in the window in Waterstones.

Then a load of emails landed on my phone so I did what a lot of other people seemed to be doing and went to the supermarket café for a cup of rather unsatisfactory coffee and a slice of cake.

I went and bought a few more things I didn't need and some stuff for washing delicate woollens in the hope that I would ever get the crusty soup deposits out of my cashmere sweater. And then I saw a stand full of Ordnance Survey maps and I bought the one that covers the area of Sally's house. This isn't in any way the sort of thing I would normally do. I don't quite know what was coming over me. I even flicked through a glossy magazine dedicated to all the local attractions of Dartmoor and Devon in general and was almost seduced into buying it when I saw an article about artisan bread making in Tavistock. Then I started looking around for binoculars. *Binoculars?* I mean really, do stop it.

I was past the checkout when my phone rang.

'What are you doing? Where are you? You do realise you've missed that do at the National Portrait Gallery you were so keen on going to?'

'Hi, Jassy, everything okay?' I said, steering my trolley past a small boy having a tantrum because his mother wouldn't let him have a go in the coin-operated fire engine.

'No actually. No, everything is not okay. I've had Benedict on the phone every evening since you left London. He's really upset. He says he just had a friend round to his home and you got the hump.'

'I didn't, I just reacted as anyone else would have when I found him entertaining a scantily dressed blonde in my frigging kitchen and tried to pass her off as just a friend.'

'So why did you just shoot off like that? What's the matter with you? Chuck him out, for God's sake! You could stay here if you want time to cool off. I mean now you're miles from anywhere. I've been ringing you and emailing you and you never answer.'

'And by the way it's not Benedict's home, it's mine and perhaps he needs to be reminded of it.'

'Then even more reason why you'd better come back. Leaving him to get on with it isn't really the best way of teaching him a lesson. What on earth's the matter?' Jassy said in an eye-rolling tone of voice.

'No, okay, right. Look, I found him with a strange woman in my kitchen. I think I have a perfect right to be annoyed. Don't you?'

'He just said he had a friend round and you flew off the handle.'

'A friend? Yes right! She was wearing my frigging apron – the one I bought in New York as a joke – and chopping up onions with my knife too. And Benedict knows I hate anyone cooking in my kitchen. I've lived there for nearly three years and never so much as turned the grill on. And there she was wobbling her breast implants all over my granite worktops!'

'Yuk! That's not a nice image!'

'Look, Jassy, that's not the point. The point is that I went back to my home, as I'm fully entitled to do, and Benedict had some tart in the kitchen.'

'Oh he said that was Tess. I can't remember her last name. She's on that late-night chat show with thingy with the beard. She gives out the drinks. You know, where the guests are sitting there talking about their latest book or film or husband. She's the one who comes round with a tray of champagne and not much on.'

'Well she had even less on when I saw her! Trollop!' I shouted.

Two people looked round and steered their trolleys pointedly away from me.

'Well no wonder you were mad with him,' Jassy said soothingly, 'but why didn't you show him the door instead of going off on holiday?'

'I just need to get away, okay? I needed some time to think.' I closed my eyes for a moment. I hadn't been thinking straight for quite some time.

'It's not the same without you here. The Gang are all missing you.'

The Gang.

I could just imagine them all sitting around our favourite table in our favourite wine bar with an eclectic clutter of bottles and glasses in front of them. All of them partying like they were still in their twenties, even though so many of our other friends had already married and had kids. The very thought of seeing the Gang was suddenly rather exhausting.

I tucked the phone under my chin, got to my car, opened the boot and started putting my shopping in.

'Are you still there?'

'Yes, Jassy, calm down. I'm not having a holiday; it's more of a working mini-break. I've been writing and it's been going well. I just want to finish off a couple of things. What day is it?'

'Um, um, Tuesday.'

'Right well I'll come back at the weekend. If you see Benedict—'

'He's bound to drop in.'

'—tell him I'm still furious and he'd better not have any more friends like that in.'

'Okay, stop shouting. You can always come and stay with me you know. You're very welcome.'

I thought about it. Remembering Ralphie's lascivious growling at my sister '*Come here, you, I'm going to bowl a maiden over*,' in the next room was not something I wanted to repeat.

'Look I'm probably over-reacting. Let me think about it. I'm a bit messed up at the moment,' I said.

'I'll say! Where are you anyway?'

'In the supermarket car park.'

'Look, just come back. Otherwise Benedict is going to drive me mad.'

'So it's okay if he drives *me* mad?'

'Well he's your boyfriend. Stop being so difficult! Get rid of him. Hang on, Ralphie's just got back. He's been out to fetch his dry cleaning.' She giggled. 'We got chocolate body paint on his DJ trousers. You would have howled. We'd been—'

'Please, Jassy, I don't want to know.'

'Promise me you'll be back at the weekend? And by the way we've got an invite from Penguin for Samira's book launch. Waterstones. Piccadilly.'

'Yes I promise.'

*

I got back to Barracane House as dusk was falling, and for the first time the dark shadows of the little outhouse and the stunted trees looked a bit forbidding. I hurried inside and put some lights on. As I brought the last bag of shopping in I saw a handwritten note had been pushed through the letterbox. Now this was rather exciting.

'Sorry to have missed you – I wondered if you would like to meet up for a drink in the Cat and Convict. They do good food too. It's only a couple of miles down the road. I've drawn a map for you. If so, I'll see you there about seven. Joe Field.'

I hadn't expected that. What a marvellous idea! And after my spectacular cooking failure, eating out would be a great alternative. But what should I wear?

In London I would have fished out some spiky shoes and

something from the latest go-to designer. There was always a bit of jostling for position with that in the Gang. The men seemed to get away with the usual shirt/chinos/jacket/stupid knotted scarf combo, but for we girls it was always a tense little moment when we saw what the other girls were wearing and whether we had scored more points on the cool/trendy/sexy/enviable ... Oh boy, all of a sudden even the thought of it sounded draining.

I just chose some simple jeans (7 for all Mankind – I mean I do have standards) and a pale blue sweater (Brora – cashmere) and left Barracane House just before seven. I was feeling quite chilled out but I still wasn't going to arrive first. I mean I wasn't desperate or anything.

I'd done a bit of remedial work on my hair (on the cusp of complete chaos) and my incipient black eye (not as bad as I'd feared) and set off for the Cat and Convict.

*

It sounded like a lot of modern pubs that take on a silly combination of names in order to sound whacky and end up being pretentious and tiresome, but I was pleasantly surprised. A framed notice in the hallway told the tale of a convict who had escaped from Dartmoor Prison in the nineteenth century and escaped capture because he hid in the barn with the pub cat.

Inside, the place was already quite full with a lot of country tweeds and waxed jackets heaped up on the coat stand by the door. You wouldn't do that in Notting Hill.

There was a preponderance of low beams, dark furniture and what looked like half a small tree burning in a massive inglenook fireplace. The successor to the cat of legend was asleep on the lintel above it, surrounded by pewter tankards and brass candlesticks. As I walked in, every head turned to look at me. Not in a threatening or unfriendly way, just sort of naturally curious.

'There you are.'

Joe was at my side, and he led me over to a table that was close enough to the fire to be warm without singeing my clothing. He already had a pewter tankard of beer with his name engraved on the side. Evidently he was a local in every sense of the word. I sat down as relaxed as a first-time buyer asking their bank manager for a mortgage.

'What can I get you?'

'Red wine would be lovely.'

I sat and enjoyed the warmth of the fire for a few minutes until he returned with my drink and two menus.

'Hungry? They do some great food here if you are. Especially the pies.'

'I haven't had a pie since I left school!' I said, slightly faint with the thought.

'Then this would be a good time to try one,' he said. 'The steak and ale is a house speciality.'

I thought about eating a pie in front of him. I get a bit

funny about eating in front of people, in case they think I'm greedy I suppose. Stupid.

I looked down the menu for something less fattening. A salad or a light bite. There wasn't anything. There were, however, a lot of things I absolutely love: proper comfort food, like cottage pie and fish and chips. Chilli and lasagne. Things I'd not had for a very long time. I've been on a diet for about twenty-five years, if I think about it.

'I'll have the cottage pie,' I said at last.

Joe nodded approvingly and went to order.

I saw him exchanging a joke with a man behind the bar who was as wide as he was tall and they both turned and glanced at me. I looked away and watched as the cat got down from the mantelpiece by a circuitous route involving a plate rack, a shelf, a bookcase and an armchair before it stopped on the hearth and washed its paws.

Joe came and sat down again and the cat strolled over to wind itself round his legs. He reached down to scratch its ears.

'Friend of yours?'

Joe grinned. 'I like most animals, don't you?'

'I suppose so, but there aren't many in my life if I'm honest. The occasional designer dog maybe?'

'Designer dog.' He looked thoughtful. 'So you're a writer?'

I nodded and sipped my wine.

'And what do you write?'

'Romance. Some chick lit. I've done some medical and some psychological as well. And dabbled in erotica ...'

Damn, why did I have to say that? Why did I say the word *erotica*?

Would he have read *Housemistress and Headmaster*?

Bloody hell, I hope not. My publisher had put a particularly suggestive cover on that one. A close-up of glossy red lips and very white teeth biting a man's hand. It had done brilliantly in America; they couldn't get hold of it fast enough.

He grinned. 'Really? That's fascinating.'

Quick, change the subject.

'And you're a farmer. A sheep farmer? That's hard work I bet.'

'It is.' He leaned back in his chair next to the fire and sipped his beer. 'My father and grandfather before me too. Although these days a lot of the hard graft is done by my farm manager and his brother. And my mother and my step-father are still at the big farmhouse and Will does a lot. When I get a bit of free time I sometimes write freelance magazine articles. So what are you writing at the moment?'

'I'm working on a book called *Choose Yes*. I finished the first draft last year and now I'm editing. My editor wanted me to tweak some changes to the plot by the end of last December and I'm nowhere near finishing. I keep having to put her off with different excuses.'

'What's it about?'

This was embarrassing because I kept reworking it and now even I wasn't entirely sure.

'It's about a woman who swaps houses for the summer

with a doctor. She was single then I made her a jilted bride and now she's a widow. My editor thought it would work better. The hero is a paediatrician – terribly noble and altogether wonderful. When they eventually meet up of course it's love at first sight, whoop de do and happy ever after. All that bollocks.'

He laughed. 'You sound rather jaded about it if you don't mind me saying.'

'Well, life's not like that is it?'

At that moment the barman came over with two massive meals and placed one in front of me. Then there was the required exchange about cutlery, sauces and did we need more drinks.

'Not seen you in here before,' he said, wiping his hands on a tea towel before offering me a meaty paw to shake. 'Pete Skinner, pleasure to meet you. Friend of Joe's are you? That's nice.'

'Otherwise why would she be sitting with me?' Joe laughed.

Pete raised his bushy eyebrows and tilted his head. 'I'm just saying; bit of a surprise though if you know what I mean.'

'Thanks for that, Pete,' Joe said.

Pete wound the tea towel between his hands and then flicked it gently at the cat to shoo it off. 'I mean there'll be some that will have summat to say, I'll bet.'

'Thanks, Pete,' Joe said again, his voice carrying a warning.

Pete laughed and went back off behind the bar.

The meal looked and smelled delicious and was about three times the amount I would have normally eaten.

'So you don't believe in love at first sight?' Joe said after a few minutes.

'Good heavens no,' I said. 'I suppose that makes me a bit of a hypocrite. Selling books crammed with love and happy couples when I don't believe a word of it. Pretending there is a Mr Right out there. That perfect someone. If you just think about it the chances are unlikely and the divorce statistics speak for themselves.'

He blinked a bit and looked away for a moment. Then he grinned. 'So you haven't met Mr Right?'

'Not a chance,' I said, realising with a surprise that it was true.

The funny thing was as I said all this I knew I didn't believe it. Deep down I wanted there to be a particular, special, wonderful person.

Benedict was nice-looking, well spoken, educated and clever with what my mother would have called 'good prospects'. He had a lot of positive points. There wasn't any one thing about him I could violently object to. Even after two years there was nothing terrible. However, recently there *had* been lots of little things, which were adding up to a series of arguments that got less and less reasoned and more and more heated as I released my irritation about his bike, his hypochondria and his inability to load or unload the dishwasher. And then I'd caught him with a half-dressed woman in my kitchen. I think anyone would find that off-putting.

'This meal is fantastic,' I said, hoping to change the subject, 'and this place is everyone's dream of a country pub. The décor, the look of it. You'd never get anywhere like this in London. It's all chrome and spindly bar stools and meals served on blocks of wood or bits of slate.'

'I told you it was a nice place. And they brew their own beer in the basement. The building is at least four hundred years old, maybe more. There was a rumour one of the big chains wanted to buy it only recently. There was uproar.'

'I bet.'

We carried on eating and chatting until eventually I had to concede defeat; in the battle of woman versus food, food had won.

'So, I didn't think you'd be in tonight, Joe?'

I looked up as a young woman stopped at our table, one hand on Joe's shoulder. She watched me with narrow, suspicious eyes.

Oh heck! The girlfriend? The *wife*?

Joe looked up unconcerned.

'Hello, Ellie, how are you?'

'Oh fine, had to get the vet out to Maggie the night before last.'

'Is she okay?'

'I think so. Got the sheep sorted? They say the weather is going to turn.'

'Yes Jim and Ken did that yesterday.'

Ellie stood looking at me.

'Aren't you going to introduce me?'

'Of course. This is Louisa. She's staying in Barracane House for a few weeks. She's a writer. You might have heard of her.'

'*Have* I heard of you?' She looked at me with flinty grey eyes, her antagonism obvious.

'Lulu Darling, I usually write romances. But occasionally some medical or family saga.'

Too much information; I was prattling.

Ellie screwed her face up in thought. Even then she was remarkably pretty. She had a thick, blonde plait that hung down over one shoulder and she took hold of the end of it and stroked it against her cheek.

'Nope I don't think so. Oh hang on I think I might have *tried* to read one once. It wasn't quite my thing. I prefer real books.'

No, I expected you to say something like that.

'Ah well, you can't please everyone,' I said cheerfully.

She gave me a sweet, nose-crinkling smile, pulled out the chair next to mine and sat down.

'You don't mind do you?' She leaned across a little bit, just enough to block my view of Joe, and put her pint on the table. 'How did you get that black eye? Been fighting?'

I touched my cheekbone defensively. 'Oh it's nothing – just a little bump.'

Ellie turned away to speak to Joe. 'I was hoping to talk to you about Ivy.'

'Yes, go on,' Joe said.

'You don't mind?' She shot me a look.

'Well ...' Joe said.

'Good. I was talking to Isobel the other day. She says Penny Barron has a grey. Lovely temperament. She wondered if you'd be interested.'

'Yes I might be, but I'll talk to her about it. After all it's up to Ivy in the long run.'

Ellie took a pull at her cider. 'If you like I'll go with her one day next week – she could have a look. Have a trial?'

'Look, Ellie, I'll ring Penny and have a chat, okay. And thanks.'

'It's no trouble, honestly.'

Joe leaned forward to look at me. 'Sorry about this.'

'I'm fine,' I said, wondering if it was acceptable to accidentally tip the remains of my meal over Ellie's feet. And who was Ivy? And Penny?

Pete returned with his tea towel tucked into his belt.

'All done are we? Didn't finish, eh? Looks like the little lady doesn't have much of an appetite. Not for my cottage pie anyway! Them cottages takes a lot of catching too I don't mind telling you. Ha ha ha!'

'Delicious, Pete, as always.'

'Dessert menus is it?' Pete said, wiping his nose on his tea towel.

There should be a hygiene certificate somewhere. I wondered what it said.

'Um not for me thanks,' I said.

'Well it's your loss, me duck. There's toffee apple crumble on too. Betty's best I call it.'

'So what shall I say to Penny?' Ellie said. 'I'll be seeing her next week. She's bound to ask.'

'No toffee apple crumble for you?' Pete said. 'You knows you likes it.'

Joe stood up. 'No, not this evening thanks; in fact I think we've got to go. I've got to be back by nine.'

I looked at the clock. It was only eight twenty-five. He'd had enough.

'Oh yes,' Ellie said, darting me another look, 'of course.'

Joe paid the bill. I followed him outside and he walked me over to my car. I'd parked it ready for a swift getaway, facing the exit in case the evening turned into a disaster. Of course it hadn't been a disaster; Joe was a lovely man. Easy to talk to, good company in fact. But—

'I'm sorry about Ellie,' he said at last as we came to a stop beside my car.

Other vehicles surrounded it now that the car park had filled up. Most of them were massive four by fours. They made my little sports car look like a baby trying to join in with the adults.

I shook my head. 'You don't have to apologise. I've had a lovely evening.'

I just wondered who Ivy was. And what was Ellie to him?

'Good, I just wanted to find out more about you. You're a one-off.'

I reached into my bag to find my car keys. 'Is that a good thing?'

Joe laughed. 'Oh yes. Are you all right?'

'Of course.' I felt silly and brittle.

I opened the car door and slung my bag into the passenger seat.

Joe put one hand on my arm and I looked up at him.

The night around us was dark and frosty and his breath steamed on the cold air. He had a red scarf this time, tucked in to the collar of his coat, and it scraped gently against his stubble as he shrugged his shoulders against the chill. 'Thank you, it's been a great evening. I've enjoyed your company.'

'Thank you. It was lovely. I really enjoyed it too.'

'Louisa—'

I wondered for a mad moment if he was going to kiss me. Why would he do that? He wasn't the sort of man to do that. Was he?

Suddenly, I hoped he was.

I wanted him to kiss me. I wanted to feel his lips on mine. I wanted ...

No I didn't. What on earth was I playing at? I had a partner. I needed to get home, put on some warm pyjamas, make some hot chocolate and get into bed.

On my own.

I wanted a good night's sleep, undisturbed by my usual complicated dreams of being back in school and trying to hide a burn mark in my sweater. Just before I came out I had discovered yet another plot chasm in *Choose Yes*. Tomorrow I would concentrate on solving it. I wanted nothing more than that.

I absolutely didn't want this big bear of a man to put his arms around me, press me back against my car and kiss the breath out of me.

Of course I didn't. I was already in a relationship. I had Benedict.

'It's fine, absolutely fine,' I said. I could feel a stiff smile stretch across my face. He took a step back and the moment was lost.

I got into my car and waved goodbye to him as I pulled out of the car park and my little car dived into the dark night.

Chapter Six

I got my wish.

No not that wish, the other wish.

I drove back to Barracane House, made some hot chocolate and went upstairs. It was only nine thirty. At home I'd be thinking of going out. I had this ridiculous feeling that Joe might suddenly arrive at the house with explanations and apologies and I didn't want that.

So I closed the bedroom curtains and put all the lights out and got into bed. I settled down with my laptop and was astonished to see that for once I had some Wi-Fi.

Several emails arrived, most of them junk of course but two were from Sally, my agent, who was politely but firmly enquiring how I was getting on with my rewriting. There was one from Jassy reinforcing my need to return to London as we had been invited to a private viewing at the National Portrait Gallery at the end of the month. Ralphie had man-flu, Benedict was being a complete pain and she was sick of fielding his questions about where I was and why I was being like this.

Then there was a long email from Benedict himself, saying

how unfair I was being and how it wasn't his fault. I'd misunderstood the situation apparently. I wouldn't have thought there was much to misunderstand. Still if I was honest I did feel rather miserable about it too. I sent him a short email saying I would be back at the weekend and then I closed my laptop.

The room was warm and comfortable and pretty too in shades of grey and dusky pink. Sally certainly had good taste when it came to interior décor. Either that or she had a friend who did. The curtains at the little windows were thick and cosy, the quilt on the bed was handmade and just the right side of charming without slipping over the edge into fussy.

Soon I was going to pack up all my stuff and leave. I would spend the rest of my time here writing and being impressively productive. Sally would be thrilled and forgive all the weeks I had spent messing about and not getting anything done.

I fell asleep just after midnight and woke with a start at eight o'clock. I was still in the same position I'd been in when I fell asleep. Why couldn't I sleep like this at home? In London I had black-out curtains and triple glazing so not a sound from the street below ever disturbed me. My bed was large and warm and orthopaedic as Benedict had occasional back trouble and yet there I woke up every couple of hours, restless and uncomfortable. Of course it hadn't helped that for all his healthy lifestyle, dairy-free diet and adhesive nasal strips Benedict sometimes snored loud enough to rattle the windows.

*

I did my best for the rest of the week, trying to wrestle with my feelings about Benedict and the future and at the same time not think about Joe. But I had a job to do. I was a writer who took the job seriously. Sally was waiting for me to deliver this book. I had stacks of food in the house; I didn't need to go out. The weather was gradually getting colder by the day – even though at this time of year it should have been getting warmer – so I didn't really want to.

That morning I woke just after seven o'clock and went downstairs looking for tea. Something had changed. It was still quite dark outside but the light was different. For a few minutes I couldn't work out what it was. Then I pulled open the kitchen blind.

In the night it had snowed. It had snowed a lot and it was still snowing. Should it snow like this in March? Outside in the drive my car was little more than a series of mounds and bumps covered over with a thick white blanket. Childishly excited, I ran to the sitting room and pulled back the curtains. There was a fabulous panoramic view down the valley that was now blurred by the snow falling.

I couldn't see any hedges or roads and the air had a strange yellowish tinge that suggested the storm was not over. I opened the front door, pulling my dressing gown around me, and shivered. Not so much from the cold as the excitement. I hadn't seen any decent snow for years and I couldn't remember a snowfall like this one. The air was very still with only the tiny sound of snowflakes rustling onto the ground. There were no birds, no animal tracks, no distant sound of dogs barking; nothing disturbed the silent morning.

I went back inside and had some breakfast. This sort of weather called for hearty stews and home-made bread. I didn't have the wherewithal for either so instead I had a sachet of instant porridge.

I was supposed to be going home soon; back to London and parties and private viewings and real life. If this snow carried on there was no chance that would happen and suddenly I grinned. I wanted to go back to London, didn't I? I needed to go back. People were expecting me. Benedict wanted me back. We had things to talk about. But some demon inside me whispered *you can't – you might be stuck here for a bit longer.* The prospect didn't seem to bother me at all.

I cleared up and surveyed the contents of the fridge. There was some long-life milk in the cupboard, plenty of tinned food stores and some bread in the freezer. I'd have to restock when I got the chance. It was going to be another adventure. A sort of strange childish escapade that involved being marooned for an indefinite time.

I prodded the dying embers of the fire and stirred it into life with some kindling. There weren't many logs left. I'd have to go out at some point to fetch more wood from the shed. Sod it – I wasn't looking forward to that.

I meant to settle down and get a good morning's work in but instead I kept looking out of the window, hoping it was still snowing. I wondered what would happen to Joe's sheep.

I remembered him talking about Jim and Ken sorting them out. That would be a relief. Even with a tractor it wouldn't be much fun traipsing over all these fields. And the poor sheep too. Didn't their feet get really cold?

I went to make more coffee and rummaged in the back of the store cupboard until I found some biscuits. I went back to my place by the fire, opened a packet of chocolate digestives and ate one. Then I had another two. I never ate biscuits at home. What was I doing? I'd be the size of a house at this rate.

Oh well.

I did a bit more editing and found another place where the plot went up the creek. I don't know how I hadn't noticed it before. There was no way my heroine would take three days to drive from Oxford to Kendal unless she had a disastrous sense of direction or was going in a pony and trap. I'd have to dispense with the overnight stop in Chesterfield where the hero came to her hotel room and took her to paradise and back. Which was a shame as I'd rather liked the sex scenes I'd written. Then I looked at a book of maps and realised if she was stopping in Chesterfield she probably *did* have a terrible sense of direction.

I gave a sigh and redirected her to Knutsford. The climactic (in every sense of the word) meeting with the hero would have to wait until she got to Kendal. I didn't want her to spend a night of bliss in a motel on the side of the motorway. And that meant I would have to reschedule the showdown with her ghastly mother.

There was a sharp rap on the window and I nearly fell off the sofa with the shock. I got up and went to see who it was. It was Joe. He was back!

He stood on the doorstep muffled up in a thick tweedy coat and a woollen beanie hat.

'You okay?' he said, excited and smiling broadly.

His face was red with the cold and he stood stamping the snow off his boots for several seconds, resisting my invitations to come into the house.

'Just called in to see you were all right. I knew we were forecast some bad weather but I don't think anyone expected this.'

'I'm supposed to be going back to London tomorrow,' I said.

I persuaded him to come into the hall where he stood dripping melted snow onto the flagstones. He pulled off his beanie hat and patted down his hair where it had ruffled into unruly curls.

'You won't be going anywhere tomorrow if it stays like this,' he said cheerfully. 'The roads are difficult between here and Exeter. Little car like yours, well you'd never get through.'

'No I suppose not.'

We both took a moment to think about this.

'I was worried that you might not have much stuff here: wood and milk, that sort of thing. Ivy wondered if you'd like to come over for dinner tonight?'

Ah, Ivy must be his wife. So had she known I'd met up

with him last night? Perhaps she did. Perhaps they had an open relationship where she occasionally went off with sheep shearers and he chatted up stray women? No don't be ridiculous.

'That's very kind of her, but how—'

'Well it's midday; I could come and get you later on. This snow isn't going to last long. I've got the sheep to see to and a few things to sort out, but I could fetch you in the Land Rover. About seven. Okay?'

He began pulling his hat and gloves on again, ready to leave. It was a fait accompli.

'I don't know—' I said.

'Go on, it'll be fun.'

He gave me a slightly crooked smile that made me feel a bit funny inside. I wanted to object; to tell him I had a significant other. I wasn't the sort of girl who liked being told what to do. And I certainly didn't like being pushed into a speedy decision. He needed to know that.

Instead I smiled. 'I'll see you at seven o'clock then.'

'Great, see you later.'

Well that told him.

I watched him tramp off down the lane, his boots crunching into the snow. I would see him again later and the thought suddenly made me feel rather giddy. For heaven's sake I wasn't a teenager. Perhaps my blood sugar was low?

I ate another two chocolate digestives just in case.

I supposed Ivy was the brisk, no-nonsense blonde pocket

Venus I had imagined. I expected she would produce a hearty stew made from their own lambs and their own vegetables and probably an apple pie made from their own apples. There might even be hand-thrown plates, hand-blown glasses and hand-made cutlery. There would be a table hewn from a local tree and a cloth woven from their own wool.

Right, I was getting a bit hysterical and silly here.

But I was certainly curious.

*

Just before seven o'clock I pulled on every warm garment I possessed and my cute, embroidered gloves that were fashion items with as much warmth in them as a tea towel. I didn't have any warm headgear, so I borrowed a maroon bobble hat from the cupboard under the stairs that proclaimed me a supporter of the Washington Redskins, whoever they were.

I heard the distant rumble of a heavy vehicle coming up the lane. During the afternoon the snow had stopped and the lowering clouds had disappeared over the moor leaving a clear and cold sky. It was nearly dark and Joe's headlights pierced the gloom in a very reassuring way as he pulled up next to the house.

He leaned across to open the door of the four by four for me and I clambered up beside him. It was surprisingly warm in there. Heat was blasting out onto my feet and after a few minutes I pulled off the woolly hat and the useless gloves and tucked them in my pocket.

A short while later he slowed down and took a sharp turning to the left. We drove carefully up a single-track lane. It was incredibly dark and I could see random snowflakes blowing against the windscreen. We stopped by a farmhouse, which was big and built from dark stone. There was a light on over the front door and as I got out of the car I heard the sound of dogs woofing behind it. The barking increased in volume to a furious level and then a high, female voice called for them to stop being silly. Who was that then? Ivy?

'Don't mind the dogs. I'll put them out in the kitchen. Come on, let's get inside.'

I followed him into a hallway that had the sort of old flagstones that would have cost a small fortune in any reclamation yard in London. From there we went into a sitting room bright with an open fire in a massive inglenook fireplace. There were tapestry sofas and thick curtains closed against the darkness. It looked absolutely perfect. Every piece of furniture was dark wood and held the patina of old age and generations of polishing.

'Not a very nice night,' he said.

'No.' I was suddenly shy in a way that I hadn't been since I was seven.

'Can I take your coat?' he said. 'Ivy will be down in a minute. She's gone up to have a bath. She's a bit under the weather.'

Who the hell is Ivy? Why didn't I have the nerve to ask?

'Oh wow you should have said something; I wouldn't have come at all if I'd known. She doesn't want to be catering for guests if she's unwell.'

Joe shook his head. 'She's fine with it. I told you it was her idea.'

I felt awful. I imagined the pocket Venus lying mournfully in her bath, one hand over her eyes. Would she have Jo Malone bath oil? Or would she make do with something less fancy? Sheep dip or something?

Joe returned with two glasses of red wine – not three – and handed one to me. Perhaps Ivy was off wine? Or perhaps she was a recovering alcoholic? The sort who would say things like '*No, none for me thanks. It's been three years and two months and four days since I touched a drop. I feel so empowered these days. Alcohol is a poison you know, and so many empty calories too. I'll just have a glass of Appletiser.*' And then she would watch with hungry eyes as we swigged back our glasses of toxins.

'Something smells wonderful,' I said. It did too.

'Beef stew. After all, I know you're not a vegetarian.'

'No I'm a carnivore through and through,' I said, toasting the prospect with my wine. I could almost imagine the shudder Benedict would have given if he'd heard me. It was eighteen months since I'd had a bacon sandwich, thanks to him.

'Excellent. Come and relax.'

The minutes ticked past and we talked about the snow and he told me about the worst winters he had known.

Had Ivy drowned or gone to bed?

I wondered if he got lonely or if Ivy ever wanted to seek out the bright lights, but I didn't ask. Out in the hallway a clock chimed the hour.

'Is Ivy all right?' I said at last.

'She'll be down in a minute.' Overhead the floorboards creaked. 'There you are, she's coming down now. I expect she's in her best pyjamas in your honour.'

What? *What?* Had I walked unknowingly into something weird?

A few seconds later the door opened and a little girl came in.

'Come and say hello,' Joe said holding out an arm to her. 'This is my daughter Ivy.'

Chapter Seven

Ivy ran into his embrace and looked over at me shyly. She was perhaps about seven, small and neat with the sort of flawless prettiness that deserves to be captured forever in a watercolour portrait.

'Hello,' I said.

'Are you Louisa?' Ivy said. 'The one who had a flat tyre?'

'Yes. Are you feeling better?'

'No.' She leaned her head in towards her father so that her dark hair fell across her face. 'I've got a headache.'

Joe hugged her. 'I'll get you your next dose of Calpol and some hot chocolate. That always makes you feel better doesn't it?'

Ivy nodded and Joe put his glass down and went out. Ivy slipped back into Joe's chair and looked at me.

'There's a girl called Louisa in my class.'

'My little sister couldn't say it. She could only say Lu.'

'What's your sister called?'

'Jassy. Her real name is Jasmine.'

'Where is she?'

'At home in London.'

Ivy gave a heavy sigh and rested her head on her hand. The log in the fireplace shifted and crackled.

'I'd like a sister,' Ivy said.

All sorts of ideas went round my mind at this point. The principal of course was where was Ivy's mother? Was she somewhere in the house? In the attic perhaps like a mad Mrs Rochester? Or had she left with Alan the shearer? Before I could ask the little girl some leading questions, Joe returned.

'Come on, my lovely, let's get you up to bed. I've got your hot chocolate and your medicine upstairs. You do feel rather hot.' He put a hand to her forehead. 'Come on, say goodnight.'

Ivy looked over at me from her position under Joe's arm. 'Night.'

'I hope you're feeling better soon,' I said.

'Thank you.'

Secretly, I was a bit relieved. She seemed a sweet little girl but I've not really had anything to do with children. I've certainly never wanted any of my own and now I'm nearly forty I suppose the possibility is receding fast. Oh well.

I sat and sipped my wine, enjoying the comfort of my place by the fire. Outside there was a sudden blast of wind against the window; evidently the weather was no better. It was nice to be somewhere that felt so – so safe. That was a strange word to come up with.

Joe returned, closing the door softly behind him.

'Is she all right?' I said.

'Yes, just a bit of a cold I think. Every time they go back to school they bring home a load of new germs.'

'What a ghastly thought!'

He settled back into his chair and looked over at me. 'I'm guessing you don't have children, Louisa?'

'No.'

Why did I suddenly feel uneasy, as though I had to explain myself to him? I didn't have to tell him that I'd never met any man I would have been happy entrusting with my genetic future. I'd dated a string of highly intelligent, well-heeled and ultimately unsuitable men of which Benedict was the latest.

A sudden realisation struck me.

Perhaps that's why I wasn't really that upset that I'd found him with another woman. Because Tess had been my get out of jail free card. I didn't have to do that awful thing my friends talked about: *going to the next stage.*

When you'd found out everything you wanted to know about the other person there would always come a night when you ran out of things to talk about and so did they. If you weren't careful one of you would ask the world's most horrible question. *What are you thinking about?* Perhaps the only acceptable thing left to say – to fill the yawning silence – was *I love you*.

Then, when the novelty of saying that wore off and you got fed up of telling each other how wonderful you were, you got engaged.

Then there would be a complicated wedding to plan

together, an expensive honeymoon in Dubai or the Maldives when at least one of you would get food poisoning or sunstroke and then a few weeks or months later the proud announcement of a pregnancy. That would effectively signal the end of carefree nights out with the Gang in the latest bistro and the start of one partner's complaints about the other's parenting involvement, arguments about money and a bitter stalemate would exist until eventually the poor kid would be shuttled between divorcing parents.

'What was all that about?' he said, laughing.

I looked across at him, aware I'd been silent for quite some time.

'Sorry? What?'

'Your face was a picture! I don't know what you were thinking but it looked very complicated.'

'Sorry, I suppose I was miles away. I wasn't thinking anything important.'

'Come and have something to eat,' he said. 'Bring your wine.'

We went through to a room that was everything a house hunter seeking a country kitchen could possibly want but it wasn't a designer image like Sally's. There was a built-in dresser laden with mismatched plates and bowls and a cream Aga nestling in an inglenook – the sort of Aga that was well used, chipped around the edges and had tea towels on the rail and socks drying on the top. On the floor in front of it the two sheepdogs were stretched out with a tabby cat curled up on one of them. The table was in the middle of the room and was solid and marked with countless scratches and grooves from years of wear. There was a pile of books and catalogues at the far end and a child's school bag and lunchbox. Two wooden benches stood on either side and there was a carver chair at the head.

'Oh God, this is gorgeous!' I said, and I meant it. It made my kitchen in London look sterile and dull, and even Sally's kitchen in Barracane House with all its designer touches and matching everything seemed faintly embarrassing in comparison.

'It's a bit of a shambles,' Joe said with a rueful expression, 'but it works.'

We sat down and he served up a hearty beef stew and dumplings. The meal was probably six trillion calories per serving but it was superb. I had a second helping and he asked me some more about my writing and I asked him about sheep although most of the time I didn't actually listen to his answers. I was fascinated by the shape and strength of his hands, and the way his hair fell over his forehead. I don't think I had talked quite so much for a very long time. And he actually listened and wanted to know about me.

'So how many books have you sold?'

'I don't actually know, lots.'

'Hundreds? Thousands?'

'Hundreds of thousands.'

'So why are you here? Why is someone like you here?'

I bristled. 'Someone like me? What does that mean?'

He leaned back in his chair and looked at me. Then he shook his head and smiled.

'It doesn't matter.'

'You mean a city type like me? Why am I here in the back of beyond playing at the country life?'

'I didn't say that but yes, I suppose so.'

'I don't really know, but I like it here for some reason. And I wanted some peace. I wanted to get away from ... from a situation. This seemed the best way. I'm planning on going back on Saturday.'

'A man?'

'Partly.'

'It's fine, it's none of my business.' He stood up and began clearing away the plates.

No it wasn't.

It was odd; I didn't want to discuss Benedict. He had no place here. He didn't compare with Joe any more than the two sheepdogs dozing in front of the Aga were like my friend's designer dog with its popping eyes and ridiculous little outfits. Does that dog enjoy being dressed up as Santa at Christmas, Uncle Sam on the Fourth of July or Batman at Halloween? I'm not convinced.

'I haven't done anything for pudding, but we could take some cheese into the sitting room and sit by the fire?'

'That would be nice; I really don't need any more to eat though. That was a great meal. You're a good cook.'

Tell me about Ivy. Where is her mother?

'Well I've had to learn. I'm not one to live on ready meals and I've got Ivy to think of.'

We went back into the sitting room and he put some more wood on the fire making it crackle and spit behind the guard. Then he came to sit next to me; not so close as to make me feel uncomfortable but close enough to be interesting.

'Tell me about Ivy,' I said.

'She's my daughter, pony mad, determined, very sweet and seven going on fifteen sometimes.'

'So Ellie was talking about a pony for her? I think I was a bit in the way.'

Joe shook his head. 'You weren't in the way at all. Ellie is an old friend. I've known her most of my life. I went to school with her brother. We were in the Young Farmers Club together. She's just always been there. I'm sure you have friends like that?'

I thought about it.

Well no actually. Not many.

'A few but most of my friends are people I've known for five minutes in comparison. People who live the same sort of life I do: fun and frivolous. Parties, book launches, exhibitions. That sort of thing. A couple of celebrities, one TV chef famous for his healthy, gluten-free vegetarian recipes but who is in fact obsessed with sausage sandwiches and Haribo. And no I can't divulge his name! Some are writers. A couple are old school friends. Once a month we gather like a flock of starlings wittering on about writer's block and *Sunday Times* rankings while taking up a large table at Julie's restaurant and knocking back wine like there is no tomorrow. But friends I have known all my life? No not really. Apart from Jassy, I suppose. Does one's irritating younger sister count as a friend?'

'She should,' he said.

'Then Jassy is a friend. She's just been reunited with her husband, Ralphie Sutton. They got married last year with an archway of cricket bats as they came out of the church – most of the England team were there – and miniature cricket balls on the wedding cake. They were all over the papers. You will have heard of him if you follow cricket. He's a commentator for the BBC. He's just got back from the West Indies tour.'

'Nope, never heard of him.'

I laughed. 'Don't ever tell him that, he would be mortified.'

He laughed. 'If I ever meet him I'll do my best to pretend.'

The chances of Ralphie Sutton meeting Joe Field were unlikely. Ralphie was a high-class metrosexual man with the grooming products to prove it. It was impossible to imagine him in the middle of the country unless he was doing some fancy fashion shoot for country tweeds and complicated watches and there was a five-star hotel stay involved. He was the sort of person who bought the *Countryfile* calendar as his contribution towards Children in Need and thought that qualified him as ecologically involved. I felt a sudden twitch of annoyance.

'More wine?' Joe topped up our glasses and raised his in

a toast to me. 'The roads will be cleared in the next day or so. I had a message from a chap who farms not far from here. He's got his snowplough out and he's already started clearing the road. You'll get back to safety.'

'I suppose.'

'But—' He stopped talking suddenly as there was a thump from upstairs and the sound of running feet.

He looked up at the ceiling. 'That's not like her. I'll just go and check Ivy's okay. Don't go away.'

He put his glass down on the table and went upstairs. I took off my shoes and curled my feet under me. Don't go away? How would I? Why would I? The fire was perfect, the flames glowing and flickering. I wondered what the snow was like outside.

I closed my eyes. What it would be like to live here? Would it be wonderful and fulfilling? Or was I being unrealistically fanciful? It was probably a life of hard work and a lot of mud. If it were that great everyone would be doing it wouldn't they? Chickens in the gardens and village fetes. No big cities, or chic wine bars. Farmers' markets and local pubs. No massive museums and exhibition halls. No V&A, no Harvey Nicks. No independent boutiques and bookstores. Community shops and greengrocers. I couldn't quite imagine it. But even so ...

I heard Joe coming back downstairs. He'd taken his sweater off and rolled up his sleeves.

'She's really not well. She's just thrown up everywhere. I'm just going to tidy her up, take her a drink of cold water.'

I stood up. 'Can I help?'

What could I do? I'm hopeless when I'm ill, I'm even worse with other people. We've already established I'd have made a terrible nurse. And someone else's vomit? I don't think so. The thought of a load of child's bedclothes covered in sick was too horrible to contemplate.

'No, you stay there. I'll get her sorted out. I'm sure she'll settle down.'

He went off upstairs and I sat back down, resting my head against the cushions and almost drifting off for a moment. Poor Ivy, I'm not particularly maternal but no one wants to see a child ill.

Joe came back a few minutes later.

'She's got a really high temperature.' He looked worried. 'Perhaps I should phone the doctor.'

'Why not?' I said. Although in Notting Hill, it would have been just as much use to send up a smoke signal or shout out of the window.

'Louisa, will you come and tell me what you think?' he said.

'Yes, of course,' I said.

What possible use would I be?

I followed him up the staircase, which was unbelievable: wooden and carved into a thousand plants and leaves. It would have been worth a fortune in some London shop. And yet here it was just so right; a part of the house and the history it held.

He led me into Ivy's bedroom. It was very warm, the sort of warmth that was unexpected until I realised the heat was coming from the little girl in the bed. The curtains were closed and there was a light on the bedside table that was covered by a pale green shade painted with gambolling ponies. Along the wall under the window was a built-in bookcase filled with paperbacks and untidy sheaves of paper. The edge of each shelf was edged with silk rosettes of several different colours – red, green, blue and gold – that had been attached with drawing pins.

At first glance it looked as though Ivy was asleep. There was a sour, hot smell in the room that seemed all wrong. She opened her eyes as Joe went to sit on the chair next to her bed.

'Daddy?'

'Hello, sweetheart, I'm here.'

'I've got a bad head. I don't feel very well.'

'Would you like some water?'

Ivy shook her head. 'Can you turn the light out? It hurts my eyes.'

'In a minute.'

Joe put one hand across his daughter's forehead.

'There's been a nasty bug going round the school, hasn't there? I thought we had got away with it. Maybe not.'

I stood at the foot of Ivy's bed gnawing at a thumbnail, wondering what to do. 'Perhaps we could sponge her with a cool, damp cloth?'

I remembered this from *The Angel in Ward B*. There had been someone with a high temperature and only devoted attention from my heroine had saved the day.

'Good idea,' Joe said.

He went into the bathroom and came back with a wet flannel. He held it to his daughter's forehead. After a moment he looked up at me, his blue eyes clouded with worry.

'She's so hot, Louisa. I'm worried. It's even worse than when she had chicken pox.'

I ran downstairs and fetched a bowl from the kitchen filled with iced water. And then Joe rinsed out the flannel and sponged Ivy's throat and arms. She was wearing clean cotton pyjamas with pictures of birds on them. She looked tiny, lying in her single bed.

We stayed there for a few minutes rinsing out the cloth and sponging her forehead. Something was definitely not right.

'Can you carry on doing this? I'm going to phone the doctor,' he said, handing me the flannel.

Oh bloody hell.

I took the cloth and carried on dabbing the cold water onto Ivy's forehead and throat. She opened her eyes and looked at me. 'Where's Daddy?'

'Downstairs, he'll be back in a minute.'

'I don't feel very well.'

'I know, I'm sorry.'

'Can you turn the light out? It hurts my eyes.'

'Okay, in a minute.'

I sponged her neck and moved the neck of her birdy pyjamas so they didn't get wet. There was a mark like a small red splotch just below her collarbone and when I looked there were several others on her arm.

Something about this triggered a memory and I went into the bathroom where I found a glass. I took it back and pressed it against the mark. I wouldn't have known what this indicated but one of my creations – Staff Nurse Emma Bannock in *The Darkest Hour* – certainly did.

Joe came back into the room. 'Is she okay?'

'No. You need an ambulance.'

'You think she's that bad?'

'Look at this rash. I think it could be meningitis.'

Joe watched as I pressed the glass against the mark again. 'Christ, I think you're right.' He put his hand on his daughter's head.

He raced downstairs and I could hear his voice, low and urgent as he spoke to someone.

'Okay, we are lucky; the main road has been cleared and gritted and there's a four by four rapid response team who were working nearby. Someone had fallen over and broken an ankle. They'll be on the way in a few minutes. But I've got to get her downstairs.'

Chapter Eight

The rest of the night was a blur. About twenty minutes later we saw the lights of a vehicle coming slowly up the lane. It looked like a cross between an ambulance and an armoured truck. There were two paramedics inside, high-vis jackets luminous in the moonlight, and they came into the house with all sorts of paraphernalia, oxygen and a load of tubes and bags. They were marvellous.

In just a few minutes Ivy was in the back on a stretcher with Joe following in his Land Rover. They left the house, making their way back up the lane, the vehicle lights rocking as they negotiated the ruts and piles of snow. At last the lights of the two vehicles disappeared altogether and there was nothing out there again but a deep, dark silence.

I closed the front door and went to put some more wood on the fire. I sat on the sofa in front of the blaze, huddled in a blanket I found on the back of a chair. What should I do now? I couldn't walk home, and even if I was daft enough to try I couldn't leave the house unlocked. They might be hours, or even days. I had no idea. I had nothing with me except some breath mints and a lipstick. Should I stay here or find a bedroom?

I felt so helpless and so sorry for the little girl. And for Joe, my heart went out to him. This was what happened when you were a parent. The terrible fears and worries that presumably never ended.

Kids were a pain; everyone knew that. Why did anyone bother having them? We'd all heard people moaning about their children. They had tantrums in supermarkets and made unreasonable demands. They got addicted to computer games and sent photos of their bits to each other. They kicked back and became sullen and uncommunicative. They lied and nicked stuff and rebelled.

But now I began to wonder; there must also be a bond, unbreakable and true. A love that should be unbreakable anyway. Otherwise what was the point? Wasn't that what families were all about? I thought about my parents, a couple who had argued since the day they met but obviously really loved each other and after forty-three years still couldn't bear to be apart. And Jassy, maddening at times but kind, loyal and sometimes too honest for comfort. There was no doubt we shared a sisterly love.

It wasn't the sort of fleeting, perishable thing I felt for Benedict. Not the casual, designer-decorated love he had declared for me with expensive jewellery and unexpected Bollinger when he won in court.

I went out to the kitchen to make a cup of tea. I sat at the table while the sheepdogs slumbered on and the cat – after giving me a filthy look – forced its way between them.

I suddenly realised this house was a place filled with love. There were pictures taped to the fridge, photos of Ivy dressed in riding gear. Ivy at the seaside. Ivy in school uniform. There were things in the fridge for her packed lunches, on the table was a wooden bowl filled with her hair scrunchies and ribbons. Her mug, decorated with ponies and IVY painted on the front was upended on the draining board waiting for her return.

I thought about all the awful things that meningitis could cause. For the first time in many years I closed my eyes and I prayed.

*

Just after seven o'clock the next morning Joe came home. I had been asleep on the sofa in the sitting room, covered by a blanket. I woke as he came in and stood up. He looked at me and smiled.

'You're still here. I'm glad.'

I hardly dared to ask. 'Well? How's Ivy?'

'I'm sorry I had to abandon you like that – I wasn't thinking.'

'It's fine, I'm fine. But Ivy?'

'They say she's going to pull through,' he said. He rubbed his hands over his face. His voice was just a bit wobbly. 'I had a long chat with the doctor and they caught it in time. She's on an antibiotic drip. She's sleeping but she's going to be fine. I've just come back for an hour's sleep and then I'll take her some clean clothes and a few of her things.'

'Oh, Joe, thank God!'

He pulled me into his arms and hugged me. A proper man hug that was unexpected and wonderful. I relaxed against him and I heard him give a shaky laugh, a sound that rumbled through his chest. He rested his chin on the top of my head.

'Thank you, Louisa – if you hadn't been here I don't know what I would have done. I don't know what would have happened. I can't bear to think about it.'

'Are you okay? Do you want anything? A cup of tea?'

He leaned back and looked down at me and then suddenly his expression changed. I felt his arms tighten around me.

'I don't ... I can't ...'

And then he kissed me.

I could feel him trembling.

I felt the hardness of his muscles against me and for a moment I was distinctly wobbly too. He was more marvellous and gentle than any man I had known and the feel of his hands on me left me breathless.

At last he pulled back and buried his face in my hair.

'Louisa, what are we doing?' he said.

'I don't know, I don't know,' I said, and I clung to him.

It was the drama of it all, the fear he had felt through the night as Ivy battled. I'd heard about this sort of thing. It had happened in at least two of my books. A life-changing event: the death of a parent (*I Know Everything*) or the aftermath of a tsunami (*Five Miles to Midnight*) brought on this sort of emotional reaction. I'd read somewhere that this sort of thing led to unplanned sex, unexpected pregnancy and all sorts of turmoil. There was a proper term for it but I couldn't remember it. All I knew was I really, really didn't want him to stop. And I wanted more. A lot more.

Oh yes, now I remembered. *Comfort sex*, that was it.

I shouldn't be doing this. I really shouldn't.

But he held out his hand to me and I took it. He led me to the bottom of the beautiful, carved staircase and I followed him. We went upstairs and into his bedroom and I went willingly. I could hardly wait.

He didn't turn the light on in his room but the curtains were still open and the early dawn light, reflected off the snow outside, was brightening the room.

I unbuttoned his shirt. I put my hands flat against his warm chest, feeling the steady beat of his heart under my fingers.

'Louisa,' he whispered, his breath warm on my face, 'I haven't done this for a very long time.'

'What? Taken your shirt off?' I whispered back.

He laughed and I breathed in the scent of him. Masculine and strong, a mixture of soap and the cold morning air.

I dropped his shirt onto the floor and ran my hands over his arms and his shoulders. He shivered with pleasure and I felt his fingers pressing into my back.

'I mean this,' he said.

'But you can't have forgotten. It's like riding a bike isn't it?' I said.

He kissed my eyelids very gently. 'It's nothing like riding a bike.'

Slowly at first and then with increasing urgency we discovered each other. His mouth touching my cheek, my neck, my breast. I pushed my hands into his warm hair and held his head as he softly bit my shoulder, his mouth tracing the hollow of my throat.

His hands explored my body, touching and teasing and I felt my heart thudding as he stirred sensations in me that I hadn't expected. I twisted in his arms, hungry for more, and he pushed me down on the bed, his mouth on mine. Outside the sun rose above the snowy fields and at last he was where I wanted him to be. Near me, above me, inside me.

Just for a moment there was nothing but his need for me. My need for him. Being together, turning my body with his. Meeting him and matching him.

I had written about moments like this.

So many times.

But never understood how it felt.

I'd been pretending. I'd been wrong. I'd been blind.

*

He pulled the quilt over us and held me then for a long time, his arms comforting and warm.

'Louisa,' he said at last and he kissed my hair.

No one had called me Louisa for years. No one had ever said my name quite like he did.

'I'm so glad,' I said.

He chuckled. 'Which particular bit are you glad about?'

'I'm glad about Ivy, that she is going to be okay. I'm glad about—'

What could I say?

'I'm glad about this.'

'You're sure?'

'I'm sure. Aren't you?'

He laughed then. 'Of course!'

I felt a sudden chill of something.

Of course, he had said. *Of course* he was all right. Why wouldn't he be?

He had found a willing sexual partner to help relieve the stress and tension of the last few hours. His mind had been on his daughter; he'd had a terrible time.

Of course. Worried sick about Ivy and when he got home, crazy with lack of sleep and anxiety, I'd been there, pulling his clothes off. What a tart.

What day was it? Saturday? Thursday? Wednesday?

'I'm going back to London today,' I said, 'if I can get the car as far as the road.'

'I'll help you,' he said.

Yes.

I moved out of his arms and wrapped myself in a blanket, suddenly shy.

'How long will Ivy be in hospital?'

I looked around for my hastily discarded clothes: my shirt on the landing outside the bedroom, my trousers on the floor, my knickers on the windowsill.

'I don't know yet. She'll be there for a while I expect. I'll find out more later when I go to see her.'

'You must be exhausted,' I said.

He looked it. His face was dark with stubble and there were shadows under his eyes.

He ran one hand through his hair. 'You could say that.'

'I must go home and let you sleep.'

'I'm sorry. I'll take you.'

I wanted to be able to say, *No don't worry, I'll walk*, but of course I had no idea how far it was or which way to go. And I could hardly ring for a taxi. And was he sorry I was going or sorry he had to drive me?

I scrambled into my clothes and went downstairs to wait for him. Five minutes later we were outside and on our way back to Barracane House. The snow was dazzling in the early morning sunlight, glittering and glorious. But it was thawing. There were patches of mud on the lane where the Land Rover had churned up the snow. We got to the house and I could see that my car had shed its layer of snow already and as the sun rose, melted snow was dripping off the bumpers. I'd get out of here if it killed me.

He stilled the furious noise of the car engine.

'If you have trouble, I'll give you a hand. I'll come back on my way to the hospital to make sure you're not having any problems. Is that all right?'

'Of course. Tell Ivy she's very brave.'

He leaned forward to kiss my cheek, a moment that was somehow awkward. Why had I done this? Why had I been so easy, so terribly available? Was it because he was different from all the men I had ever met? Not just because his shoulders had been broad and hard under my hands and his skin had been warm and scented with the sweetness of hay. Something between us was unlike anything I'd ever known. The emotion had been deeper and more meaningful. I couldn't understand it. I needed to think.

I went into the house and closed the door behind me and let out a manic scream of frustration.

Damnation.

*

I changed the bed, washed the sheets and left them to dry in the utility room. Then I hoovered, dusted, washed up the mugs and plates I'd used and put everything away. It was as though I wanted to hide the fact that I had ever been there.

I was packed up and ready to go within a couple of hours. I scoured every room for my stuff. Books, paperwork, notes on my floundering plot. My laptop and chargers. I emptied the waste paper basket and put my recycling out into the right bins.

Then I realised I was sweating and needed a shower. If nothing else I wanted to wash away the reek of sex and Joe and change all my clothes again. I almost felt like throwing them away with all the empty wine bottles and plastic food trays.

I had to leave soon though; if Joe was going to return I didn't want him to find me here. He'd want to come in and talk to me and tell me about Ivy and then he might kiss me again and then who knows how I would resist him?

I wouldn't, I know I wouldn't. He'd look at me with those beautiful blue eyes and I'd have my knickers off in double quick time. How shaming. The very thought of him feeling me, touching me, offering me his body, licking and tasting his ...

Shut the fuck up FFS! Shut up! *Just Shut Up!*

I was in a committed relationship. I was with Benedict. Our friends called us Benedict-and-Lulu, almost as though we were an entity – that's how we were. I'd thought our relationship was different. For want of a better word, more permanent. I made myself think about him and just for one crazy moment I couldn't remember what Benedict looked like. Yes of course I could. Tall, lean, dark-eyed, good-looking with a broad grin that could be cheeky, occasionally sexy.

I remembered being with him in Edinburgh for Hogmanay, at Ascot when he had to pull one of my stilettos out of the turf. Yes he could be fussy about food but I made myself remember his enjoyment of life, fine wine, the life and soul of many parties. A liking for handmade suits and silk ties. A weakness for Swiss chocolate. I felt quite sentimental, and sad knowing something in me had changed. If he knew what I'd done ...

I was ashamed of myself. And astonished that I could behave like this.

I got my stuff out to the car and wedged everything in as best I could and prayed for the car to start and get me out of here.

Twenty rather hair-raising minutes later I reached the main road. I seemed to be the only traveller risking the gritted roads. Occasionally I passed a lorry or a milk tanker and by the time I reached the motorway the roads were clear and wet and pointing reassuringly towards London.

*

I got back to Notting Hill at nearly four o'clock. The flat was empty but then I hadn't told him I was on my way back. I wouldn't expect Benedict for at least a couple of hours. Saturday afternoons were spent watching sport in the over-themed wine bar that he liked to refer to as The Pub. I knew what a proper pub looked like now, and it bore no resemblance to Dizzy's with its carefully distressed wooden bar stools, marble-topped tables and faux advertising signs for pre-war cigarettes that had once seemed so retro and original. He would be with his pals, watching some sporting event that they didn't fully understand on the massive televisions.

I dumped my bags in the hall, looked around and felt my sentimental mood fade and my irritation levels rise. The place was an absolute shambles.

For a start there was some knobbly rustic bread covered in a mouldy fur *on top of* the bread bin. The laundry basket had been brought out of the bedroom into the middle of the living room and was so full the lid wouldn't close. What was Benedict expecting? That the staff would sort it out while he was away? There was a similar problem with the kitchen bin where the lid was open and a couple of eggshells had been carefully balanced on the top of the pile. *On top.* Why? *Why* couldn't he see that the bin needed emptying? Was he going to carry on balancing stuff like a children's game until the whole lot toppled over?

Right.

Tired as I was, I set to and started clearing up. It never ceased to astonish me that someone who was in some ways such a fuss arse could also be so slovenly. In the bedroom there were clothes everywhere. I'm afraid I lost the plot a bit. I found some black bin liners and filled them all with shirts, sweaters, nasty pointy Italian shoes, hideous Lycra bike gear, gym gear, one of his fancy suits and even his poncey Panama hat, bought for an afternoon's showing off at The Oval with Ralphie.

I dumped the lot in the hall and then started to tidy up

his other stuff. Two books on Albania because he thought it might be a cheap holiday, various toiletries. His teeth whitening trays left on top of the bookcase, vitamin supplements and a pot of hair unguents on the coffee table. I swear he had twice as much stuff as I did. Oh yes and his Andy Warhol print that I had always hated, the one of Mick Jagger looking particularly unattractive – that came down off the wall and I stuck it behind the sofa.

By the time I had finished I was knackered and could quite easily have fallen asleep on the floor but I guessed he would be back before too long.

Right on the dot of six thirty Benedict came back. Very slightly pissed and very pleased with himself. He came barging in the front door with a couple of cronies guffawing behind him. I guessed it would be Percy and Toby but most of Benedict's friends were interchangeable, so I could be wrong. Except Toby has taken to cultivating a thick beard in a sort of irritating hipster way and at the same time shaved his thinning hair so that now it looks as though he has his head on upside down.

'Hey my little lady has come back!' Benedict carolled as he saw me. 'I wasn't expecting you! Where have you been? What are all the bags in the hall? Doing some housework?'

'That's what girlies are there for!' Percy said. 'Lucky you!'

'No I'm just tidying up,' I said ignoring Percy. 'What have you been doing while I was away? The place looked like it was burgled.'

Benedict looked around, puzzled. 'But ...'

'Got a drink, old man? Don't know about you but I'm in the mood for some fizz,' Percy said, lurching towards the kitchen.

I went to stand in his way.

'Not now, Percy. Would you mind leaving and taking what's his name with you? Benedict and I have something to discuss.'

'*Hello!* You're on a promise, me old chum!' Percy chortled. 'And you're a lucky fellow.'

'Lulu is looking lululicious! I know I would!' Toby said, looking even more like a Woolly Willy toy I'd had as a child where the beard and hair were made with a magnet and iron filings.

'Would what, Toby?' I said, putting my arm out to stop him going into the kitchen.

He flustered a bit. 'Well you know.'

'No, do enlighten me. Would what?'

Benedict interrupted at this point. 'Better go, chaps – I think the little lady and I have something to clear up.'

He encouraged them out of the door and turned to face me, his eyes wide with innocent outrage.

'What was all that about? You made me look a right idiot!'

'You are a right idiot. This is my flat and you've left it looking like a slum just because I've been away. And stop calling me the little lady.'

'I've been feeling under the weather, and really busy with this case, you know that!' he said, outraged.

'It's Saturday. You haven't been at work *today* for God's sake. You could have done something this morning.'

'But it's the weekend!'

'And?'

He blustered around for a few seconds and then just repeated himself.

'But it's the weekend.'

I turned away and went into the kitchen to pour myself a glass of wine.

'Benedict. I've just driven back from Devon. It was snowing. I'm tired, I'm hungry and I just wanted a quiet evening. I didn't want to spend hours cleaning up after you just because you can't be bothered and you think your weekend is more important than mine.'

He gave a little confused shake of his head. 'What the hell's got into you?'

I took a sip of my wine and put the glass down on the worktop. I couldn't go on like this for much longer.

'I'm fed up with this, Benedict. I'm beginning to wonder ...'

Panic flittered across his face for a second. Then he came towards me with his best puppy dog look and a rueful pout. I think it was supposed to soften me up. It didn't.

'I'm sorry, poppet, don't be cross. I had one of my headaches. It might even have been a migraine. I've missed you. I wasn't thinking.' He put his hands on my waist and rocked me gently from side to side. 'Don't be cross with me.'

'And don't call me poppet either,' I said, pushing him away.

This was the point where I should start to calm down. But I didn't. Perhaps I had a guilty conscience? I deserved to. After all I had enjoyed sex with another man, hadn't I? If I had proof that Benedict had slept with another woman I'd have been absolutely furious. I'd have slagged him off something rotten to anyone who was prepared to listen.

I was a hypocrite. I suddenly felt thoroughly ashamed of myself.

'Just don't do it again,' I said rather weakly.

'That's my girl. There's my little Lu.'

He was pulling me in towards him. I know what this signalled: some bedroom action. Suddenly there was nothing I wanted less. Unless it was cleaning out the dishwasher filter.

Benedict made a little crooning noise. 'Look, I'll open a bottle of bubbly and we'll do some snuggling. I've missed you so much. I bet you've missed me too. Stuck in the back of beyond with no company and no one to cuddle up to. I know you, Lulu, you're not happy because you need a bit of attention. That's it, isn't it?'

Joe.

Suddenly I thought of Joe.

And that was all I could think of. Being in bed with Joe. Being in Joe's arms.

Benedict mistook my silence for agreement and moved in to kiss me.

'Let's have some champagne and just for once we'll order

a takeaway – your choice. And we'll do that thing with the ice cream. And you'll be yourself in no time.'

I came to my senses and gently pushed him away.

'I'm really tired.'

'I know, my little Lulabelle. C'mon, a little bit of jiggy and you'll be my girl again.'

I was outraged. '*A little bit of jiggy?* You're astonishing!'

'Hahahaha! So I'm told!' Benedict struck a Usain Bolt lightning pose.

'No I mean no, I'm not in the mood.'

'Oh, Lu, sweetie, calm down. We can work through this. I can see you're upset but – well you were a bit to blame, you know.'

'How?'

He stuck his hands in his pockets and shrugged. 'Well I don't know, I'm a chap. You can't just leave a chap to get on with it and go away all the time.'

'You've somehow acquired some sort of disability?'

'No, you're just being silly now. Look—' Benedict ran his hand through his hair '—can we just start again? You're right I should have tidied up but I didn't and I'm sorry. I wasn't expecting you. Okay. Now let's open the bubbly and say no more about it. You can tell me all about what you've been doing.'

What I've been doing.

I wondered how the evening would pan out if I told Benedict the truth.

Actually, Benedict, last night I had the best sex of my life with a farmer.

'Nothing very thrilling. Some writing, a bit of editing. Tell me what you've been doing,' I said, desperate to turn his attention away from me and what I'd been up to in the last twenty-four hours.

He perked up at that and started to rabbit on about what Percy had said and what Toby had done and their continuing problems with parking now that the car park near their chambers had been dug up to sort out the Victorian drains. This expanded into how clever he was to ride a bike to work and how he thought he needed to upgrade to something a bit lighter. By which I suppose he meant more expensive.

We drank champagne and Benedict ordered a curry that turned out to be bland and disappointing. He blamed me for that too, because I didn't want anything too spicy. Then we watched a depressing programme about plastic bags and how they were ruining the environment and I went to bed, leaving Benedict snoring on the sofa.

Chapter Nine

The following day was Sunday of course, which usually meant a morning in bed followed by brunch with the Sunday papers. This time I was up early, encouraging Benedict into the shower by hoovering the living room rather clumsily, bashing against the sofa and waking him up.

We got to Dizzy's just before midday and some of the usual suspects wandered in a few minutes later. First came Toby and the odious Percy and his equally irritating brother Leo. By then I was so clenched up with indecision and guilt I was practically mute. I buried myself in the colour supplements and pretended I was hungover because then I could legitimately exclude myself from the conversation without being marked down as stroppy or hormonal.

Something was going to have to change. I could feel it in the air. Something in me was different although I couldn't put my finger on exactly what it was. This life – London and bars and overdone partying, shallow senseless gossip. Expensive taxis to clubs and cafés. The noise, the dirt, the jostling crowds. The terrible feeling that there should be more than this but not knowing what. Not knowing what I wanted.

I carried on reading an article about tattoos and wondered why anyone would have one considering the possibility of infection, dodgy graphics or bad spelling.

'Lululicious is jolly quiet today,' Percy said at last, his voice booming out across the table. 'Late night then was it? Happy reunion, Benedict? Hahahaha!'

I sent him a withering look.

'I'm off to get a refill,' Leo said. He stood up, knocking his head against one of the low-slung pendant lights. He did this with monotonous regularity and never seemed to learn.

Percy held out his pint glass. 'Same again, eh?'

'Get it yourself, you lazy sod!' Leo said, rubbing his head ruefully.

'Well that's charming isn't it?' Percy said looking around for sympathy.

Someone behind the bar turned up the volume of the music playing. It was something noisy, pounding with a heavy bass and some screeching woman singing over the top of it.

I could feel the tension rising inside my head. If it carried on I was going to lose it. I was going to throw myself onto the floor and kick and scream like a toddler having a tantrum. There was a new server behind the bar who was annoying me on several levels. Her blue and green hair. Her pink Doc Marten boots. Her tattoos. Even her nose stud infuriated me.

Percy and Benedict started bickering about who was going to get the next round of drinks in, citing the night before last when Percy had bought a bottle of champagne and Benedict countered by reminding him about the many rounds of shots they had shared at Twickenham.

The door opened and my sister came in, yelping with excitement to see me, closely followed by Ralphie and his sister Maud.

'You're back!' Jassy exclaimed. 'I'm so relieved! You had snow didn't you? I was afraid you'd be stuck in the back of beyond for the rest of your life! Poor darling, was it really awful?' She came over to kiss me and then of course Ralphie, oozing charm and an impressive Caribbean tan with white owl eyes where he had kept his sunglasses on, came over to give me a hug and tell me – as he always did – how *gorgeous* I was looking. Which was a lie because I knew perfectly well I didn't.

*

We got back to the flat just before five thirty with the prospect of meeting up with the Gang later for cocktails. I wanted to be left alone. I really couldn't be bothered. If I closed my eyes I could almost see the sitting room at Barracane House. The wood burner, the lovely views down the valley, the comfortable bed. Oh God what was I thinking? What was the matter with me?

Benedict was in a fine humour, loving and pleasantly tactile. He stood behind me and kissed my neck while I unlocked the front door. Now in the past this would have put me in the mood or at least halfway there. This time I brushed him off like a troublesome mosquito.

Benedict sighed. 'What's the matter? Come on, you're still upset about something.'

'Oh I don't know. I'm just a bit off,' I said.

'Well I can tell that.'

He walked over to the television, unbuttoning his coat and dropping it over the back of a chair. Then he slumped down with the TV remotes in his hands, kicked off his shoes and started flicking though the channels.

'I'm not feeling great,' I said. I walked over to the window and looked out at the street below.

'Hmm?' He didn't look up. 'Time of the month?'

'No, Benedict, and you don't get extra Brownie points when you say that you know.'

'Huh?'

'There are other reasons why I might be feeling out of sorts.'

He looked up at me then, his head turning sharply.

'Christ on a bike, you're not up the duff are you?'

'No, Benedict. But wouldn't that be a lovely way of discussing it if I were,' I said waspishly.

'Thank heavens for that,' he said and turned his attention back to the screen.

He was watching football. In a few minutes he was engrossed in it. 'I don't suppose you'd get me a beer would you?' he said.

Like a muppet I went to the fridge, pulled out a beer and uncapped it for him.

'There's a good girl, now come and snuggle,' he said, patting the sofa cushions next to him. I didn't move. I stood watching the cars in the street, the people hurrying to get out of the rain.

'I think I'll sell this flat,' I said at last.

Until that moment I hadn't known I was going to say any such thing.

He didn't react.

'I said I'm going to sell this flat.' Repeating it seemed to solidify the thought in my head.

This time I got through. His head whipped round.

'What? Sell this flat? Why the hell would you do that?'

'I need a change,' I said.

'Change? But where would we go? I mean where is better than Notting Hill? I hope you're not thinking of the house, dog and garden thing because it wouldn't work for us – you know it wouldn't.'

'No I'm not thinking of that. I mean a real change.'

'And this flat is so convenient,' he said.

'Convenient for you, you mean?'

'Well yes, but you too. I mean all our friends are here. We know all the shops. There's never any problem with ... you know.'

'What?'

'Stuff. Deliveries, taxis,' he said, 'noise, vandalism. Drunks.'

'Well that's not true. Maudie found someone asleep on her front step the other day.'

'Did she? Good grief.'

He was only listening with half his attention now, his eyes swivelling back to the television.

'And I would like somewhere with a bit more space. Perhaps a second bedroom or a separate dining room.'

'Well maybe, but it's an awful drag having to find somewhere isn't it? Oooh that was definitely off side!'

'Or a garden,' I said, brightening at the idea, 'yes I'd like a garden.'

He snorted. 'Don't be ridiculous!'

'Why is that ridiculous?' I said.

'Because there are people who do gardens and there are people who don't. People like us. Weeding, mowing, planting stuff, getting rid of green waste, there's no way I'm doing that.'

'Well no I don't imagine you would. You can't bring yourself to take the recycling out,' I muttered.

'Well then? I'm not interested in a garden. Maybe a roof terrace with a hot tub. That might do. Oh, ref! Did you see that?'

I sighed. 'I do want a garden,' I said stubbornly after a few minutes. On the street a taxi driver had got out of his cab and was waving his arms at someone blocking his lane. 'I want to live somewhere peaceful, somewhere with a view. Where I can see the stars at night.'

Benedict turned to look at me, his face creased with incomprehension.

'What the hell are you on about? Since when did you care about that? Do you really think I'm going to move into some bijou little terrace with a picnic bench and some terracotta pots and strings of fairy lights along the fence? Have you lost your mind? You're *not* pregnant are you? You're absolutely sure?'

'No I'm not!'

'You're acting as though you're going crazy. Everyone wants to live in Notting Hill. There isn't one person in the country who wouldn't jump at the chance.'

Joe wouldn't.

I tried to imagine Joe here, living in this flat with its echoing chrome stairwell and the glass balcony that was big enough for one chair but not two. The kitchen that had a massive American fridge freezer because it looked cool but had no space for a tumble dryer. The high-end dishwasher with the irritating little slots for cutlery in the top. The living area with a fifty-inch television on the wall above the white pebble gas fire. Compared with Barracane House or Lower Tor Farm – Joe's farm – it was fake, smug and embarrassing.

'Then why doesn't everyone live here?' I said foolishly.

'Because everyone can't afford it,' Benedict said in a *duh* tone of voice. 'Look you're just being silly, all this dodging backwards and forward to Devon – you're just tired and disoriented.'

'Disorientated,' I muttered.

'That too. Now look, fetch me another beer, have one yourself if you like, then come and cuddle up to me.'

I got as far as the kitchen and opening the fridge door. The bottles of pretentious overpriced beer were stacked up on the metal rack. I suddenly remembered the Cat and Convict and the beer brewed there, foaming in Joe's pewter tankard.

I shut the fridge door and poured myself a glass of red wine. Then I went to sit down in the chair opposite Benedict. After a few seconds he looked over.

'Got my beer, sweetie?'

'Nope,' I said.

He pulled a face.

'Get it yourself,' I said.

Benedict stood up, shaking his head, and went to the kitchen. 'My word you are in a state aren't you?'

He came back, slumped into the sofa, took a pull at his beer and turned up the television a fraction.

'This isn't really working, Benedict,' I said.

After a moment he looked over. 'What? What's not working?'

'This. All of this isn't working,' I said.

He put the beer bottle down on the coffee table with a thump. 'Oh for fuck's sake, Lu. Can we talk about this some other time? You're obviously tired and hormonal.'

'I'm not,' I said. 'I'm going to sell this flat and I'm going to move somewhere nice.'

He looked incredulous. 'But this is *nice*. What's not *nice* about this?'

'It's not what I want. Not any more.'

He came over and sat on the arm of my chair and stroked my hair.

'Look, I don't want to move, Lu. I like it here. I like living here with you. I don't want to live somewhere "nice" when I already live somewhere fucking marvellous.'

I was suddenly calm and clear-headed. I was going to take control.

'I'll be putting the flat on the market soon. So you'll have to decide what you want to do.'

At this point he was sufficiently alarmed to turn the television off and he moved to sit opposite me, perched on the edge of the coffee table. He took my hands in his.

'Lu, just sleep on it okay? You're in a funny mood. You're overtired. You're not thinking straight. I don't want to move and nor do you, okay?'

'Well you're going to have to.'

'Where? Where is this insanity taking us?'

'Me. It's taking me. You need to think about it.'

'What?' he said, outraged.

I stood up and pulled my hands away. 'Like I said, this isn't working. I'm sorry.'

'You can't do this! I have rights too. I pay the electricity bill!'

'And I pay everything else. Don't make this any more difficult than it already is.'

Benedict took another long swig of his beer. 'Is that what all this is about? You want me to pay rent or something?'

'It wouldn't have killed you to offer.'

'Then I will.'

'It's not just that. It's everything,' I said, sipping my wine. I felt odd and edgy; my insides were clenched with fright at what I had started. But I couldn't stop now. I'd taken the first step towards something.

Benedict sighed. 'What the hell do you want?'

'I want to sell this place and move somewhere with some character. With some soul. A community where people give a damn.'

'How can you think ... *Soul?* Are you serious? Be careful what you wish for, Lu,' he said, laughing.

I gave him a withering look. 'I'm going to give you a month to find somewhere.'

'What?' he shouted.

'A month. You've got lots of friends and loads of contacts.'

'Bollocks! But what about us?'

I gnawed at a hangnail. 'I'm not stupid, Benedict. That blonde the other day – she wasn't the first, was she? You're telling me she wasn't a friend with significant benefits?'

'Oh for God's sake. And stop biting your nails.'

'They're my nails and I'll bloody well bite them if I want to!' I said. 'Look, Benedict, it's obvious, you want something different and so do I.'

He finished his beer and put it down on the table with another loud thump. 'Fuck!'

'I'm going to have a bath,' I said.

'Well I'm going down the pub. Don't wait up, will you?' he spat. 'I'll probably crash with Percy tonight. I've got a shit day coming up tomorrow, a really hard day, but don't let that bother you. You just carry on having your silly little fantasies about the grass being greener.'

Seconds later the front door slammed shut behind him.

*

I went into the bathroom, locked the door behind me and gave a little fist pump of triumph. I'd known what I wanted to achieve but I hadn't known I had the willpower to stick to it. After two years together I'd realised Benedict had perfected the knack of making me feel uncomfortable simply because I disagreed with him.

We'd gone to Barcelona when I wanted to go to Carcassonne.

We'd spent last Christmas in London when I'd wanted to meet up with my parents in France.

We'd missed countless exhibitions and book launches because he didn't fancy it.

We'd been to too many parties where he had flirted with other women.

At the furthermost corners of my mind I had feared that he would talk me round. The old me would have given in or been persuaded.

I liked this new me. I'd been firm; I'd said no and I'd meant it.

After a long soak in the bath I went to see if there was any decent food in the kitchen. As I might have predicted there was no milk, no cheese, and the bread (organic, seven-seeded and still in its ecologically friendly paper bag,) was rock hard and slightly green. There is something to be said for preservatives sometimes. But on the other hand there were some organic free-range eggs from deliriously happy hens somewhere in Berkshire, a recently opened packet of smoked salmon presumably from some equally cheerful fish in Scotland and a nicely chilled bottle of champagne.

I made some scrambled eggs and smoked salmon, put the television on and watched a programme on quilt making in New England that I would never have got away with if Benedict had been around. Particularly as there was football on another channel. But then isn't there always?

I opened the champagne with a view to getting through it all. And the more pissed I got the more I thought about Joe. His height, his broad shoulders, his kindness, the way he'd kissed me.

I wished I'd taken a picture of him.

I wished I'd not leapt into bed with him.

That wasn't true. I'd leap into bed with him again at the drop of a sock.

I went to get changed into some comfortable pyjamas and a dressing gown and returned to my champagne. It was going down very nicely indeed. I went to see if there was anything else to eat and found only a bag of kale, some wrinkled tomatoes and half a pot of tahini. I cursed Benedict for the untidy, neurotic, health food freak he had become and started to trawl through the cupboards, even the ones that were hardly ever used. I didn't cook so why did I imagine there would be anything interesting in any of them? There weren't even enough dishes or plates.

Was it possible to order a takeaway of milk chocolate, Wagon Wheels and whole milk? With a side order of sliced, white bread with extra gluten and some actual butter instead of the churned axle grease Benedict insisted on?

I thought about Joe's kitchen and the beef stew he had made, the warmth and cosiness of his kitchen with the sheep-dogs and the cat forming a tangled, furry pyramid in front of the Aga. Benedict would have had a fit if he'd seen that. The perceived lack of hygiene, the air thick with saturated fats and calories and delicious smells.

My mobile rang.

'Jassy.'

'Hi, I was just ringing to see how you're getting on.'

'Great thanks – Benedict and I have split up.'

I heard her shocked intake of breath.

'Really? God! What happened?'

'Not much. At the moment I don't care, I'm drinking a bottle of champagne.'

'Yes I thought you sounded a bit slurred,' Jassy said. 'Tell me what happened?'

'I deserve to be slurred,' I said, taking a swig of champagne.

'I've put up with Benedict and his sludgy breakfast smoothies for too long. I told him I'm going to sell the flat and move somewhere else.'

'You're joking!' Jassy breathed, horrified. 'Sell the flat?'

'I'm serious. I just realised I don't want this any more, I want something else.'

'What? FFS. What in the name of all that's holy could possibly be better than what you've got?'

I put her on speaker, knocked back my champagne, and refilled the glass. 'There must be loads of things. I don't really know.'

'Then you should sleep on it. Don't do anything.'

'That's what he says.'

'Well perhaps he's right. Look, you've been wrestling with *Choose Yes*. Sally's been on at you hasn't she – maybe that's it?'

'Maybe,' I agreed.

'So don't do anything you can't undo. I mean if nothing else this is going to completely bugger up my birthday dinner, just when I thought it was sorted.'

'I'm not staying with Benedict for the convenience of your seating plan,' I said.

'I didn't mean that.'

'Calm down, I know you didn't. I'm nearly forty, Jassy.'

'Oh God. Spare me. It's not the frigging biological clock speech is it?'

'No, of course not.'

'You know you'd be a shit mother. Just like me.' Jassy made the sort of noises associated with lighting up a cigarette.

'Thanks for that. Why can't I find a man? A *man* man who can do manly things with bits of wood and mend engines and doesn't mind mud. And doesn't watch me eating Crunchies with a sad look on his face.'

Jassy snorted with laughter. 'You're round the bend. So are you coming out tonight? We were going to meet up with the Gang at nine thirty. Probably at that new wine bar down by the market: Billy's or Bunty's or something. You coming? You can drown your sorrows a bit more.'

I thought about it for a minute. It would mean changing out of my pyjamas, slapping on some make-up, putting proper shoes on, calling an Uber because it was now raining, and squeezing around a table with seven or eight noisy people who would know nothing about Devon or how cold the night can be. They would be banging on about the congestion charge and talking a load of crap about pollution and plastic bottles. They would have no idea that really clean air is crisp and clear as water. That the night sky is endless and full of wonderful things.

I suddenly realised I was too hot. Maybe that was why I didn't usually wear PJs and a dressing gown. They might be needed in Barracane House where no room was draft-proof and the wind whistled through the letterbox, but they certainly weren't necessary in a well-insulated, zero-carbon flat like mine. I shrugged off the dressing gown and topped up my glass. The champagne foamed over the top and I dabbed ineffectually at it with a tissue.

'Are you still there?' Jassy said.

'Yes I've got you on speakerphone. No I'm not coming out. I'm heading for an early night actually. I'm in my PJs.'

'Lulu, it's only quarter to eight!' Jassy said, confused. 'Are you ill?'

'No, I'm just tired. All that driving and stuff. And ...'

I hesitated. I'd seen some sentimental post on Facebook once that said, *Your sister will always keep your secrets safe*. Should I tell her about Joe? Should I confide in her about how I dragged him into bed? No chance, not if I wanted to keep it a secret from the rest of London. She'd see it as some sort of unwise bucolic romance and I'd find myself in her next book.

'And what?' she said.

I couldn't stop myself from talking about him. 'Do you remember Joe Field? The neighbour who fixed my puncture?'

'The chap who popped off and popped back?'

'Yes him. Well his daughter – he has a daughter Ivy – was unwell and she had meningitis and we had to get the rescue services out.'

'Wow, how do you know?'

'I was round at his house and she threw up and I went upstairs to see her and she had that rash—'

'Hang on! You were round at his house?'

Bugger. Why did I say that? TMI.

'Yes he invited me round for a meal.' I must have been pissed to let this nugget of information slip.

'Oh did he indeed? Well look at you! A rural interlude as soon as my back is turned!' Jassy's voice rose several octaves into a squeak.

I knew it. 'No it was just—'

'But he was rather gorgeous as I recall. Rather hunky and *big*.'

Well yes he was certainly ... *shut up.*

'Anyway, that's why I'm tired. I haven't been sleeping well (*for various reasons*) ambulances and stuff and all that driving. I need some sleep.'

'Wow, and is she okay?'

'Yes, I think she's going to be fine.'

'Well what shall I say if Benedict turns up looking for you?'

'Jassy, I don't care. Tell him I've got smallpox or something.'

Jassy rang off and I carried on knocking back Benedict's champagne. More out of cussedness than anything. I didn't really want it. Apart from anything else it was giving me heartburn.

I did a bit of channel hopping and eventually found a gritty police series set in Los Angeles where a sullen detective was in hot water for shooting someone who had clearly deserved it. He was definitely manly, I thought. With his stubble and LAPD badge and gun. I bet he could change a tyre. Even his smart and sassy ex-wife seemed to find him irresistible.

I did a bit of hiccupping, dragged myself off the sofa and

went to the bathroom to find some heartburn tablets. There were none in my cabinet so I looked in Benedict's. For all his healthy, ecological lifestyle and bike riding and gluten avoidance he suffered from heartburn all the time. I found three packets and a bottle of some vile pink gloop. And behind it was an unopened pregnancy test.

Really?

Had I bought this?

I took it out and looked at it, wondering if I was going mad. Or had in fact already gone mad and forgotten.

Nope, there was no way this was mine.

I looked at myself thoughtfully in the cabinet mirror. I didn't look that good actually. A bit blurred and pale. I went to sit on the sofa and tried to think.

So let me get this straight: someone had bought a pregnancy test and left it in Benedict's bathroom cabinet.

Had they had 'an accident'?

Or was she trying to get pregnant? Was he? Were they? He'd always made it perfectly clear he didn't want children. I didn't think I had either. His horror at the possibility of me being pregnant had been obvious. So what was this doing here? Who had bought this? That blonde – what was her name? Tess?

But they can only have known each other for five minutes – *hadn't they?*

God I was stupid. Who knows how long this had been going on? Certainly long enough to have to think about pregnancy. Planned or otherwise. But we had always agreed we didn't want children. How many times had he rolled his eyes at some baby crying on the tube or a toddler kicking the back of his seat on a plane?

I felt tears prickling my eyes. I took a deep breath.

Bastard.

I picked up the champagne bottle and drained what was left in it in one long, throat-stinging swallow. Horrible.

There, that would teach him.

*

I stayed awake long enough to get into bed and I woke at about five thirty bursting for the loo. There in the bathroom bin was the pregnancy test. So I hadn't dreamed it then?

I went back to bed and dozed for a bit and then I went to find some aspirin and a glass of water. And then I snoozed a bit more. Hunger got the better of me at about six thirty and the thought of the bakery down the street – the air thick with the scent of cinnamon and sugar – called to me like a siren song.

I was out and back within ten minutes carrying a large full-fat latte with two sugars and a selection of Danish pastries. A cinnamon swirl, a croissant, a pain au chocolat and a maple pecan thingy. This was a sugar crisis of epic proportions.

I kicked off my shoes and sat in bed to have my breakfast, propped up by Benedict's hypoallergenic pillows. I thought some more about what I was going to do. Things I was going to say to him. What possible excuses could he come up with?

I woke up again just after nine o'clock, covered in flakes of pastry and shards of icing. I needed to get myself sorted out. I couldn't spend the day eating and lounging about. Particularly as I didn't have any proper food in the house. And I might not have a daily commute that was longer than twenty steps but I did have a book to sort out and an increasingly irritated editor and agent to placate. I was also rather sticky and had a wedge of pain au chocolat stuck to my face. I'd end up with type two diabetes as well if I carried on. I needed to get a grip.

I made myself a list.

1) Throw out all B's hideous food.

2) Buy nice, proper food. And some wine.

3) Change the bed!!!! Consider buying new sheets. And pillows. And duvet.

4) Phone Sally to thank her for use of house ~~and her neighbour~~ and apologise in a grovelling way for lateness of book.

5) Get book finished.

6) Stop fantasising about Joe – just stop it!

Right. That should keep me going for a few weeks. First things first. I went to find that bag of kale and chucked it down the waste disposal.

Chapter Ten

Later that day I took my hangover into the nearest estate agent and made an appointment for one of their valuers to come and give my flat the once-over. Christy Church was someone I had seen many times, pounding the streets in her sensible brogues, and she seemed more than delighted to take me on; after all, as we agreed, my place was in a well-maintained block and in a highly desirable area. She didn't envision any trouble at all selling it and estimated six to ten weeks maximum before she got an acceptable offer. I handed over a spare set of keys and went off to find coffee and some paracetamol.

Sitting in the café window I watched the traffic stopping and starting and getting snarled up and drivers honking at each other. It was a miracle anyone ever got anywhere if it was always like this. I pulled apart a raspberry muffin I had somehow ordered as well as my cappuccino and thought some more about what I was going to do.

I checked my phone every couple of minutes, wondering if I was going to get a flurry of messages from Benedict. If he had spent the night on Percy's hard leather sofa his back was probably killing him and he'd be in the mood to try reconciliation. On the other hand he might have had more comfortable places in mind where he could lay his weary head. Bastard.

I finished, paid the bill and hopped on the tube. There was someone who *was* sending me a battery of text messages and I couldn't avoid her any longer.

*

'So when am I to expect *Choose Yes* – any time soon or is it going to be another six months? The publishers are screaming at me. I hope you realise that.'

I flopped down into one of her armchairs. 'I'm sorry, Sally, really I am. I had a bit of a crisis and well – I got distracted. You know how it is.'

She harrumphed a bit. Perhaps I hadn't been grovelling enough yet?

'I thought that's why you went down to Devon again. To get your shit into some sort of order? How was the house by the way? It must be five months since I went there. I don't know why I keep it on sometimes. Henry thinks I should sell it and buy somewhere in France. We last went to Devon for my cousin's hen weekend just before Christmas. Catrin wanted to go to Jamaica and I told her straight, I didn't have the time and she didn't have the money. Her wedding is already getting completely out of control what with bloody scrolls and fairy light curtains and frigging almonds in gauze bags. I've told her no one wants them. People will be suing her for broken teeth and cracked dentures. Anyway, four weeks Saturday it will all be over and she'll be Mrs St John Payne. Can you believe that? No one is called St John these days are they? Where the hell did she dig him up? Still if he's what she wants, who am I to argue? Three husbands. I'm no expert.'

'In answer to your original question, Barracane House was fantastic, Sally. Needs a few draughts fixing but it was great. I bet it's even better when it's not snowing.'

'Ahh did you have snow? Fuck. I've always wanted to be there when it snowed.'

'It didn't last. Just long enough ...'

I stopped. Any minute now I was going to put my foot in it and talk about him. I didn't want to talk about him.

'Anyway, *Choose Yes*. I thought you said it was going well?'

Sally paced around the office and went to look out of the window. Far below the traffic along the Embankment was the usual stop-start jumble, brake lights gleaming in the dull afternoon.

'It was going well,' I said, 'it was going very well. I just came back because of – well, various reasons.'

Sally sighed. 'So go on, what's happening now?'

'I split up with Benedict. I came back earlier than he was expecting and found him with a little blonde companion. He almost talked his way out of that but now there's a pregnancy test in his bathroom cabinet that is nothing to do with me.'

'No! What a complete bastard!'

'Quite. He stamped off to stay with a friend and I haven't spoken to him since.'

'Good riddance by the sound of it. Never mind him. *Choose Yes*? What's happening there?' Sally tapped her nails against the grimy window. I knew what the problem was: she wanted a cigarette.

'I'm still working on it. I've done a massive rewrite on it, changed the perspective and strengthened Darcy's journey to include some more about her determination to make the business work.'

'Yes yes yes, this all sounds excellent, Lulu, but when can I get my hands on the bloody thing? I've had to invent a lot of reasons for the delay. Poppy over at Finch and Murray was being her usual enthusiastic self but I could tell she was tetchy. You're going to miss your slot if you're not careful.'

I was suddenly rather irritated. 'So I miss my slot. So what, Sally? What is Poppy going to do? Come over here and give me a smack? I don't think so. I've given them stuff over the years that's made them a fortune. I've never missed a deadline. I think just for once they might cut me some slack.'

'Don't sulk,' Sally said. She opened the window, letting in the noise from the traffic below us and with it a gust of rain. She closed it again with a grunt of annoyance. 'This must be the most miserable spring on record. I'll have to go up on the roof to the hut. Bloody smoking regulations. What's the matter with people? Everyone seems to have basic human rights but me. Why haven't I got the right to frigging smoke when I want to? I own this office, I should be allowed to smoke in here.'

'Then smoke,' I said. 'I'm not stopping you.'

'Complaints from the management committee,' she said. 'Do you want to come up with me?'

'No, not really. Why don't you take Jassy and me out to lunch any more? We used to have some great times. Remember?'

'Publishing's not like that now and you know it,' Sally muttered. She was already pulling on her raincoat and digging about in her handbag for her cigarette case. 'So when can I have this much changed and much promised work?'

I thought about it. I still wasn't satisfied but I couldn't put up with all this nagging.

'End of the week,' I said.

'Definitely?'

'Definitely.'

'Right. Well look, I'm going up onto the roof with all the other criminals for a cancer stick. You go and finish your blasted heroine's journey and I'll see you on Friday. Yes?'

'Yes, yes, give it a rest.'

I left, taking the stairs down the five flights from Sally's office as a sort of nod to exercise. I liked Sally; I liked the relationship we had. She was without fail moody, rude and impatient and Jassy and I were her favourite clients. God knows what she was like with the rest of them. She had the reputation of an attack dog and half the editors in London were terrified of her.

Outside it was getting dark and the afternoon was cold and wet, an English spring at its worst. Why did we always seem to get rubbish weather these days? Was I just imagining my childhood winters had been crisp and cold with every Christmas a white one. Spring a time of sunshine and blossom? I stood for a moment and looked up at the sour sky, tinged to a nasty jaundiced colour by the streetlights.

Devon wasn't like this. Devon had proper starry skies and proper weather and proper men.

Sod it!

I had been doing so well in my attempt to not think about him.

I crossed over and looked down at the river Thames, which was flowing sluggishly, a flotsam of cardboard and sticks wedged against Waterloo Bridge. I could do with a cigarette too if I was honest.

I thought about the progress of *Choose Yes* and felt slightly sick with dissatisfaction. I'd been wrestling with it for months now. I wasn't used to this at all.

Usually the idea became the plot, which became the book. This light-hearted tale of love and happy-ever-after in Oxford amongst the dreaming spires now seemed pedestrian and more than slightly tedious. Perhaps I was too close to it? Perhaps I had read it too many times? I was sure there was at least one more plot hole but to be honest I couldn't be bothered to go looking for it. The copy-edit would sort that out. But was Darcy still a sweet and attractive character or had I now messed about so much that she was, as I suspected, smug and irritating?

I walked along by the side of the river for a few minutes, getting colder and wetter and more miserable.

I collected a couple of bags of groceries, hailed a taxi and went home. I cleared out the rest of the ghastly food Benedict had left in my fridge, wiped all the shelves and sprayed them with the special biodegradable, planet-loving cleaning spray that didn't clean at all as far as I could tell. Instead it left a greasy slick over everything. Then I organised all my additive-rich food inside and made a sandwich. That took care of a couple of hours and I tried to decide on the best place to write. The sofa seemed too soft, the chair in the window too hard. I had a small desk in an alcove where I had successfully churned out thousands of words before now. Today I couldn't settle to anything and I had a mountain of work to get through before Friday. I began to panic.

I calmed down by making some proper coffee in a cafetière and chucking the decaffeinated stuff Benedict liked down the waste disposal. I did a bit more fiddling about with my book and phoned Jassy. She didn't answer and I remembered she was going to some exhibition at the Natural History Museum and had probably turned her phone off. I did a bit of sighing and then went out onto the balcony to have a cigarette. If I was hoping to sell the flat quickly it wouldn't do to have it smelling like a giant ashtray. I wasn't actually sure that I was enjoying smoking again. Which was just as well as the price seemed to have rocketed in the last few years.

I plumped up the sofa cushions and straightened the rug in front of the white pebble gas fire. Then I tweaked the carefully chosen ornaments that Benedict had put on the coffee table next to it. Two glass things we had bought in Murano and a weird sculpture of three things that were supposed to be ducks. Benedict had bought it for me as a birthday present last year when I had been hoping for a cashmere sweater.

I'd dropped enough hints. And I'd dropped the catalogue into his briefcase with the corner of the right page turned down and even the colour and size ringed in red biro.

I went and found a plastic box and packed all of the ornaments away. Then, getting into the swing of things, I went through the whole room picking up stuff that was his. There was a lot. I ended up with two boxes and three black bin liners full of his books, magazines, clothes, maps, chargers and discarded bike-themed gadgets to show him how fast/slow/accurately/brilliantly he was pedalling. Twat.

I had some more coffee and sat out on the windy balcony in my coat to have another cigarette. Perhaps I would develop a terrible nicotine addiction and a rattling cough? I would lie on a couch, pale and wan like a modern-day Mimì from *La Bohème* and blame Benedict. My phone rang. It was my estate agent who already had the lively cough I had been imagining.

'Christy Church here from Church, Barratt and Glym. Do you have a moment?'

'Of course!'

'I want to send one of the chaps round to take some measurements and we are going to need some better photos. When's convenient?'

I looked around. It looked a bit shambolic actually what with my tidying up and chucking out.

'Tomorrow afternoon?' I said, 'I'm having a bit of a—'

'Good. One thirty,' she said. 'We have the spare set of keys you gave us; you don't need to be in. In fact we prefer it if you are out. People get very precious about things and Barry likes to move things, you know. Get the place looking stylish.'

'Of course,' I said.

Never one to waste words, Christy ended the call and suddenly and totally unexpectedly, I began to cry. Proper crying too. Huge sobs and tears and snot and everything. I sank down onto a chair and howled. I cried so hard I gave myself a headache. I hadn't cried like that since I was a child. Probably when some guinea pig or other had died or escaped. Or when Jassy had got the boy I'd been after. That happened a lot.

What was I doing with my life? Was this it? Producing a series of books about love and kindness and tenderness and people meeting their soul mate. Their Mr Right. The love of their life?

I didn't know about any of those things. I might just as well write about life on Mars or ghost hunting or world peace.

They were just as unlikely as finding the one man in the universe who understood me, cared for me and who didn't smell, have any disgusting habits or look like Donald Trump.

God, crying is really exhausting if you do it properly and I don't think the cigarette helped. It made me feel worse than if I hadn't bothered. I sat in the chair for a while after I eventually stopped producing my own personal tsunami and tried to calm down.

*

I was back at Sally's office on Friday afternoon feeling far from happy with life. There was something about this latest book that I knew wasn't right. But I didn't know what it was any more than I knew what was wrong with me. I was half hoping Sally could at least sort out the book, and I didn't have to wait long. She opened the email I had sent her the previous evening. When I sat down in one of her stylish but uncomfortable chairs she didn't waste a moment.

'Thanks for coming in. You look shit by the way. Are you ill?'

'Bit of a cold coming, I think,' I said. Evidently all that time messing about with Touche Éclat and eye shadow had been wasted.

'Look, Lulu, you know I'm one of your biggest fans,' she said.

Oh boy, this didn't sound good. That was the sort of sentence inevitably followed by the word *but*.

'But I have to say this one, what's it called *Choose Something?*'

'*Choose Yes*,' I said stiffly.

'Well it's not quite what I was hoping for. I'll be honest, there are chunks of some of your other books in this one. Now usually that doesn't really matter but this time, well ... I've had a look through and for a start you've already used the name Jake Collins.'

'Have I?'

'In *Best Before Date*. I know you have because it made me think of Jackie Collins. And the sex scene in chapter seven is practically word for word the same as a sex scene in *Five Miles to Midnight*. Did you realise you've just swapped snow for sand? Again I think you could get away with it to some extent, but when both times your MC is wearing – and I quote word for word – *nothing but a smile as big as her need for him. He pulled her down on to his body, hot hard and ready for her, insatiable and knowing.* Then I think you've come a bit adrift.'

My mind whirled.

'Did I?' I said, feeling a bit sick.

I never had conversations like this with Sally. She'd supported me, found me publishers, cut me deals all round the world. It was my – what was it? Seventeenth book? I couldn't actually remember. Eighteenth?

'I thought we were friends,' I said rather pathetically.

Sally made a noise of sheer exasperation. 'Of course we are bloody friends, you daft mare! This has nothing to do with being friends and you know it. This is to do with business. Your business. My business. Can't you see that?'

'Yes,' I said rather sulkily.

'Don't sulk.'

'I'm not.'

'You are. I'm doing this for your own good. Look you're a great writer, you've got a massive fan base, you shift thousands of books. And I want this one to be just as good as the other nineteen.'

'This would be my twentieth book? I didn't realise,' I said.

Sally shook her head at me and sat down with a bump. 'Jassy is working on her fifteenth. She's like you used to be. The Darling sisters. Churning out bestsellers like a well-oiled machine. What's the matter?'

'I don't know,' I said, 'perhaps I've got ...'

Sally held up a hand. 'Don't give me any crap about writer's block. You always said there was no such thing. Two years ago we did a whole live Twitter feed on there being *No Such Thing as Writer's Block*. It created a massive thread.'

'Yes all right.'

'So?' Sally said.

I held my face between my hands and closed my eyes. 'I don't *know*. I feel like I'm in a fog. I can't seem to concentrate. I used to be able to get the words out like a machine gun. Now I'm hard put to string a sentence together. That's why I went to Devon remember? That and Jassy's knee.'

Sally thought for a moment. 'Perhaps you need a proper holiday?'

'I hate holidays; you know I do. Anyway, I think my passport is about to expire.'

'No one hates holidays. Renew your bloody passport. Take some time off. Think about things and recharge the old batteries.'

I sat and gnawed at a thumbnail for a few seconds.

'Old batteries. That's rich. Do you know I'm nearly forty? I know I only admit to thirty-six, but I'm actually thirty-nine. If I carry on like this I'll soon be younger than Jassy. I'll be forty in August.'

'So?' Sally said with a dismissive flick of her hand. 'Who cares? Lots of people knock off a few years.'

'But *I know* I'm going to be forty in August. I care. Nothing changes that. I wrote my first book when I was nineteen. What am I doing?'

'Is this a *why are we all here* moment?' Sally said, tapping a packet of cigarettes on her desk. 'If so, please spare me. We're here to produce books that people buy, Lulu. We've both bought houses and flats and shoes and meals at the Ivy because of it.'

'But what about me?' I said.

'Aren't you happy? Aren't you pleased you have achieved so much?' Sally pulled out a cigarette and looked longingly at it. 'Oh fuck this. If anyone complains I'll say it was you.'

She went and opened the window and lit up, taking in a deep drag of nicotine with a face that registered near ecstasy.

Perhaps I should have one of hers if it guaranteed such pleasure?

'Well? Aren't you?' she said.

'I don't know. I really don't know.'

Sally sat on the window seat and smoked her cigarette, looking thoughtfully out at the Thames.

'I wanted to be a doctor you know,' she said. 'I had all sorts of unrealistic ideas about what it would be like. I'd have been useless at it. I couldn't do chemistry. I went to a girls' grammar school and the science teaching was crap. Brilliant if you wanted to be a teacher or a civil servant but ... well, never mind. Then – here's a funny thing – I wanted to be someone like you.'

'Like me?'

'I wanted to *be* you at one point. Not now obviously because I've married Henry and we have Enid. But some years ago – before I met Henry – I thought that if anyone had it all, it was you. Clever, popular, talented, attractive, successful. And now you're telling me I was wrong?'

'Look, Sally, I'm not so stupid to think a man would solve my problems but I have had a succession of Benedicts. The last one – like Elvis – has just left the building. Jassy has Ralphie. And no I wouldn't want Ralphie Sutton if I were paid. I don't have a Henry. And I don't have an Enid. How is she by the way?'

'Fine. Nearly six. Growing up fast. A nightmare and a delight in equal parts. That's what you get for having a child when you're forty-three so just think about it.'

'Goodness, is she really?' I shifted in my chair, trying to think. 'I have to find something else. I can't seem to focus. Maybe I have executive burnout. Perhaps writer's block actually does exist? And I'm selling my flat. I've told Benedict he has a month to find somewhere else.'

'Bollocks. I know! Go to India and visit an ashram. Learn how to meditate and find your inner whatsit. Isn't that what people do when they have a midlife crisis? Or unlock the secrets of the universe by giving some dodgy shaman in Thailand your bank account details and PIN. That will solve all your problems. There's nothing like having no money for making you focus.'

'Fuck off.'

'Charming.'

Sally stubbed out her cigarette on the windowsill and turned to look at me.

'Seriously, Lu, take some time off. Get over Benedict. You don't have to sell that flat just to get rid of him do you? But you do look shit. In fact you look as though you've spent the last few days crying. I can stall the publishers with this book. I'll tell them some old spiel about you exploring a new genre or researching the Pilgrim Fathers or something.'

I turned away so she couldn't see how close I was to crying again.

'Maybe,' I said, rather crossly.

'There we are then, that's settled. Go away from London. Get away from all this. Use Barracane House all you like. It's going to mean we will be late delivering the next book, but I can sort that with the publishers. Ask them to cut you some slack. Maybe I'll pop down at weekends and see how you're doing. I know! I'll bring Enid. That's a great idea! No sooner do I get her back into school than they spring a holiday on me. I never have any idea what I'm going to do with her. Why is it that the more expensive the school is the shorter the terms are? I keep meaning to keep a log of how many days she actually spends a full day in the classroom. Nature studies and she's out in the grounds looking for beetles in her official fifty-quid wellies. Art appreciation means a ruinously expensive outing to the National Portrait Gallery. Home economics means a trip to Waitrose using the official twenty-quid school clipboards. A couple of days in her company will knock all this nonsense out of your head.'

*

Barracane House.

Devon.

The damp, wind-scored moors.

That incredible feeling of being in the right place.

Joe.

Chapter Eleven

I got back to my flat just before three o'clock. It was a dark, depressing afternoon with freezing rain splattering onto my legs. Bloody English weather. Maybe I did need to get some sunshine.

I changed the sheets, packed a couple of cases, cleaned out the fridge into a cardboard box to take with me so at least I would have a few vegetables and bread. Then I sent a couple of emails and rang Benedict. Of course it went straight to answerphone so I left him a long message telling him to get on with finding somewhere else to live. Eventually I was cut off by the beep so I phoned back and left another message, not quite such a polite one this time and again was cut off. So I phoned back for a third time and told him I'd found the pregnancy test in my bathroom and then called him out for the unprincipled rat that he was.

Then I got back into bed. No I didn't expect to either but it looked too fantastically appealing not to. I slept for a couple of hours and then jammed all my stuff into my inadequate car and set off for Devon. I was just in time to catch the worst of the rush hour. That was clever of me.

Instead of bowling off down the motorway into a Hollywood sunset I found myself stop-starting and swearing my way along the A4 until I reached the M4. And then I stop-started and swore all the way to Reading thanks to the road works and a couple of minor accidents that had been moved onto the hard shoulder ages ago by the look of them. Still, it didn't stop other drivers from slowing down to have a good look. People are so stupid sometimes – what are they hoping to see? Blood? Body parts rolling across the road?

Eventually the traffic thinned out and I got to the giddy heights of fifty miles an hour before I realised I was starving and wanted the loo so I would have to stop again. I pulled into the next services and enjoyed, if that's the right word, the delights of a Friday night motorway service station at its finest. The car park was nearly full and the place was heaving with cross-looking people and crying kids on their way to hell by the look of them. Then I realised it was the start of the Easter holidays. Brilliant. Couldn't have timed that better if I'd tried.

I even considered turning back and leaving it for a day or two before I made my move, but then I saw an information display TV warning of a pile-up and delays on the Eastbound M4 going back into London and thought better of it. Instead I enjoyed the proximity of a furious-looking father, his harassed wife and their two ghastly children. They sat in near silence chomping down huge burgers and buckets of fizzy drinks that would no doubt necessitate another pit stop before too long.

Occasionally the father would shoot a glare at his offspring when they started squabbling and his wife would slap one or the other before it could degenerate into a full-scale row.

I rammed down a weak overpriced latte and a bland overpriced cheese and pickle sandwich, and nursing incipient indigestion hurried back through the rain to my car and pressed on towards the West Country.

Bristol and the Almondsbury Interchange was another joyful experience and delayed me by another hour until I got past Gordano services and ploughed on into the growing darkness.

What in the name of all that was holy did I think I was doing? Until last year I'd managed to avoid going to Devon at all. Now it was as though I was pinging backwards and forwards on elastic.

I knew I was doing the right thing. It might seem ill-planned – well more like un-planned if I was honest – and impulsive but this was something that I would not regret doing. This time I was not being dragged along behind Jassy. I was not escaping from London or my boredom or from Benedict's pathetic attempts to make up. I wanted to go. I was deciding to do this for me.

Still, it was bloody miles. I didn't remember Devon being so far last time. Surely someone had moved it or something. Just as I thought I must be nearly there I would see a signpost with another unfeasibly large distance outlined on it. By ten thirty the roads had cleared but I think my hands had fused to the steering wheel like a couple of crab pincers. I would probably have to call the AA and be surgically removed from the car at some point.

I reached Barracane House just before midnight and stumbled around by the back door, my legs almost numb, looking for the key, hoping against hope that I had put it back in the right place when I'd left last time. Eventually I had the bright idea of switching on the torch in my mobile, which made things much easier.

Once inside the house I made a lot of noise and switched on several lights. Well there might be a party of mice enjoying themselves somewhere and if there were I'd rather not see them. The Aga was still keeping the winter chill off the house and I put the central heating on. I'd insisted I was going to pay Sally during my stay so I didn't care about boosting the electricity bill. If I hadn't been so tired I might have had a glass of wine or put a match to the wood burner. Instead I lugged my cases upstairs and went to bed.

The sheets were cold and smooth under my back and for a few minutes I lay in the darkness and wondered if there was a hot water bottle somewhere that I could use. I tried to weigh up the benefits of going downstairs to find out against the definite disadvantage of having to find my dressing gown and slippers but having decided I would buy an electric blanket, I settled it by falling asleep.

*

I woke to another very black and wet morning. I pulled back the curtains and sat up in bed with my first cup of tea. The view was of nothing but the darkness. It was both a bit worrying and at the same time rather exciting. Outside I could hear gusts buffeting against the window and the occasional harmonica-like howl I recognised as the wind negotiating the letterbox.

Once I had sorted breakfast out, I would drive over to the local supermarket and stock up. I would buy lots of healthy food. Fresh vegetables and fruit. Perhaps I should get skimmed milk and low-fat stuff so I didn't improve on the writer's arse I was developing. Then I would drive into Stokeley and look around. I knew there were some baker's shops there. They might sell doughnuts, not that I wanted one. Or some organic seeded bread. I definitely didn't want that, the mood I was in.

I finished my tea, showered and dressed. By the time I had decided what to wear it was getting light and I could see outside to the battered and dull landscape that surrounded the house.

Half an hour later I battled – and I do mean battled – my way against the wind and into my car. It couldn't always be like this, surely? This had to be a one-off. A sort of once-in-a-lifetime Michael Fish moment?

I was unfairly annoyed with Devon for a second. I wanted it to be as I had imagined it. Distant moorland stretching romantically on towards the horizon. Wind-blasted trees and strange rocky outcrops. A lone bird stretching its wings against the cerulean sky. Instead it just looked rather dull and neglected. High on the slope above the house there were some scrubby-looking ponies standing with their backs to the wind, their tails blowing over their haunches.

I drove down the lane and out to what passed for a main road. This just meant two cars could safely pass without one of them having to scrape their paintwork on the hedge and pull in their wing mirrors. Eventually I found a road wide enough to have paint marks down the middle and an actual sign indicating that Stokeley was a mere five miles away. Speaking as someone who has been known to go out in my (smart) pyjamas for milk from the shop at the end of my road, this seemed quite startling. Five miles! Still it was a nice enough drive with hardly any traffic on the road and some lovely if rain-smudged views out of the window.

I wasn't quite as controlled as I had intended once I got to Superfine Supermarket – *We love your food as much as you do.* And several items with dubious health benefits sneaked into my trolley. And I did find an electric blanket, which filled me with unexpected delight. I was feeling quite perky by the time I got to the checkout where an assistant in a regulation purple check overall and a name badge identifying her as Maureen inspected my purchases with admiration as she scanned them through.

'Love a bit of cheese I do,' she said, 'but them doctors dared me to eat it. Dared me. And bread? Don't talk to me about bread. I could eat bread all day. My boy said to me: *Mum, you're an addict you are*. A breadaholic.'

She picked up the packet of Wagon Wheels that was trying to coyly hide under a pack of baking potatoes. 'And I haven't dared have one of them since I was a child. Although I did have one the other day come to think of it. And they were half the size, as I remember. Half! Or perhaps I'm twice the size and that's what's changed.'

Eventually we got to the end of my shopping and Maureen moved on to the next customer who had a trolley filled with ready meals and biscuits.

'Chocolate Hobnobs,' I heard her say with a drool of regret, 'my doctor dared me to eat those. Dared me.'

It seemed there was a lot of food in the store that posed an imminent hazard to Maureen's well-being and I quickly wheeled my stash off in case some of it had an adverse effect on her.

Making my way back home I looked out for signs that I might remember from the last time I'd been there. My heart did a little leap of triumph as I passed the Cat and Convict. There was a chalkboard outside advertising *Friday night Curry and a pint of Cat's Piss.* It sounded less than great but what would I know? It couldn't be far now, and it wasn't. A mile or so down the road I saw a metal signpost, painted white and green – Lower Tor Farm.

I took a deep breath and swung my car into the driveway. I waited for a few minutes, wondering if Joe would see my car and come out to greet me. But nothing happened. I opened the car door and got out. I could hear the sound of dogs barking somewhere but no sign of life otherwise.

I went up to the front door and knocked. It was a large, iron knocker, heavy and shaped like some sort of pixie or dwarf or something. I could hear the sound of it echoing in the hall. I could imagine it. The flagstone floor, the dark wood coat stand and the door into the kitchen open and welcoming. Perhaps there would be a stew in the Aga for when Ivy returned from school, the meat melting with the hours of slow heat. Minutes passed and nothing happened. I knocked again, louder this time.

'B'ain yer.'

I turned, startled for a moment. A man came round the side of the barn, Joe's two sheepdogs at his feet.

'Hello? Sorry?' I said.

He came a few steps closer, flicking the peak of his battered tweed cap at me in greeting.

'B'ain yer, missus. Gorn backalong.'

I was going mad. The man sounded as though he was talking English and yet I couldn't understand a word.

I repeated the words. 'B'ain yer.'

'Thas wor I sed. Joe b'ain yer.'

'Oh! Joe's not here? Do you know when he will be back?'

My companion flicked the tweed cap again and stuck out his lower lip.

'Carn't say.'

'Later today?' I said encouragingly.

'Ooo no. I shun think so. Gorn.'

I understood that all right. Bugger.

'Well if you see him, would you tell him Lu – Louisa was here. I'm back at Barracane House.'

I almost rummaged in my bag for one of my cards to give him, but then thought better of it. Instead I posted it through the letterbox while the man and his canine bodyguards watched me with interest.

'B'ain yer,' he said again rather slowly as though I was simple.

'No I do understand, but maybe he'll be back later. I mean when does Ivy get home from school?'

He thought long and hard about this one.

'School holidays innit?' he said. 'I'm arter doin' them sheep.'

I translated this. Sod it. They could have gone off anywhere. Scotland, Spain, Turkey, Neptune for all I knew.

'I'll come back,' I said speaking slowly and slightly louder as though the old man was deaf. 'I'm at Barracane House.'

'Happen you is,' he said with a nod, 'happen.'

Great, I'd come here in a burst of enthusiasm, driven for hours, fought my way down the motorway and Joe wasn't here. Instead I seemed to have encountered the village character. My imaginary reunion with Joe had gone all wrong. To add to the charm of the moment one of the sheepdogs went and peed on my front wheel.

If this had been one of my books Joe would have come out of the house, perhaps he would have been dressed in jeans and a checked shirt. No, it was freezing. He'd have his thick Aran sweater on and the waxed jacket. Some battered leather gloves perhaps and a lamb tucked under one arm. No he wasn't posing for a country clothing catalogue, FFS.

He'd stop, look at me in surprise and then grab me and swing me round with delight. But then he'd have to drop the lamb and that wouldn't be very kind would it?

'Louisa, I didn't expect to see you! How wonderful! I can't stop thinking about you.'

No that was ridiculous.

'Louisa! Sweetheart! How I have longed for this moment!'

Even more ridiculous.

I realised that the old man was still watching me. I gave him a brisk farewell and got into my car, hoping against hope that I would be capable of turning it round without scraping anything or running one of the dogs over.

Back in the kitchen I unloaded my shopping. Perhaps Joe would get home, see the card through the door and drive straight over here to see me?

Nope.

I made a sandwich and ate it standing at the sitting room window watching the lane to see if he was coming to see me. I then ate a Wagon Wheel and watched the news. The usual load of death, deceit and disaster and ugly people caught doing things that were unequivocally wrong or incompetent but loudly protesting their innocence and claiming lessons would be learned.

I drank the best part of a bottle of wine and watched a film about a man saving some people from a tsunami. His children never once rolled their eyes at him and he formed an unbelievable relationship with a pneumatically enhanced woman who wore designer swimwear and little else. Then, cursing the fact that I'd forgotten about the electric blanket, I went to bed.

I stayed awake long enough to have a debate with myself as to what I would do if Joe turned up to see me in the middle of the night. Would I let him in and take him upstairs with a seductive smile? Or would I shout abuse out of the window and slam it shut?

Oh for heaven's sake, of course he wouldn't turn up in the middle of the night. If nothing else he had Ivy to consider. And it was blowing a gale and the rain was splattering against the window like gravel. And I had no reason to think that he might – I mean why would he?

Chapter Twelve

I spent the next few days unable to settle to anything. I thought about Benedict and wondered if he was all right; if he'd moved out. All the thoughts I'd had about writing and chilling and relaxing while going for long country walks and breathing in all that clean air didn't materialise into any action at all. And why had I ever thought they would? I mean long country walks and I have always been strangers. The best I can claim is I once walked for miles across Hampstead Heath because I was promised blossom, birdsong and a great pub that did fantastic seafood at the end of it. All I got was sore feet and mud on my new, sensible shoes. And the pub was closed for refurbishment.

Anyway, that's not important. Eventually I got into some sort of routine. Breakfast, sometimes a trip out to Stokeley in order to support local businesses (like the bakery), and then drove home what I thought of as the long way round past Lower Tor Farm. There never seemed to be anyone home and I didn't dare risk driving in to see if Joe was back because I just knew the old codger with the tweed cap would appear and start up again about Joe being backalong or whatever it was he'd said.

In the afternoons I did some more writing, drank large amounts of coffee, ate biscuits and generally messed about. I'd found some distraction in the form of glossy cookery books on the kitchen bookshelf, presumably tomes given to Sally by hopeful publishers and by the look of them never actually opened or used. I decided to give it a go. I don't mean complicated things, but I did make some more soup, taking particular care to screw on the blender lid properly this time, and a stew, which turned out better than expected. I wasn't going to start making bread or pastry or anything. Still, it made a nice change from sticking ready meals into the microwave. Particularly after I'd checked the ingredients of one and found that actual food products as we know them were pretty low down on the list.

I got to day five and realised it was a long time since I had actually spoken to anyone other than the old bloke in the tweed cap, who might have been the local lunatic for all I knew, and various shop assistants. How long did the Easter holidays go on for? Surely Joe and Ivy would have to come back soon?

I wrote all morning, wrestling my heroine into a passionate confrontation with the hero that unfortunately ended with me sitting looking out of the window trying to remember and write down what Joe had done that had made me almost melt. Then I wandered into the kitchen and flicked through the biggest and glossiest cookery book on the shelf, depressingly entitled *Meals for Singles* – I bet that wasn't a bestseller.

I mean you might as well call it *Even Billy-No-Mates Has To Eat Something Other Than Crunchy Nut Cornflakes Sometimes.* The cover illustration showed a perky redhead perched on a bar stool apparently eating a Michelin-starred meal off some elaborate china. By the smug look on her face she was not expecting to be alone for long and doubtless the appeal of her solitary meal was already attracting some hunky blokes to her door. I mean no one sits on a bar stool in full make-up, stilettos and what looked like a Dior vintage frock just to enjoy some toast and Marmite.

I picked up the next one: *Cakes for Lovers*. What the hell did that imply? Making a certain type of cake that would attract a lover? Or a particular cake would satisfy a lover more than another sort? It reminded me of the old Tom and Jerry cartoons when a hot pie is left on the windowsill to cool and someone sneaks past and nicks it. Perhaps I would make a cake? There was no doubt I liked cake. Maybe now I had got to grips with soup I would unleash some untapped talents for baking and what they confusingly call pastry work on *MasterChef*.

Maybe I would – God I was hopeless. Why wasn't I getting on with some writing? That was why I was here after all.

For want of something better to do I found all the stuff I needed and the right cake tins as well, which was nothing sort of miraculous. And then I made a Victoria sponge.

It took me a very long time.

I mean ages.

Weighing things out and cracking eggs and then spilling

sugar all over the floor, which is probably the most annoying thing that can happen in a kitchen, short of pouring boiling oil over your own feet. This meant I had to get the hoover out and it took me a good twenty minutes to remember where it was, plug it in, change the bag, which was strained to bursting point, and remember how it worked. Then I had to look at another book because I only had the Aga to cook in and it didn't seem to have any temperature control.

By now an hour and a half had passed and all I had to show for it was a load of flour over the front of my favourite jeans and some residual crunching underfoot.

Eventually I encouraged the blasted cake into the hotter of the two ovens and I set to clearing up the devastation I had left in my wake. It looked as though there had been a badly behaved playgroup through the kitchen. It wasn't like this for Nigella. She just seemed to swap one cashmere cardigan for another through choice not because she was filthy dirty.

At last I sat down with a very large glass of red wine and realised my feet and my back were aching. This cake-making business was exhausting too. How come Mary Berry looked so trim and clean when she finished cooking? All she had to do was wink at the camera and say *this is a bit of all right*. Perhaps unlike me she remembered to put the flour guard on when she started the KitchenAid? Maybe she had a team of people to scrape the cake mix off the wall?

*

By the time it was done it was nearly seven thirty and I was shattered. I went upstairs and had a shower and put on my warmest pyjamas (SpongeBob SquarePants) and a man's tartan dressing gown Sally had left hanging behind the bedroom door. I even had some slippers; rather disreputable things Jassy had bought me for a joke at Christmas that looked like gorilla feet, hairy and with claws. So I looked a sight. Still when I went back to the kitchen the cake was just about cool enough to wedge together with some raspberry jam. I looked at it with a critical eye and compared it to the picture in the book. There was of course no comparison. Mine looked as though it had been run over. Mary Berry would have wept.

I cut myself a chunk and refilled my wine glass and went to sit next to the fire. Just as I took a bite – I mean the exact second – someone rang the doorbell.

It seemed the *Cakes for Lovers* had worked its magic. There on the doorstep – dressed in a waxed jacket and wellington boots – was Joe Field. And I was still chewing. I had to. Far from being as 'fluffy as a cloud', my cake was claggy, clogging up my palate, gluing my teeth together and resisting my attempts to swallow it. We stood and looked at each other for a second.

'Bwaro,' I mumbled.

'Hello,' he said, running a hand through his curls. He looked me up and down, his expression rather puzzled. 'Are you going to bed?'

I swallowed hard. 'I've been making a *cake*,' I said as though it was an obvious reply.

'Ah, of course,' he said, biting his lip. He was laughing at me – I know he was. And why wouldn't he? I always seemed to be covered in food.

'... and I got a bit messy.'

'Yes, I see. I saw your card through the door.'

'I would invite you in, but well, you know,' I said.

'Of course not, I thought I'd just pop by and see if you were okay.'

The man was always popping. How could I get him to stop? How could I get him to come in at a time when I was dressed, clean, relatively sane and sober? And where had he been?

'I'm fine!' I said a bit too enthusiastically.

We stood in silence for a moment and then we both spoke at once.

'I've been ...'

'You could ...'

'So you're settled in?' Joe said at last.

'Yes. I needed a change. I was finding life a bit hectic,' I said.

'Yes I can imagine. Lots to do.'

'How is Ivy?' I said.

'She's great. She gets tired easily but you wouldn't know we'd had all that drama. My mother called in to sit with her while I came over.'

'I'm so pleased! That's fantastic news.'

His face softened and he smiled. 'Yes. Ivy was asking about you too. Wondering how you were and where you were.'

'Was she? That's amazing! I didn't think she would remember me.'

He shook his head. 'Oh Ivy notices everything. She's taken rather a shine to you.'

We stood and shuffled a bit and I thought well blow it, he's seen me in all my glory I might as well invite him in.

Too late. He spoke first.

'Well I'd better get back. I just wanted to ... you know ... call in and make sure you were okay.'

I fought down the rather lovely memory of him with his shirt off the last time we had met and felt myself blush.

'Brilliant! Lovely! Yes I'm absolutely fine. Very happy indeed,' I said, trying to hide my gorilla slippers by half closing the door.

He stepped away. It was only afterwards that I realised he probably thought I was closing the door on him. That's how daft I am.

'That's good. Of course you are. Well, I'll be off then.'

'Super!'

Super? Since when did I say things like that?

He gave a tight little smile and turned and walked away. A second later I heard a vehicle start up and the gleam of headlights shone out across the darkness. Whatever he was driving sounded pretty heavy duty; maybe it was his Land

Rover. Not one of the poncey Chelsea Tractors you get in Notting Hill with leather seats and air conditioning and Yankee Candle air fresheners hanging from the rear-view mirror, but a throaty roar of something that was probably much muddier and had a bale of straw and a sheepdog in the back.

Buggeration.

I dawdle about the Devon lanes for days waiting for an unexpected sighting of the man, and when he eventually turns up I am dressed like an oversized child, have a gob full of cake, am devoid of any make-up and am wearing gorilla feet slippers.

Just brilliant.

Chapter Thirteen

I was probably coming across as slightly crazy, possibly even weird. It seemed that just about every time Joe saw me I was doing something stupid, wandering about with no shoes on or covered in food. Perhaps I should calm down a bit. If I was going to stay here for any length of time I ought to behave like a normal, local person. What did local people do?

I went and had a shower while I thought about it. Then I narrowly avoided spraying under my arms with some hair-spray instead of deodorant, went downstairs and prepared a civilised breakfast. Toast and marmalade and coffee. I didn't spill anything or drop anything down my front. I could do this. I was after all old enough to know the difference between being a delightfully kooky young woman in the manner of Goldie Hawn at her best and a slightly off-putting eccentric who couldn't be relied upon not to make a scene in a pub.

Of course! I would go to the pub!

I was going to be here for some time so I would make the Cat and Convict my local hang-out. I would be friendly and approachable and take an interest in whatever it was that people did here. Perhaps there would be a fete in the offing or a Women's Institute Sale of Produce? Good decision. I would start today.

I made a pact with myself: I would spend all day working on *Choose Yes* and as a reward for good behaviour I would go to the pub for dinner. I would eat sparingly and sensibly through the day and that would mean I could have something gloriously filling later. And not have to wash up afterwards. And maybe Joe would be there. Or not. It didn't actually matter, did it?

I stuck to my plan, made myself a cafetière of coffee and went to sit next to the wood burner. It was such a great place to work, warm and comfortable, and when I needed something to look at and think, there were few things better to look at than a fire. I got right into my writing in a way I hadn't been able to do for a very long time. Although somewhere along the line I managed to eat half a packet of custard creams.

There was some sludgy-looking soup left over from my last attempt to be domestic, so I had that for lunch. I was doing well. Apart from the salt and vinegar crisps. But they were part of a multipack and everyone knows they aren't as full as single ones. #*Clutchingatstraws*.

At five thirty I set off for the Cat and Convict. Then I turned the car round and went back home to pick up my laptop so I could check my emails while I had the chance for reliable Wi-Fi. If I was the only one in there because there was something more interesting going on that evening I wouldn't have to read old copies of the parish magazine.

I'd almost set off again when I remembered my laptop was almost out of charge so I went back for the charging cable. Honestly you wouldn't think there were so many things to consider. I'm sure life wasn't so complicated back in London. But then in London there weren't roads with grass growing down the middle, unexpected views of moorland and distant glimpses of snow, packed hard against the rocks on the horizon. I stood for a moment watching a buzzard soaring above me, circling lazily in the still evening air and felt a jolt of pure happiness shoot through me.

In the Cat and Convict there were a few people already there propping up the bar, and some nice tables free. I went to sit down near a handy plug socket and opened my laptop.

''ere she is! Nice to see you agin.'

It was Pete the barman, standing next to me, wiping his hands on what looked suspiciously like the same tea towel he had been using the last time I was there.

'Oh hello. It's Pete isn't it?' I said, trying to look approachable and pleasant and not as though I was still worrying about his Food Hygiene Rating certificate.

He stood grinning broadly at me for a moment and then handed me a menu.

'Once seen ne'er forgit!' he said. He sounded pleased to be remembered. 'So what kin I getcha, me duck?'

I translated and thought for a moment. 'A large glass of red wine and—'

'Pie du jewer is snake and pigmy,' he said, chuckling at himself, 'just kidding you, me duck. Steak and Kidley I means to say. With mash, chips or bless me, *both* if you'm feeling adventurous?'

Pie and chips. Yes, and Joe wasn't there to watch me eat it. Perhaps I'd risk it.

He brought me back about half a bottle of wine in a large glass and ten minutes later a pie the size of a small hatbox accompanied by a glistening pile of chips and an apologetic-looking salad garnish, which Pete nodded at with some pride.

'There you is me duck. I know you ladies like a bit of greenery.'

Oh well.

Over at the bar three elderly men were silently downing pints of beer and staring at their reflections in the mirror behind the bar. Another was reading something on an iPad and a fifth was doing a crossword. Pete decided to lighten the atmosphere with some piped music and switched on a selection of country and western music that had the beer drinkers frowning in annoyance until one of them yelled at him to turn it off.

'Jes tring to raise the tone,' he grumbled, 'and mind yewer language, Dick Marrick, ladies present.'

The men all turned to look at me and I blushed over my pie and tried to chew daintily.

'Waiting to see Joe Field I'll be bound,' Pete said with a cheerful wink.

'Who is?' asked one of the beer drinkers – distinguished by his jaunty maroon knitted waistcoat.

'You'm blind as a white cat with a blue eye,' Pete said, wiping the bar down with his trusty tea towel.

They all turned to look at me again.

'Oh!' said the waistcoat wearer. 'I see.'

Pete turned the music back on – a selection of slightly less frantic oldies – and the beer drinkers went back to their self-appraisal. The man with the crossword read out a clue and the others sucked their teeth and offered inaccurate suggestions.

Pete came out from behind the bar, his tea towel tucked into his belt.

'Now how are you getting on, me duck? Few more chips with that?'

I swallowed my mouthful. 'I'll never finish all this lot, but thanks all the same.'

He dabbed at the next-door table with the end of his tea towel. 'Joe Field don't often come in mid-week.'

'No?' I tried to look disinterested. 'Never mind.'

'More likely tomorrow lunchtime, what with Ivy in school and that,' he added with a meaningful look.

'Really?'

'But sometimes he comes in of a Friday evening when young Ivy's off at Brownies. Curry night, Fridays are. Curry and a pint of Cat's Piss. Very popular that is. I'll mention you was looking for him when I see him, shall I?'

'God no! I mean no thank you,' I said, taking a gulp of my wine.

What on earth was I doing here? Making a fool of myself. It would be all over the local paper if I weren't careful.

Obsessed and sex-starved London exile looking for love. Lulu Darling, ~~35~~ 39, was seen in the Cat and Convict yesterday pretending to work on her laptop but in fact hoping for hunky farmer Joe Field to turn up and take her back to his farmhouse where he would ...

Would what?

What was I hoping to achieve? More of the same? More hot sex? I thought about it for a second. Worse things could happen, I suppose. But really, I just wanted to see him, talk to him. Find that feeling again, the one that had made me do this in the first place.

I realised Pete was still hanging about, rubbing at a couple of the gleaming horse brasses hanging from the mantelpiece on leather straps.

I put my knife and fork together. 'Thanks, that was really great.'

Pete picked up my plate. 'Puddin', me duck?'

'No, no I'm full; I couldn't manage anything else. Just the bill please.'

He took my plate away and I opened up my laptop again. A couple of emails pinged in. Discounted holidays in India, final reductions on some overpriced handbags.

The bar was filling up now with some jolly-looking people and an older, tweedy couple who seemed to know everyone. They had brought in two muddy spaniels that were obviously torn between wanting to lie by the fire and being only too aware of the pub cat lurking on the chair next to it.

The woman removed one of her tweed layers and came to warm herself in front of the fire. She threw me a friendly look.

'Evening. Raw out there isn't it?'

'Very,' I said.

I typed a few words, aware that she was watching me.

'Not seen you in here before, just visiting?'

In my usual London haunts no one would dream of asking such a question, so it was a bit unsettling.

'Um yes, I'm staying up the road for a few weeks. Working.'

'Just – I think I know you? Have we met?' She pulled off her gloves and extended a cold hand. She was probably in her sixties, very slim with bright intelligent eyes and a nose glowing red with the cold. 'Isobel Trevose.'

'Lulu Darling.'

She grinned. 'Lulu Darling? I knew it! The writer? I thought I recognised you. How marvellous. I'm such a fan.'

She turned to where her companion was ordering drinks and almost fell over a spaniel crouched behind her feet and casting terrified glances at the cat.

'William! Come over here. You'll never guess who this is!'

By now of course everyone in the pub had turned and were unashamedly staring at me.

Maroon Waistcoat pushed his spectacles up his nose.

'Who is she then? Not that Holly Willoughby, is it?'

Isobel's companion came over, pulling off his fleece hat. He stared at me a bit, looking nonplussed. He was very tall and his ruffled grey hair stood up like a crest.

'Sorry. I'm sure I should know ...'

'It's Lulu Darling, Will! The writer! I've got all her books. Well, I did have until I gave them to the church jumble.' She rolled her eyes at me and then peered down at my open laptop. 'Honestly, men! Are you working on your next masterpiece?'

'Well, sort of.'

'What's it about? No, don't tell me, I want it to be a surprise. I've only just finished one – the one where the girl fell down the cliff and had to be rescued. And then she met that man with the Labrador and she thought he didn't like her because he ignored her on the train and then she found out he was deaf. That one.'

'*Listen to My Heart*?'

'That's the one. I thought it was terrif. And before that I read the one about the doctor who knocked the nurse on the bike down. And she was concussed and kissed him in the ambulance.'

'*Best Before Date*?'

'Yes and then ...'

Will put a glass of red wine in her hand.

'Izzy love, I think you're probably interrupting Miss Darling's train of thought.'

Isobel took a slurp of wine and stared at me, her eyes round. 'God, I probably am. I'm terribly sorry.'

'It's fine, really. I was about to go anyway. I was just doing some tinkering. I've been writing all day. I needed to get out and I'm not a brilliant cook.'

'The food here is great isn't it? I say, you wouldn't come and talk to our book group would you? We meet every other Thursday. We've just started a new book, the last one was dire. *A Girl in something. Girl in a Garden? Girl in Hysterics?* I can't remember – that shows how good it was. But anyway I'm sure we would all like to hear you instead. Some of the books we read are really hard going with hardly any plot to speak of. The one before last was just a series of pretentious ramblings about an old man with Alzheimer's talking about the war and how he led a bombing raid on Dresden when in fact he'd been in prison for desertion. Connie was incandescent. Her uncle was one of the Few. What do you say?'

'Um I don't know,' I said, feeling a bit winded by Isobel's vivacity. Will meanwhile had gone to sit at the adjoining table and pulled a packet of pork scratchings out of his coat pocket. He threw one each to the spaniels and they caught them with an ease born of long practice. The cat hissed at them.

Isobel clapped her hands together. 'Well, look, think about it. I'll leave you in peace. We meet in the Village Hall this week at two thirty; you'd be awfully welcome, even if it's just for a chat. We've never had a celebrity before. Although Sue brought her mother along once – she was engaged once to someone in a group. The Tremeloes, I think, or it could have been the Merseybeats, I can't really remember. She had some great gossip though once she'd had a couple of glasses of vino.' She reached into her handbag, pulled out a card and handed it to me. 'That's me, give me a ring if you like.'

She went to sit down at the adjoining table and I packed up my laptop, coiling up the cable.

'We've not driven you away have we?' she called across.

'Wouldn't blame her,' Will said.

'No not at all, I was on my way home anyway.'

I made my excuses and got as far as the door before I remembered I hadn't paid the bill and had to go back.

Pete took my money and I dropped the change into the half coconut shell by the till marked 'tips'.

'I see you made a friend,' Pete said, nodding his head towards Isobel. 'That's nice. You want to ask her about Joe – she'd know.'

'I'm fine, really it's not important.'

Too late. Pete shouted across the room to where Isobel and Will were studying the menu.

'Izzy me duck, where's yon Joe got to? Young lady here would like to know.'

'No I wouldn't, I mean it's really not important,' I said, feeling rather hot and bothered.

'Joe? Who wants to know?'

Pete pointed at me. 'You want to ask Izzy. She's his mother after all.'

I turned back open-mouthed. Isobel pulled a funny face and waggled jazz hands at me.

'Guilty as charged,' she said, 'we'll both have the chicken pie, Pete.'

Chapter Fourteen

Over the next couple of days, I read through *Choose Yes* again and was frankly appalled. No wonder Sally hadn't liked it. It was cobblers. I should have known better. I couldn't quite understand how it had happened. I was well known for being able to churn out at least one publishable book every year; I'd never had any problem before. I knew what my readers liked and I gave it to them. Sometimes with a medical slant, sometimes a hint of mistaken identity, adultery or unexpected illness. Everyone was happy in the end; the Amazon reviews were always very cheering. Well, nearly always. There's always someone who likes to dole out snide comments and one star when they obviously haven't read the book at all and couldn't produce one themselves if Jilly Cooper held their hand all the way through.

I had taken Sally's hard copy of the blasted book to work through and a box of sharpened pencils. Page by page I crossed things out, scribbled notes, screwed up pages in disgust and then had to smooth them out again. It was really boring. I mean, the book was boring and that's unforgivable.

Eventually after a couple of days I came up for air and realised I needed to do something drastic. Right. What? How drastic?

I was out of milk and bread and biscuits, three things I couldn't do without, so I went out shopping first thing, wondering if Superfine did home deliveries. Apparently not.

Maureen, the assistant I recognised from my previous visits, was there and ready to chat despite the fact that my trolley contained several hazardous foodstuffs.

'Hello again,' she said, examining a chocolate Swiss roll that had found its way into my shopping. She chuckled. 'I remember these. My old mum used to think they was puddin's and she gave 'em to us with custard.'

Brilliant idea, I thought.

'And when we told her they was cake she was mortified. How have you been? Not snowed in that time?'

'No, all fine,' I said.

'Busy day is it?'

'Oh, you know,' I said with a bit of a shrug.

I hardly ever tell people I'm a writer because more often than not the person hasn't heard of you and then it gets embarrassing. Or they have a story to tell about a friend who wrote a book and couldn't get it published. Or they think you earn as much as J.K. Rowling and look at you sideways.

Maureen wasn't about to give up. 'So back to work now?'

'Yes, cup of tea and a Penguin. That will keep me going.'

Maureen looked carefully at the new pack of propelling pencils I'd bought. They were really pretty with patterns of leaves and shells and I never could resist.

'What do you do, me duck? Are you a teacher?'

'No, I'm a writer.'

'Writer. That's nice. I like a good book.'

'Oh yes?'

'Murder. I like a good murder. I can't be doing with all the sloppy stuff. Love and such. My sister lent me a book about a girl who met a billionaire and all they did was argue for two hundred pages until the last chapter when he ups and proposes. Now how can that work eh? You tell me.'

'Difficult,' I agreed, shoving my shopping into bags and wondering how I could change the subject.

'So what do you write?' Maureen said, peering at the calorie values of some ice cream tubs.

'The latest one is a bit of a horror,' I said truthfully, 'but I'm trying to do something about it.'

*

I got back to Barracane House, unloaded my shopping and realised it was Thursday. There was something I was going to do but for a while I couldn't remember what. I made coffee and had some elevenses and scrawled across a few more pages of *Choose Yes* before I remembered Isobel's book group – that was it. I'd been invited to go along by Joe's mother. An opportunity I couldn't really miss if I wanted to find out more about him.

At two thirty I parked outside the village hall, watching half a dozen women filing in carrying books and a couple of cake tins. Inside there was a general hum of chatter that halted quite dramatically when I came in.

'Oh my, you came after all! Look, everyone! It's Lulu Darling! The one I told you about!'

It was Isobel Trevose, hurrying across to greet me, then introduce me to everyone and usher me to a chair next to hers all in the same breath.

'Janice, Mary, Trisha and Hilary. And this is Connie and the one with the plate of flapjacks is Sue.'

The other ladies sorted out teas and coffees and put the cakes out onto plates, sat down, introduced themselves and then looked at me hopefully as though they were expecting me to do tricks or reveal the secrets of the universe.

'So, Lulu, tell us all about yourself,' Isobel said.

'Nothing like putting her on the spot,' Sue said and they all laughed.

'What are you all reading?' I said instead.

Isobel picked up her paperback and showed me. '*Hector's Walk* by Jessie Clara Jones. It's had such rave reviews. Have you read it?'

'No, I never seem to have the time to read other people's books these days,' I admitted. 'I mean I get sent a lot of books but I hardly ever get round to reading them.'

Isobel dropped the book on the table with a dismissive hand. 'Well don't start with this one. We're finding it very hard going aren't we, ladies?'

There was a general hum of agreement.

'Lulu, tell us how you got started as a writer. I'm sure we would love to know, wouldn't we?' said another. I think it was Connie, distinguished by brightly hennaed hair and an orange batik scarf that clashed quite alarmingly.

There was a lot of nodding at this.

I've done this a lot. Hearing about how writers got their toes on the publishing ladder endlessly fascinates people. I've told the story so often I could do it in my sleep.

'I was in my first term in university and I ran out of money after a fortnight. My parents were in China – they were going through the period when they described themselves as travel writers. I think it was just an excuse to keep on travelling. My younger sister Jasmine was at boarding school so she was no use. So I sent a load of my short stories to a magazine editor my father knew and he bought four. In those days you got paid almost immediately, well I did anyway. Perhaps he was just being kind. And he asked me to do some more. They eventually bought a dozen and I made enough money to get through the term without admitting I'd spent my entire term's allowance at the student union on beer and fags.'

Everyone laughed.

'And then he called me in for a chat – he looked like Father

Christmas and his name was Cornelius Maximillian-Alexander – he suggested I write a book. So I did.'

'Just like that?' Sue said.

'Pretty much. And I sent it to him and he sent it on to someone he knew. I didn't have an agent or anything; things were different all those years ago. And then I got an agent – Sally Gardener – and, touch wood, I'm still with her. And then three years later my sister Jassy wrote a book and Sally took her on as a client too and we became this sort of brand – the Darling sisters.'

'You make it sound so easy,' Janice sighed. 'Do you know, I think I might give it a try. I mean with this book being so, well, awful. I bet I could do something just as good. Gosh I hope the author isn't a friend of yours.' She suddenly looked worried.

I laughed. I'd met Jessie Clara Jones at some book launch or other last year and it was mutual dislike at first sight. Particularly after she'd made some disparaging remarks about *chick lit* and *self-published writers* as though they were the scum of the earth. She was the sort of writer who sits up and begs for praise before she's got her coat off and then commandeers the whole room with a lot of self-deprecating tosh until everyone is shouting at her how marvellous she is.

'Well no, but Jessie Clara Jones had a massive hit with her debut and an even bigger one with the following book. I mean you must remember *Knowing Nancy* and the follow-up *Baby Fall*? Well I'm sure *Hector's Walk* will be another bestseller, despite the reviews being a bit mixed. She's got the backing of one of the best publishers in the world and there's been a bidding war for the film rights of *Knowing Nancy*.'

'So what are you writing now?' Sue asked.

'I'm doing a structural edit of *Choose Yes*. I'm nearly six months late delivering it to the publishers. That's why I'm here, trying to get it whipped into shape.'

'And is it going well? No distractions?' Isobel said.

Well, only your son.

'I'm getting there,' I said with a smile. The sort of smile that's supposed to convey how in control and cool I am. I wasn't sure it worked.

'Perhaps we could help?' Janice said, helping herself to a flapjack and pushing the plate towards me. 'What's the problem with it?'

'You're very nosey, Janice,' Mary said.

'Yes? And?' Janice said, taking a bite of her cake.

It was quite good fun actually. Once the talk had veered away from me and on to what makes a good read. The general consensus was it needed to have 1) a heroine who was a bit weird but still interesting 2) a good plot and 3) a satisfactory ending.

I suddenly realised *Choose Yes* didn't have any of these things. Why not, for God's sake? I knew how to create captivating heroines. I could write decent sex scenes without making readers feel queasy but I'd left my main characters still arguing about whether they loved each other or not. No wonder Sally had given me an earbashing. The chatter went on around me as I drank my coffee, gnawed at a rather gritty flapjack and I wondered how to address the problems with my wretched book. The very thought of it was exhausting.

About an hour later after some desultory talk about the problems of fly-tipping, the new recycling bins and various questions about Jessie Clara Jones that I had to avoid answering for fear of legal ramifications, I realised the meeting was breaking up. Janice and Mary were pulling their coats on and talking about what they were going to cook for their evening meals.

Isobel locked up the hall and walked with me to my car. 'So you've met my son?'

'Joe? Yes, he changed a tyre for me when I first came here.'

Her face changed and her eyes widened. 'Oh my God, it's you! You're the woman who saved Ivy's life! Oh my stars! How can I have been so slow? Of course! Lulu! *Louisa.* I didn't put two and two together, I must be losing the plot.' She put her arms around my shoulders and hugged me. 'Thank you so much. If you hadn't said something I don't know what would have happened. I can't bear to think about it.'

'I'm glad I was there,' I said. 'Really it was the paramedics who did the hard work, getting through the snow.'

'Honestly I shall have a few words with Joe when I see him again! Why is it that men only give one half of the story and nearly always leave out the important information?'

At last we had got on to Joe.

'So he's your only son?'

'Yes, he's lovely. Although as his mother I would say that wouldn't I? And when his father died he was absolutely splendid. He took over the farm even though he was barely out of his teens and he did just about everything. I mean Will helped as much as he could but he had his own place to run. Sorry, I should explain, Will is my second husband; we married nearly fifteen years ago. Look, you must come round for dinner. No, I won't take a refusal. We'll come and get you one evening soon and you can come over and let us thank you properly.'

'Really there's no need ...'

'Nonsense! My only grandchild! There's every need! Now—' Isobel started to rummage about in her cavernous handbag and pulled out a diary and a pencil '—next week is a nightmare, the week after is worse, um, um, what about tomorrow? Yes tomorrow. Friday. Are you busy?'

Of course I wasn't busy; after all, I was staying here on my own in an area of the country where the number of people I regularly talked to could be counted on the fingers on one hand.

'Then that's settled. We'll come and get you. No, don't argue – Great Tor Farm. We live at the end of a muddy track and it's easy to miss especially in the dark. Your poor little car would never cope with it. Seven o'clock? Fine.'

I got into my car and she got into hers and then she got out again and rapped on my window.

'You're not a vegetarian are you?' I shook my head. 'No – thank heavens for that! Right, I'll see you tomorrow evening!'

Chapter Fifteen

I was rather excited at the prospect of meeting some new people and finding out more about Joe and Ivy and of course the question that had never been satisfactorily addressed: Ivy's mother.

I got a bit more of the dreary editing work done that morning then went to choose my outfit for the evening. It wasn't easy. A pair of tailored black trousers, a white cowl neck sweater and a grey herringbone jacket. I finished off with some black suede ankle boots. Then I realised the trousers were rather tight around the waist courtesy of all the junk I had been eating and to think of wearing black trousers and a white cashmere sweater to a place where I'd already been warned about the mud was sheer madness. Not to mention the suede boots. I changed into some dark jeans and a white T-shirt topped off with a leather jacket. I looked like a Rock Chick manqué.

Then I tried a dress and heels (ludicrous), a skirt and matching jumper (dull) and eventually went back to the jeans, the white T-shirt and a cheerful red cardigan. By the time I had sorted that out it was nearly six thirty so I went downstairs to watch out of the sitting room window for Isobel to arrive. At six thirty-five I went to find a sneaky glass of red wine to give me a bit of Dutch courage, which is ridiculous when you think I've been to gala evenings at the Mansion House and Hampton Court, even a thing at Sandhurst when I was dating a man who looked like Tom Cruise but who turned out to have obsessive-compulsive disorder and had brought his own cutlery in a Tupperware box.

I finished my wine, washed up the glass in a rather guilty way and put it back in the cupboard. Five minutes later I saw a four by four making its way up the lane so I went to fetch my coat. The front doorbell rang and I went to answer it.

There on the doorstep, looking more blisteringly attractive than even I had remembered, was Joe.

'Oh,' I said rather faintly, wondering if he was going to kiss me and whether he would smell the alcohol on my breath if he did.

'Hello,' he said and he grinned at me, 'my mother sent me to fetch you.'

'Did she?'

Suddenly, as piercing as a knife blade, all I could think of was the way it had felt to have his body on mine, his warm breath on my throat, his hands in my hair.

He leaned forward and kissed my cheek and then he looked at me his eyes sparkling, and I could tell he was remembering exactly the same things. I turned out the light in the hall so that he couldn't see me blushing.

'Ready?' he said.

I picked up the bottle of wine and chocolates I was taking and followed him out into the dark evening. Not the muddy Land Rover this time but a rather smart four by four with leather seats and the heating full on. Joe opened the door for me and waited while I tried to get in elegantly. He got in and looked over at me, his eyes glowing.

'You look lovely,' he said.

I resisted the temptation to say something stupid and said, 'Oh. Do I?'

I mean that's a bit pathetic but it was the best I could do.

'You do,' he said and he looked steadily at me for a moment before starting up the car.

I don't think either of us said anything much during the rest of the journey. It took about twenty minutes to get to Great Tor Farm and I have no idea what he was thinking all the way there, but I was remembering Joe with no clothes on. His mouth on my body, his hands warm and clever. His voice in my ear, the feel of his hair under my fingertips, the way he said my name over and over. *Louisa. Louisa.*

When we eventually pulled up outside his mother's house I was so turned on I could hardly walk. It took a serious effort of will to get out of the car and make my way to the front door.

For the first few minutes I must have appeared to be simple-minded at best. Isobel looked elegant in an olive green sweater, tweed trousers and a beautiful silk scarf at her throat. She was there to meet me with a hug and the tall and equally tweedy Will kissed my cheek and called me a hero. I passed over the wine and the chocolates, then out from behind his legs came Ivy – still wearing her bright yellow Brownies T-shirt – who cannoned forward to hug me round the waist and butt my hipbone with her head.

'I'm so pleased you're back,' she said a bit breathlessly. 'I wondered where you'd gone.'

I put my hand on the top of her head and was surprised how nice it was to feel her warm hair under my palm.

'I'm glad to see you too, Ivy,' I said.

'We went to Cornwall for a holiday.'

A small brown terrier launched itself down the stairs and busied itself circling my feet with excited snuffles and yips.

Will scooped it up. 'Sorry about Frank, he gets a bit excited. Come into the kitchen.'

I followed him into a big, warm room with what I was coming to recognise as a regulation Aga cooker. Will dropped the little dog into its basket, which of course it immediately left in order to drag a tea towel off the Aga rail and run around the kitchen with it.

'Ignore him, he's showing off,' Isobel said, taking a swipe at Frank as he careered past her. 'I hope you don't mind, we usually eat in the kitchen because it's warmer. I did think of opening up the dining room but it's so cold in there you'd have to keep your coat on.'

'This is lovely,' I said and I meant it.

It was a room that had obviously evolved over the years with a selection of beautiful old chairs around a long table and there were wooden shelves along one wall laden with blue and white china, a stack of magazines and catalogues, and a tin box marked 'seed packets'. Along the other wall was a carved church pew with a long tapestry cushion that was occupied by a cat and her four kittens.

I couldn't resist, I had to go over and look at them and they obligingly woke up and yawned before they started wrestling with each other and biting their mother's tail. Ivy knelt down in front of them, entranced.

'Daddy says I can have two of them when they are old enough to leave their mother,' she said. 'Daddy says it's more fun to have two kittens and more fun for them too.'

'I'm sure he's right.'

'I wouldn't want them to be lonely while I'm at school,' Ivy added. 'I think I'd like those two.'

She pointed to a boisterous tabby that now had one of its siblings in a violent headlock.

'They are very cute,' I said.

Well they were. You would have to have a heart of stone not to think so.

As we stood side by side, I felt Ivy slip her hand into mine. It was sweet and totally unexpected.

'And how was Cornwall?' I said.

Ivy grinned up at me. 'We went to a house right by the sea where you could see the tide coming in over the rocks.

And we had sandwiches made with fresh crab from the man who caught them. I didn't think I would like it but I did.'

'I've never been to Cornwall,' I said.

'It was lovely,' Ivy said, swinging my hand with hers, 'to see the sea and everything. Daddy took loads of photographs. You should come with us when we go next time.'

I didn't know what to say to this but luckily Isobel called across to us.

'Come on, Ivy, let's sit down and see how the casserole has turned out. Ivy helped make it. She was very excited when I told her you were coming to dinner. Will, could you grab a bottle opener for the wine, please?'

It was a lovely evening. I sat between Ivy and Will and was told all about the farm and how many lambs they had and Ivy told me about one that had to be gently revived in the warming oven of the Aga. Then she told me about the pony she wanted to have when she was feeling strong enough to look after it. She told me about school and how she liked singing and sports day.

'Ivy won two races in her school sports day last summer,' Isobel said proudly. 'She can run faster than anyone in her class.'

'I'm not sure I can run so fast now,' Ivy said thoughtfully. 'My legs don't seem so quick.'

'That's because you've been ill. You'll get better,' Joe said.

Ivy turned to me. 'Do you remember when I was ill? Daddy said you saved my life.'

'Well I think the doctors saved you. And the ambulance men, they were here very quickly so they could take you to hospital.'

'But you knew what the matter was, didn't you?'

'That was lucky,' I said.

'How did you know? You're not a doctor, are you?'

'No, but I write books and one of the books I wrote was about a nurse who looked after someone with meningitis.'

'I had a bad headache. And I was sick. I was sick all over the bed wasn't I Daddy? It went absolutely everywhere! Even on the floor! Everywhere!'

Isobel tapped on her plate with her fork and sent Ivy a warning look. 'Shall we talk about that another time?'

Ivy giggled.

Isobel raised her wine glass to me. 'Well I'd like to raise a toast to Louisa and say thank you for everything.'

I caught Joe's eye and had to look away blushing.

We finished the meal with a selection of cheeses from a neighbouring farm and shortly afterwards Ivy decided she wanted to sleep in the room she had at her grandparents' house and went upstairs to bed. We had coffee, Isobel opened the chocolates I'd brought and we sat chatting for a while longer. Then just after ten, Joe stood up.

'I'll take you home, Louisa,' he said, 'if that's okay?'

'Fine,' I said.

Fine? *Fine?*

I was so giddy with the thought of being alone with Joe

again that I perversely started to dawdle. I carried on chatting with Will about the summer weather in the area and then Isobel asked me what my life was like in London. I entertained her for a few minutes with stories of parties and premieres and did a bit of casual name-dropping. It all seemed rather trivial and she hadn't heard of half the people I mentioned. I started to talk about the book club the previous day and she told me about Janice and the problem she had been having with her alcoholic husband.

Joe was patient, sitting with his coat on, watching me whilst making a fuss of Frank the terrier who had been sitting with his nose as close to the Aga as he could get for the previous hour.

'Oh well, I suppose we'd better let you get off,' Isobel said at last, 'but you must promise to come back.'

'Of course, and thank you for a lovely evening,' I said.

Will and Isobel watched from the front door as we got into Joe's car and they waved us off. Then there was the twenty-minute drive home.

We didn't speak at all. I could feel the tension in the car building as the seconds ticked past. I watched Joe's hands on the steering wheel, strong and confident. At last we reached Barracane House. There was a new crescent moon, sharp and beautiful in the sky, seemingly balanced on the chimney. The car stopped. Joe got out and came to open my door.

I hopped out and looked up at him. His face was shadowy, half hidden by the blackness of the night.

'Do you want coffee?' I said.

How much of a cliché was that?

I held my breath while he stood watching me.

He shut the car door and took a step forward, unbuttoned my coat, put his hands inside, feeling my waist, my back, his thumbs brushing against my breasts.

'I don't want coffee,' he said at last.

'You don't?' My voice was faint with my desire for him.

'I don't.'

'Tea?'

'No.'

His hands slipped under my T-shirt and I shivered as the cold night air hit my warm skin.

He bent his head towards me, his mouth brushing my cheek, his breath warm against my ear. 'I've missed you, Louisa. I couldn't forget that night. I tried but I couldn't forget you. Your face, the scent of your hair.'

My knees began to give way. He pushed me back against the car and kissed me. Gently at first, tasting my mouth with his.

'Oh Louisa,' he said.

I heard myself whimper and I closed my eyes, blotting out his face, his shadow falling on mine in the starlight.

We went into the house and he eased my coat off my shoulders dropping it by my feet. I knew what he was thinking. I certainly knew what I wanted. I kicked off my boots; he took off his shoes.

We went upstairs to my room in the darkness, feeling for

buttons, zips, pulling at each other's clothes without speaking, dropping them on the stairs, on the landing, on the bedroom carpet. I knew the feel of the rug by the side of the bed under my bare feet. I shuffled backwards, feeling the edge of the bed against my calves. I fell backwards. He fell with me, his weight against me hard and hot.

He turned me and stroked my skin with little murmurs of pleasure. He tasted my neck, my throat. He took my fingers into his mouth and softly bit the pad of my thumb. He moved my hand to touch him. He touched me, searched for me and found me, pushing, pushing until suddenly, overwhelmed with pleasure, I cried out against his shoulder, my teeth grazing his warm skin. Still he was not done with me and he was still for a moment while I caught my breath and waited for the sensations rippling through me to stop.

Then he reached over and turned on the bedside lamp. I blinked and turned my head away at the sudden brightness. He pulled back and held my face in his hands.

'Look at me,' he said. 'I want to see you.'

I closed my eyes, turning away.

He turned my face back towards his.

'Look at me, Louisa,' he whispered.

I looked up at him above me. He locked his gaze with mine. It was the most intimate moment of my life, the connection between us absolute and private.

I felt as though I was falling, and I think I cried out, my arms around his neck.

'Louisa, ah yes.'

He gave a long, low cry and was still.

I cried then, big tears of pure emotion, spilling down my face and onto the pillow. He kissed me and held me while I caught my breath and my pulse returned to something like normal. Then he pulled me round to lie against him, my hand flat on his shoulder. I could feel his heart thudding against mine.

'I was watching you all evening, thinking about you. Remembering. Wondering if you felt the same way. I needed you so much,' he said at last.

'So did I,' I said.

He gave a shaky laugh. 'Thank God for that!'

'It's nothing like riding a bike, is it?'

'Nothing like it,' he agreed with a chuckle.

He dropped a kiss on my neck and smoothed his hand over my breasts, making me tremble.

What now? I thought. Now that we were in my bed, our bodies tangled together, his sweat on my lips. The minutes passed. I have no idea how long we lay there. Touching, exchanging little kisses.

'Good job Ken is seeing to the sheep tomorrow morning. But it's late, I should go,' he said, his mouth against my hair.

My heart sank.

'But I really don't want to.'

I kissed him. 'You could always stay,' I said, rather casually. As though I didn't really care one way or the other.

We were adults after all; we'd had sex. People did it all the time; we could be cool with this.

Every one of my brain cells, every neurone, every last strand of mitochondria in every atom in my body was willing him to stay. But I wasn't going to beg or seem desperate. Although it did cross my mind for a second.

Instead, I mentally went through the contents of my fridge and freezer, wondering what I could offer him for breakfast in the morning. There were a few croissants and a new pot of apricot jam. There were eggs from a local farm, the yolks wonderfully yellow. There was some bacon in the freezer; I could run the packet under the hot tap to defrost it I suppose. Oh and I had some mushrooms too, little button ones that I could fry in butter. I might not be able to make a cake without plastering myself in goo, but I could do breakfast. I was sure of that. But would he want cereal? I didn't have any but I did have sachets of instant porridge. Not very romantic. Not that I wanted to be romantic, but it seemed sexier to cook a man a full English than to dole out a bowl of synthetically flavoured pap. I had a fresh bottle of orange juice. Tea, coffee and plenty of milk.

Result.

Right, so ...

I drew breath to ask what he wanted to do. And then I realised he was asleep. I watched him for a few seconds, his breathing steady and relaxed, his head deep in the pillow, his long eyelashes brushing against his cheek. I bit back a smile, reached across slowly and turned out the lamp. Then I lay awake in the darkness, and thought about things.

Him obviously and me, and what the blue blazes I was doing.

I was supposed to be here to rewrite, edit, tweak my book, thrash it into shape. Whatever you want to call it I was not supposed to be having rampant sex with the next-door neighbour. A man with a daughter who wanted a pony. He had a farm and a lifestyle so far removed from mine that it was laughable. This man had sheepdogs in the back of a muddy Land Rover. He had a barn next to his house full of bales of hay. He didn't just have a farmhouse kitchen he had farmhouse everything. He was probably on first-name terms with the local vet. He'd been in the Young Farmers Club. I was certain that no other man I had ever had a relationship with had stuck his arm up a sheep's nether regions during lambing.

And Benedict. Had I properly got rid of Benedict? Theoretically I was still getting over the break-up of our relationship. It didn't seem to be too difficult.

Then just before I fell asleep another thought crossed my mind to wake me up. What the hell was Joe doing with me? A woman who up until now had thought of the country as just the space between towns. Whose only occasional windows onto rural life were *The Archers* Sunday morning omnibus – when half the time I didn't know what was going on – and *Countryfile*. Who was surprised to find that farms really smell.

Who on *Desert Island Discs* had asked for solar powered hair straighteners as a luxury.

But it had been wonderful; I couldn't deny that. I'd been attracted to Joe from the first time I'd met him. This realisation made me feel a lot better. It meant that I had an on-going relationship with him that had already lasted several weeks. On and off. It meant that I *hadn't* leaped into bed with a good-looking stranger.

That first evening when I'd run out into the mud in a pair of cashmere socks and not really noticed, I'd fancied him then. Those socks had never really been the same since, and nor had I. Since then I'd been persuading myself that Sally's holiday house was exactly what I needed, for *work* reasons of course. It was quiet, far from London and all the myriad distractions there. Like the Gang for example, shops with glittering things in the window, restaurants of every persuasion. None of these things had been stopping me from writing before, if I was honest. I'd managed to live in Islington and Notting Hill and churn out nineteen books while still socialising, going to exhibitions, eating Thai food and buying shoes. But now, what was going on in my tiny brain? Perhaps I had executive burnout after all.

Perhaps – terrifying thought – I had nineteen books in me and *that was all*?

One thing I did know. I'd been writing eloquently about the age-old dance of love and sex and lust and the earth moving and I hadn't known a thing about any of them until now. I had – as my mother always said about my writing with a dismissive snort – just been making it all up. It was like Donald Trump writing a Haynes Guide to Being President. No wonder I was floundering.

I looked over at Joe again. Now that my eyes had become adjusted to the darkness I could see his profile, and it was a gorgeous profile too. He shifted in his sleep and muttered something. I wondered what he was dreaming about and made a solemn promise not to ask him in the morning. That would be even worse than asking what he was thinking about.

And suddenly I was frightened.

Chapter Sixteen

The next morning he was still there, still asleep. I could see half of his face, turned towards me. I did a quick check to make sure I didn't have flakes of mascara on my cheeks or drool at the corners of my mouth. (It has been known.)

A few seconds later I realised in the most surprising and interesting way possible that he was also awake.

With Benedict (I know I shouldn't make this sort of comparison) sex was like a task he set himself, almost like another form of exercise. It had to be at the right time (ideally between 10.00 p.m. and midnight), in the right mood (showered, well fed and with a couple of drinks inside him, preferably champagne) and in the right place (my side of the bed).

That morning Joe proved he was more flexible than that. I don't mean that in the gymnastic sense but in the *very happy to see you* way.

He reached across the bed and pulled me in towards him. And kissed my neck. Which relieved me because I hadn't had time to clean my teeth last night what with one thing and another and there had probably been garlic in last night's lamb casserole.

He didn't say anything and nor did I, which I liked because there's a lot to be said for just getting down and dirty sometimes, without any of the polite, slightly embarrassing things one says on these occasions. And anyway I discovered morning sex with Joe was a different thing altogether. Somehow ruder because we were stone-cold sober. There was none of the build-up of an evening spent together flirting to get us going. It felt very sexy and slightly naughty too but just as successful as the night before. It was a good job I didn't have to get up and go to work because I don't think I could have concentrated on anything. I just wanted to lie in bed all day with a rather pleased smile on my face and think erotic thoughts and that's not like me at all. I'm usually drinking tea five seconds after I wake up.

Joe seemed just as disinclined to get out of bed and we lay entwined and panting for a bit longer and then I began to giggle at the thought of what we had just done and Joe began to laugh too and suddenly it wasn't embarrassing at all. And I forgot about the possible food combinations for breakfast and went and made a pot of tea and some toast instead. And we sat up in bed together watching the sun rise over the valley and had breakfast and occasionally he leaned over and kissed me and once he licked some butter off my fingers and made me feel rather wobbly and odd inside until I realised I was feeling lustful thoughts again. And I wondered if that was – you know – *normal* because I'd always thought I had quite a low sex drive. Benedict had thought so too and Charlie once even wondered out loud if I needed therapy. Bloody cheek.

A Damascene thought struck me. Perhaps it wasn't me after all, perhaps it was the company I had been keeping?

'Much as I don't want to leave, I really must get going,' Joe said at last. 'It's nearly nine o'clock. Ivy will be up and about and she'll wonder where I am. And I need to see Ken. I can't just leave everything to him.'

'Sorry,' I said.

He looked at me. 'Are you?'

'No.'

'A bit sorry?' He grinned.

'Nope.'

'That's good. Because I'm not either.'

'Did you enjoy Cornwall?' I said.

'I did. I thought Ivy deserved to do something different. She's had a rough few weeks but she's getting stronger all the time. We went to a fantastic little cottage on the north coast, near Padstow. Do you know it?'

I shook my head.

'It was wonderful. You'd have loved it.'

Would I? Probably. Perhaps this was the time to ask about Ivy's mother?

Joe kissed my forehead. 'I must go, have things to do. I need to write a thousand words on something rural and fascinating for *Devon* magazine by the end of next week. And you have a book to edit I think you said?'

'I have a book I need to pull to pieces and stick together with Gorilla Tape if I'm honest,' I said ruefully.

He got out of bed and found his clothes while I lay back against the pillows and watched him. He was nothing like any man I'd ever known. He was muscular and broad and, well, masculine. There was something quite wonderful about watching the muscles in his arms and back moving under his smooth skin. Something that almost made me want to bite him.

At last he was sitting on the edge of the bed pulling his socks on. I was feeling quite panicky inside. I wanted to be like all the women I have ever despised, clingy and needy and begging him not to go. Or at least get some sort of commitment from him as to when I was going to see him again. Quite pathetic. Any minute now I'd be asking him what he was thinking.

I drew breath to try and say something casual, like *doing anything this evening*? Or *we must do this again sometime soon*. Instead I said nothing and watched him running his hands through his hair, trying and failing to get it into some sort of order. Even that was adorable.

'Right, I'll be off.' He leaned over and kissed the end of my nose.

'Okay,' I said.

'I'll be seeing you.'

That ranked alongside *I'll pop back* as far as I was concerned. *For heaven's sake, woman. Stop being quite so pitiful.*

I pulled on a dressing gown and went downstairs to see him off. I felt quite silly. Almost as though I was his wife and I was seeing him off to work. I wondered if he would kiss me goodbye at the front door.

He didn't, he put one hand on my shoulder and winked at me.

'I'll be seeing you,' he said.

You've said that already. When?

'Yes fine,' I replied, pulling my dressing gown around myself a bit tighter.

He paused as he got to his car and looked across at me. He opened the front door and slung his coat into the back seat and then he paused for a moment and came back across the drive towards me. Fast and purposeful. He pulled me into his arms. He bent his head down and kissed me. I mean this was kissing at its best. Not just a farewell peck, this was a lot of kissing packed into a few seconds. His arms were hard and strong around me and the cold air seeped under my dressing gown, making me shiver.

At last he let me go and I had to grab hold of the door-frame to stop myself sinking to the floor.

I went upstairs and stood on the landing to watch his car driving away down the lane. Then I let out a triumphant yodel that echoed around the house. I closed my eyes and tried to get my head into some sort of order.

*

I was crazy. I was thinking more and more about him and when I might see him again and sex and snogging and, well, mostly about him. But at the same time I didn't have the wit to ask the questions I wanted answered. How did he feel about me? Apart from anything else I really liked him. I was making a basic assumption that he found me sexually attractive. What happened to Ivy's mother and was she around?

I went to have a shower and tried on some clothes, wondering for a while why everything seemed to have shrunk. I turned my back on the biscuit tin I could see out of the corner of my eye and went outside to have a calorie-free cigarette. There was no doubt about it; I was going to develop into a lardy, chain-smoking sex obsessive. Not an attractive look at all.

I went in and settled down at the dining room table with my laptop. Then I went to get coffee and a piece of toast. I opened *Choose Yes* and scrolled back a few pages to read a particularly excruciating scene of sex and seduction where my description implied the two participants had five legs and superhuman stamina. I hadn't quite thought it through.

I drank my coffee and riffled through a few sheets of the hard copy. I did a bit of crossing out and dramatic asterisk placing with a pink highlighter to make me feel I was achieving something. Then I went to make another piece of toast and spent a few minutes hunting for the Marmite. Then I sat and looked at the screen.

Get on with your bloody book, woman!

There was something I needed to do with the blasted thing. I needed to stop tinkering about with it and rewrite it. Either that or start something else, something completely new and fresh. The idea was infinitely more appealing than trying to breathe life into *Choose Yes*.

Slowly and with great care I put the hard copy of the book back into its cardboard box and closed the lid. Then I saved the changes I had made to the laptop version and closed the whole thing down with a ceremonial spin of one index finger. I opened up a new page and typed.

Chapter One

Of course life isn't quite that simple. I'm a plotter not a pantser after all. I need a plot in the same way I need a route map or an instruction book. I reached for a new notebook and a new pencil.

The Man Who Knew Her.

That was the title that lurched out of my subconscious. There was going to be a man. A man with sparkling eyes and a sexy grin. He would be kind and thoughtful. He would think about life and the planet without being an environmental bore. He would never eat kale. He wouldn't own a bicycle. He would know how to live and care for people without being a do-gooder. He would love my main character despite her flaws and faults because she would be funny and feisty; he would make her laugh. Together they would somehow make up more than just two people. They would be friends and passionate lovers. She wouldn't know it but he was the man she needed in her life. And he would wait for her to realise it.

I sat staring into space for a few minutes and read through the notes I had scribbled. For the first time in ages I felt excited about writing, I had shivers down my spine at the thought of these people, this story. This man.

*

Before I knew it a week had passed. I only went out to stock up with milk and essentials. I even tried to cut back on the amount of junk food I was getting through. I didn't try terribly hard but I did start to buy fruit instead of biscuits occasionally.

Sometimes the words flowed out of the ends of my fingers like magic. Sometimes I looked up to find a whole morning had gone past. The next day the seconds dragged as slow as a snail on tranquillisers. I didn't seem able to concentrate, to think clearly. Then one morning when I was sitting in the supermarket café with my laptop, an email arrived from my estate agent asking me to ring her urgently. Realising it had been sent two days previously I rang.

I got straight through to the nicotine-laden tones of Christy Church who was handling the sale. She's not a woman to waste time with pleasantries.

'It's been going well, the flat is in a very desirable area with all the good access to amenities one would hope for. There's been good take-up,' she said.

'What does that mean?'

'It means people are clicking into the link on Rightmove in order to read the details. There have been several brochure requests and seven viewings. I did try and contact you first but you never answer your mobile and my colleague told me you were out of the country.'

'I'm not actually out of the country,' I said.

'Then where are you?'

'I'm in Devon.'

'Well that's practically the same thing,' she snorted. I heard her gulping at her coffee. 'We had an offer through a week ago. It was a naughty chancer, several thousand behind the askers anyway.'

'Right. So?'

'So nothing. I know them. I've rejected it on your behalf. The reason I wanted to talk to you was this. Rosie was doing a viewing on Monday and she met up with your husband. He said you weren't sure about selling anyway, which isn't what I understood. Could you clarify?'

I bit down my fury. 'What husband? I don't have a husband. I've told you this before. My ex-partner is supposed to be moving out as soon as possible. I gave him a month's notice.'

'Fine, so is he looking to purchase in this area? It's a pity he doesn't want to buy you out. Still, I might have something that would suit him.'

'Christy never mind about him, I'm employing you. Can we just concentrate on selling my flat?'

'Sure, sure. So I'll be in touch and make some notes on your file when I get a moment. How soon will he be leaving?'

My heart sank. I would have to go back to London and shunt Benedict forcefully towards his final exit from my life. It was the right thing to do for everyone concerned. I could see he would be in no hurry to leave. And let's be fair, why should he? A great flat in a super location for free and just a short bike ride to work. Or whatever passed for work in the mysterious world of corporate law, mergers, and general pissing about with other people's money.

After I'd rung off, promising to ring back the following day, I realised every one else in the café was listening in to my conversation. So I went out to my car. As I got in, the phone rang again.

'Jassy! Everything okay?'

She didn't waste time with pleasantries either.

'Lulu, where the frig have you been, you silly cow? I've been trying to ring you God knows how many times. I have exciting news!'

'Go on?'

'I'm pregnant!'

I let out a joyful scream and I think Jassy did the same thing.

‘Oh my God! When is it due? How do you feel? Are you okay?’ I said.

‘I’m due on the fifth of November. Ralphie says if it’s a boy he wants to call him Guy and if it’s a girl Sparkler. Sparkler Sutton – have you ever heard anything so daft? I’m fine. A bit sick you know and I’ve had to stop smoking and drinking so I’m a bit edgy. Although the very thought of gin makes me want to retch.’

‘Good heavens! The Plymouth Gin Distillery will go out of business!’

‘I know. Bit of a shock to the system, I can tell you. Ralphie is like a dog with twenty tails. He’s been on the phone telling as many people as he can. Probably random strangers for all I know. I’ve told him it’s early days yet but he won’t listen.’

‘Blimey! Pregnant!’

‘I know! I’m so excited. I wanted to celebrate with you, *Auntie* Lulu, but you’ve disappeared again.’

‘You know exactly where I am. I’m in Barracane House—’

‘Well okay. Look, I’ve been putting up with seven sorts of shit from Benedict. *And* I have Sally on my back night and day wanting my final edits. I’m nearly certifiable. I shouldn’t have to put up with that in my condition.’

‘No of course not. Look I’m sorry, I just needed to get away.’

‘You do know Benedict has moved back into the flat don’t you?’

‘No, I didn’t actually know that. But Christy—’

'Well surprise, surprise. He has. In fact, I saw Toby the other day and he seemed to think Tess was living there too. Or that she's certainly a regular visitor.'

'*What?*'

'Well what do you expect?'

'I expected him to move out!'

'Don't be so naïve.'

'I just assumed he would. I should have changed the locks,' I said sadly.

'You idiot, you mean you didn't?'

'No. Look, I don't suppose you would—'

'Organise it? No I bloody wouldn't. I've got more than enough to deal with at the moment. I have to see my doctor every five minutes, make bookings for various things and decide where Sparkler is going to sleep. If I don't get my act into gear she will be sleeping in a cardboard box under the bed. I'm joking. Anyway I think you need to come back here, make an enormous fuss of me and sort out this mess, not just rush off to some rural idyll. A few things have landed on Sally's desk too; things that mean the Darling sisters need to shape up a bit. If we don't we're going to be yesterday's news.'

'What sort of thing?'

'Those two aristo girls? Lady Fenella and the other one, Lady Nia thingy-whatsit. You know, the pair who are always lounging about on yachts, flashing their tits at the cameras. Wardrobe malfunction I don't think so. Sally's just got them a massive advance for their piffling ramblings on life and love and eyebrow threading. They are taking over. They are everywhere at the moment. Surely even down there in Nowheresville you've noticed them? If we don't do something, our brand – you remember that? The one we went to a lot of trouble to make? – that will be down the tubes. Sally will be spending all her waking hours on them. I've just about finished the first draft. You have buggered off out of the public eye to do what? Doss around in the back of beyond with ... with ... hang on.'

Mercifully she paused to draw breath but it just gave her time to think a bit more. 'It's that farmer chap isn't it? I knew it! You're shagging that farmer. You sly cow.'

'Jassy you're not—'

'I'm almost speechless!' She seemed to have gone up several octaves. 'All that rubbish about Benedict and it was you all the time wasn't it? Do you realise what would happen if he found out? Does Sally know?'

'Does Sally know what?'

'Don't give me that shit. You know perfectly well what I'm talking about. I'm married to Ralphie – the cutest and sexiest cricket commentator ever – not that there's much competition, and you're in a meaningful relationship with – and I quote – handsome, hotshot barrister Benedict. You're not supposed to be screwing around with rustic louts the minute you are left on your own. And I've been giving Benedict earache about that Tess on your behalf, and he keeps droning on about how he didn't do anything. What were you *thinking*?'

'He's not a rustic lout!'

'So you *are* screwing him!'

I didn't answer and Jassy gave a strangled yelp of annoyance.

'Honestly! Lulu! I wondered why you kept going down there for no good reason. Now of course it's bloody obvious. You always told me you weren't that bothered about sex anyway. Take it or leave it. That's what you said only a few months ago.'

'Jassy, will you please shut up for a second.'

'Right, I'd love to hear this. I'd like to know why you are behaving like an irresponsible teenager.'

'I think I'm in love with him,' I blurted, my voice small and silly in the middle of the tirade of abuse from my sister.

'*What?*'

There was silence for a few blessed seconds.

'What did you say?' Jassy said at last.

'I think I'm in love with him.'

As I said it I could feel myself mentally curling up into a ball and cringing. But then as the silence wore on I realised it was probably true. It would explain a lot.

Was this what love was? Not being able to concentrate on anything? Thinking of him? Remembering the shape of his hands? Wanting to be with him all the time? Feeling safe with him? Wanting to talk to him? Love wasn't just mooning around feeling happy. It wasn't just looking out of the window wondering what he was doing. It wasn't just being pleased to see him. It was so much more. It was probably an overload of some hormone making me behave like a fool but there it was.

Jassy sighed. 'Oh bugger.'

Chapter Seventeen

The following afternoon saw me back in Notting Hill and the fact I was there made me more bad-tempered than I had been for many years.

I got to the flat just in time to see one of the estate agents closing the door behind her.

'Hi, Rosie, have you been doing another viewing?' I said hopefully.

She looked more than a bit pissed off. 'Well I would if they had turned up. That's the fourth time I've arranged a viewing with them and they haven't turned up or have called me with some stupid excuse. I've wasted most of the afternoon. Honestly I've never had such trouble selling a flat in this building. They usually go in no time. Six weeks max.'

'Who was it?' I said.

'Mr and Mrs Delabole. Sold their flat already, apparently desperate to move. So much so that they don't turn up.'

A sudden suspicion struck me.

'It's not Benedict is it? Who by the way is not my husband and should be moving out very soon. Christy told me he had been messing about pretending I was thinking of taking the flat off the market and not moving at all. And that is not the case. She was supposed to be making a note on my file.'

Rosie put her bag down on the floor and put the keys to my flat safely into a zipped pocket. 'I don't think this is him but how would I know?'

'No. Well do you have their number to call them?'

'Of course but they never answer.'

I pulled my phone out. 'Tell me what it is?'

'I can't do that! That's against company policy!'

'Okay you ring it on my phone. I won't look and you can delete the number afterwards.'

After a bit of humming and hahing Rosie agreed and punched the number into my phone. Then she put it on speakerphone.

After a few seconds we heard it ringing.

And then someone answered. A familiar voice. Oleaginous. Very irritating.

'Lulu! My darling! To what do I owe this honour?'

I grabbed the phone. 'Percy?'

'Lulu? How nice to hear from you!'

'That's not Mr Delabole then? How is lovely Mrs Delabole? The invisible wife you seem incapable of actually getting? Look, you devious little sod! Stop wasting my estate agent's time! Making appointments and then not keeping them.'

He was all innocent bluster. 'Lulu, Lulu sweetie pie, some mistake! I don't know what ...'

'Yes you do. If you do this again I'll be on the phone to your boss. I know him remember? Julian Weston-Baker, tall stringy character with an over-inflated sense of his own importance. Pretty much like you, come to think of it. I sat next to him at that Mansion House dinner last year. He spent the evening looking down the front of my dress but I'm pretty certain he'll remember me.'

I heard Percy take a deep breath.

'Aw, come on, Lulu. There's no need to be like that about it. It was just a bit of fun. You're upset, Lu, I can tell.'

'Percy, if you do this again or anything like this you'll regret it.'

I ended the call and turned back to my companion who was standing drumming her fingers against the wall.

'Sorry, Rosie. I might have guessed Benedict was behind this.'

She was very annoyed. 'We can't be expected to deal with this you know. I don't care who is playing the fool – it's a total waste of our time. I've got better things to do than trail over here, wait for half an hour, and then trail back to the office. It generally means ninety minutes wasted. I thought your partner was moving out?'

'I thought he was. This is just a bit of bloody harassment.'

'Well if it carries on ...'

'It won't. I'll see to it, Rosie. I promise.'

She looked doubtful. 'I'll have to tell Christy; she'll be absolutely livid. I'll persuade her to give it one more try but this is the last time. Okay?'

'I'll sort it.'

I watched as she collected her bag and shrugged on her coat.

'And now it's pissing down,' she muttered furiously, 'thanks so much.'

'Sorry.'

I went into my flat, slung my bag across the hall and closed the door quietly when what I really wanted to do was slam it off its hinges. Then I went to look in the fridge for something unexpected and delicious that I had forgotten buying. Of course there wasn't anything. There was, however, the usual trail that marked Benedict's presence: a bag of kale, a half-empty pot of hummus, and a plastic box full of slimy salad leaves. I slammed the fridge door so the bottles inside rattled. Then I went to have a closer look around the flat and every minute I found more and more to annoy me. It was obvious Benedict was very much still around and had made little or no effort to move out.

If he was clever enough to do mergers and acquisitions, restructure corporations and still have time to have affairs behind my back, then he was certainly able to pack up an Xbox and his collection of striped shirts into bags and take them away to wherever. Yes I knew I should have chucked him bodily out onto his bony arse a long time ago but I just didn't have the confidence to do it when I should have. If could I take on Ian Hislop in a debate on television *and* make him laugh, why couldn't I sort out my private life? I have no explanation.

But I couldn't be that surprised, surely. It was my fault; I hadn't been single-minded enough. If I wanted my life to change I needed to take responsibility for it.

First of all I put the latest bag of kale down the waste disposal and then I found a roll of bin liners, opened the wardrobe and started pulling things off hangers and stuffing them in. Why did Benedict need so many shirts? Why did he need so many sweaters in so many different colours? There were dozens, most of them cashmere. Then of course there were the suits, the brocade waistcoats, ties, dinner jackets, a white tuxedo still in a dry-cleaning bag, shoes on their wooden shoe trees, heaven knows how many pairs. Not to mention the chinos, T-shirts, polo shirts, overcoats, raincoats, cycling gear.

And of course the bathroom was similarly stuffed with his belongings. Special huge white bath sheets I wasn't supposed to use because I once got mascara on one, an electric tooth-brush, shaver, vitamins, toiletries, and a set of bathroom scales that he had bought at vast expense to measure all sorts of things: his weight, muscle mass and BMI. I expect there were special settings to discover the air quality, his blood group, star sign and inside leg measurement. They were something else I wasn't supposed to use, because if I did it would spoil his stored records. So obviously I got on and jumped up and down a couple of times and then I took the batteries out just to make sure.

By this time I had used up all the bin liners, it was getting dark and I was hungry. I rang Jassy and she answered almost immediately.

'Now where are you?' she said crossly.

'Back at the flat. I'm clearing Benedict's stuff out into bin liners.'

'About bloody time too.'

'There's no food in this place. Want to meet up for a drink?'

'I suppose so,' Jassy grumbled, 'although trust me a glass of bloody fizzy water with a splash of lime does not a drink make. Sparkler has a lot to answer for. Ralphie has gone to bloody South Africa for ten days. Ten days! And with me pregnant. Pigging cricket.'

'Why can't you go with him?'

'Good question. That's what I said and he went on about how he didn't expect me to take him to work and I said that's completely different; there's no reason why I couldn't write in a hotel room in Durban while he went off to watch the matches. He wouldn't have it. I'm beginning to wonder about this "what goes on tour, stays on tour" business. I'll see you in an hour okay? Maudie has been hanging around my neck every time I go to Dizzy's. I think she wants to bend my ear about that chap she's been seeing and I'm not in the mood.'

We met up in a wine bar that used to be called *Vino Vino* the last time I looked. It was the usual mishmash of chrome, black wood, and inadequate lighting that meant people were peering at their menus by the light of their mobile phones. Jassy arrived a few minutes after I did, unwinding her scarf and dropping down onto the sofa next to me with a groan.

I went and got her a glass of something non-alcoholic and she grimaced at it.

'How is Sparkler doing?' I said.

Jassy pulled another dissatisfied face. 'Making herself known. I've never felt so awful. So, Benedict?' she said.

'Not seen him yet.'

Then she fixed me with a steely eye. 'Okay, Joe Field. Tell me everything.'

'Oh *Jassy*!'

'Don't give me that. You've been cavorting with the man next door!'

'I have not cavorted.'

'You've slept with him. Shagged him. You've had sex with him – whatever you want to call it – and now you say you're in love with him. Aren't you a bit old for this, Lulu?'

'No, apparently not,' I said, fiddling with a cardboard doily that had been placed under my wine glass.

Jassy's face twisted with incomprehension. 'But you're nearly forty for heaven's sake. You're not a teenager. You have people relying on you. Your bank manager, me, Sally, your devoted fan base. I know what this is: you're having a midlife crisis. You've already bought the sports car, you've had your teeth whitened, now it's time to have a wild fling. Really? A Lady Chatterley moment with Joe Field instead of Mellors.'

'No, I can see you might think that but that's not ...'

'Well I can't think what it is then. You're talking about selling your flat, a flat that is in one of the best locations in the country I might add. Benedict says you want something nice. *Nice?* I mean come on. Have you thought this through? Where are you planning to relocate? France? A Greek island? Or are you seriously thinking of Devon with your rustic swain?'

'Look, Jassy, I know it sounds as though I'm losing the plot—'

'Well, you might say that; I couldn't possibly comment! But in my condition ...'

'Something's happened to me, something I wasn't expecting, and I don't know how to deal with it. But I don't want to live in London any more,' I said.

'Well if you want to move to the country how about trying somewhere like – I don't know – Watford or that place that always sounds so nice – Welwyn Garden City?'

'Your idea of what constitutes the countryside is a bit off I'm afraid.'

Jassy took a sip of her drink, looking crossly at my glass of Merlot.

'The least you should do is make a clean break with Benedict, don't you think?'

'Yes.'

'Then ...' Jassy paused and looked up '... now's your chance.'

I followed her gaze and saw a grim-looking Benedict shrugging his way through the door and towards us.

'You told him I was here?' I said, horrified.

'Oh for heaven's sake, do grow up.'

Jassy drained her glass and stood up to let Benedict sit down.

'Talk some sense into her will you? I'm going outside to stand next to the smokers.'

Benedict threw me a dark look. 'What have you done with my stuff?' he said.

'I'm packing up for you,' I said. 'I'm going to sell the flat and you being in it is stopping that from happening. That and your stupid antics making appointments for non-existent viewings and Percy pissing off my estate agent.'

'Look, Lulu, I'm on the track of something; any day now I'll be out of your hair forever.' He reached over, held my hand and looked at me from under his eyelashes. 'If that's what you really want?'

'It is,' I said, pulling my hand away, 'and is your girlfriend pregnant or not?'

He had the decency to look embarrassed. 'Not. That was a complete misunderstanding, nothing to do with me at all. She had a bit of a ...'

'I don't need to hear the sordid details, I really don't.'

He shifted a bit closer to me and put his hand on my shoulder.

'Let's give it another go. What do you say?'

'Oh for heaven's sake ...'

'I'll make it up to you, honest to God. No messing about ever again. I'll tell Tess we are over. And Milly.'

'Who the hell is Milly?'

'No one, absolutely no one,' he said quickly, 'just – no one.'

I sighed and I think Benedict saw this as a sign of me weakening because he moved in closer and put his arm around my shoulder.

'I've been an idiot, Lulabelle; you know I love you. But you went away and left me on my own, d'you see? I got up to mischief. Like boys do.'

'You're not a boy, you're forty-one. But of course I can see this was all my fault,' I said.

'I didn't mean that. I missed you, Lu, I really did.'

'I was only away for ten bloody days! Couldn't you keep your trousers on for ten days?'

He kissed my cheek and crooned at me. 'Sorry, Lulu, Benedict's a bad boy. He's sorry.'

He pronounced it '*sowwy*' and I shrugged him off, immeasurably irritated.

'I'm getting the locks changed tomorrow,' I said. 'You've got until the end of the day to get your stuff out.'

His expression of pleading sadness snapped off like a light bulb.

'You cow,' he said, 'how am I going to manage that? Where am I going to find a flat in a day?'

'You've had weeks,' I said. 'I've been more than reasonable.'

'And what will you do then? Jassy told me you were pissing everyone off with your insane behaviour. What next?'

'That's not your problem. I'll cope.'

He looked at me with mocking pity. 'Feeling your age, Lu? Old clock ticking is it? Tick tock, tick tock. Pushing forty, no husband no kids. Life flying south for the winter is it? Starting again at your age isn't going to be easy.'

'Do sod off,' I said.

*

The following day Benedict turned up at the flat at six thirty in the morning, wandering around with a dejected air, kicking at the black bin liners I had packed up the previous day.

'Where are you going?' I asked.

'Like you care.'

'I'm trying to keep this civil,' I said. 'There may be post that arrives here for you that needs to be forwarded on.'

'Oh don't go to any trouble on my account.' He ran a finger across the titles in the bookcase and gave a dismissive sniff. 'I hear Jassy is in pig?'

'*What?*'

'Okay, Jassy's pregnant.'

'You do have a lovely way of putting things, Benedict. I bet your silver-tongued speeches rivet the courtroom when you let rip.'

We had a brisk exchange of views about the ownership of a Le Creuset wok and then I left him to it and went to make sure there were none of his things left in the washing machine. I was further outraged when I found some rather exotic underwear, which was definitely not mine. The next hour deteriorated into a heated argument when we both used words we would undoubtedly regret. Even so I'd like to put on record that Benedict *was* an unprincipled bastard and I *am not* borderline obese.

Eventually we both calmed down and I made some coffee as a sort of peace offering. Apparently there was a removal van arriving by midday, which necessitated humping bags up and down in the lift and infuriating other people who wanted to use it, plus a great deal of door slamming and grumbling.

Actually I did feel a bit sad about the whole thing; it's never easy to break up with someone you've loved, even if I had known for a very long time that we were not going to go the distance. Benedict must have caught me looking a bit wistful and he seized his moment.

'It's not too late you know, Lu, we could put all this behind us and start again,' he said. 'We could take a holiday somewhere nice. What was that place you wanted to go? Corona or something.'

'Carcassonne.'

'We could go there and forget all about this. My back has

been terrible. I've been sleeping in Percy's spare room next to his axolotl tank. It's very unnerving waking up to see them looking at me. They don't have eyelids.'

I looked out of the window. 'The van is here. You'd better go and load your stuff up,' I said.

'You're a hard bitch,' Benedict muttered.

A couple of hours and many trips up and down in the lift later, Benedict was gone. It was such a relief even when I realised he had taken all the towels, most of the crockery and nearly all the cutlery. Still, cheap at the price I suppose.

I moved the big armchair from its place in front of where the television used to be and into the window where I had always wanted it. I sat down with a cup of tea and watched the traffic snarling up the street below as it waited for Benedict's van to finish loading and drive off. And then with a blast on its horn and a questionable gesture out of the passenger window from Benedict, he was gone.

*

It took me the rest of the afternoon to get the place straight again, and by three o'clock the man had changed the front door locks leaving me to hoover up the detritus. Unsurprisingly, my flat now looked strangely bare and characterless, although to be honest the loss of the Andy Warhol prints and the strange African carvings was an improvement in my opinion.

Now what?

I rang Christy Church and told her of the developments and then I went out to the corner shop and bought an overpriced bottle of champagne and some snacks. I spent the evening slugging it back, accompanied by salt and vinegar crisps, cheese strings and a Crunchie, all things Benedict wouldn't tolerate having in the house. I remembered he had once caught me eating a Scotch egg and nearly sent me to have my stomach pumped.

Chapter Eighteen

So what next?

I spent the next couple of days dressing the flat so that it didn't look as though half the guts had been ripped out of it. I did all sort of pretentious things like setting the table for four with matching placemats and linen napkins (Benedict hadn't wanted those). It was like an after reveal in one of those TV programmes when the house owner has left a tolerable sitting room and returns to find it with a Schiaparelli pink accent wall and wine glasses wired together to make a chandelier. I was just about finished when I had a call from Sally. My heart sank when I saw her name on the screen.

'How's it going?' she said. 'All that Devon air bringing the colour to your cheeks?

'I'm in Notting Hill. I had to get Benedict out and get the locks changed. I'm leaving it to the estate agent to sell. I'll be back in Devon as soon as humanly possible.'

'Good. And the book? How's that coming along?'

'I've dumped it for the moment and I'm on to something else.'

There were sounds of Sally lighting a cigarette. 'Oh well, I suppose that's for the best, all things considered. And I hear Jassy is expecting? How exciting. Except she'll probably be like you and lose all her focus. Do tell me all about your new work.'

'It's sort of a departure ...' I said, 'something different.'

'Okay,' she said cautiously, 'as long as it's not too different? I thought it was about time I checked in, see how it's all going. I've been so busy recently, what with one thing and another.'

'Oh yes, I heard you had signed those ghastly twins for some deathless tome on how to be an irritant under the saddle of feminine equality. What are they calling themselves – the Trust Fund Tits?'

'Now then, grumpy, they are doing very well. They are due on *I'm a Celebrity* by the time their book is ready. Everyone will be after them.'

'Sally, I'm appalled. When they asked Jassy we agreed reality TV was the same as volunteering for Dante's Inferno.'

'Yes I know. Do shut up. This is different. Look, I was ringing to say we were thinking of coming down to Barracane at some point.'

'Fine, of course. Any idea when?'

'Not sure, it all depends on the special long weekend holiday that's being planned at Enid's school. Apparently the teachers need a couple of extra training days to get to grips with the new curriculum, though why they can't do it in the holidays I don't know. I blame Brexit.'

'Okay, well I'll look forward to seeing you both sometime soon.'

'That I doubt. Enid has taken to coming out with the most irritating questions. Who would win in a fight, a sabre-toothed tiger or a poison dart frog? Who would I prefer to be stuck in a lift with, Abigail's mother or Indigo's mother? The answer of course is 1) who cares and 2) Indigo's father. And by the way thanks a bunch for sending that box set of Disney DVDs for her birthday. I've been refusing to buy them for years.'

'What are godmothers for?' I laughed.

'If I hear that bloody song from *Frozen* once more I will probably lose it. Anyway, tons to do. Keep up the good work!'

She rang off and I returned to my task, filling in the gaps where Benedict's stuff had once been and trying to make the flat look comfortable and lived in but also immaculate. I rang Jassy, told her what I was doing and then had a brief call with Christy to reassure her that the troublemakers had been dealt with. Then for the umpteenth time set off for Devon. This was by anyone's standards getting a bit ridiculous. I'd spent nearly all my life in and around London and now it seemed I couldn't wait to get away from the place.

Five and a half hours later I drove up the mud-splattered drive of Barracane House with a sense of utter joy. Everything about it from the rain-washed sky, the sturdy stone walls and the wind-blasted trees in the neglected garden filled me with unreasonable delight. Even the scrubby and untrained plant clawing its way over the porch and the iron bucket hiding the back door key seemed delightful. I think my rose-coloured spectacles must have been on high beam.

This was going to be it. This time I was going to get the first draft of my new book finished and I wasn't going to be distracted by anyone or anything. Not the view out of the window or the crystal-clear skies at night. Not the sun sending magical beams through the stained-glass window next to the front door or the prospect of moonlight on the bedroom floor. Nothing was going to distract me. I was going to be frighteningly efficient, churning out the words like a machine. I would fill that blank and challenging screen with words of such beauty and power that it was quite possible I would win the Booker prize.

First I went to find the corkscrew and wondered what Joe was doing.

*

Of course, if I was about to retreat into my writing cave, I needed to make sure I had enough supplies and wasn't going to run out of milk or dishwasher tablets or Wagon Wheels. Perhaps I would include them in the acknowledgements particularly if it encouraged them to send me a complimentary box? I wondered how many there might be in a box. Twenty? Fifty? Could I get through fifty?

I set off first thing the following morning to stock up, spending an enjoyable few minutes chatting with my old friend Maureen in Superfine, and wondering if I could include her as a character in my new book. She was in an ebullient mood as her daughter had recently brought forth twins, bringing Maureen's grandchild count up to seven.

'Little ducks, they are,' Maureen said, misty-eyed, as she scanned my shopping. 'William and Jennifer. Nice names, ain't they? William after the prince and Jennifer after some actress she likes. Kyle wants to call them Willie and Jenny but I said you can't do that, boy, them's the twins from the Woodentops programme when I was a nipper; but he didn't know what I was on about. How's the book coming along? Have they sold the film rights yet? Sixty-three pounds twenty. All adds up, don't it? I bet you only came in for some milk.'

I drove back at a leisurely pace, dithering slightly when I came to the fork in the road that could take me past Lower Tor Farm. I didn't dither for long, and five minutes later I was progressing very slowly past, craning around to see if I could see Joe. I've never been very good at steering when I'm craning and I nearly crashed into him. He was coming towards me along the one and a half cars wide road in his Land Rover and I jerked to a stop. He hopped down from his seat and came to talk to me through my open window.

'You're back then?' He looked rather pleased.

'Seems that way,' I said, blushing furiously.

He was muffled up against the wind in a thick tweedy coat

and scarf and the hand he rested on my car door was red with the cold. I resisted the urge to take his hand between both of mine and chafe some warmth into it.

'That's good. Perhaps ...'

There was a cacophony of noise from his car and he straightened up and shouted at one of his sheepdogs who must have been standing on his car horn with its front paws.

I tried to fill in the sentence.

... you would like to go out one evening?

... you could make me one of your delicious cakes?

... you'll come round to mine for some hot bedroom action?

'... we could meet up?' he finished. 'My mother was very impressed with you going to the book club in the village hall. I don't think they've stopped talking about it since. And nor has Ivy. You're a real hit with her.'

My heart gave a little jump. 'Really? How wonderful.'

'Oh yes, and Mum's got a load of extra Brownie points thanks to you.' His blue eyes twinkled at me.

'That's nice to know. I thought she was lovely.'

'She's great, and she's a godsend looking after Ivy.'

'How is Ivy?'

'Fine. Pretty soon she'll have forgotten all about being ill. Ah well.' He stood up, as though he was about to get back into his car.

'Would you like to come round one night? I mean, one *evening*?' I said.

Idiot.

'That might be fun,' he said. 'Look I'd better go. Meg gets a bit boisterous – she'll be standing on the horn again in a minute.'

What? Oh, the dog.

'Well look through your diary and let me know. I'm going to be around for a while. Any night, I mean any *evening* would do. Or – well – whatever.'

I got a bit dithery and vague at this point. Perhaps I was having a mini-stroke with the excitement?

'Are you okay?' he said, frowning slightly.

'Yes of course, I'm just a bit – you know, tired. I had a nightmare journey back here yesterday. Traffic queues and road works and hold-ups all the way.'

Lies, all lies.

'Okay, well, I'll be in touch. I'll back up into the gateway, so you can get past.'

He gave a little wave and walked back to his car where the dog was woofing and bouncing around like a wound-up toy.

A few minutes later I was home and unloading my bags, going through every detail of our conversation like a thirteen-year-old. What had I said and what did he say and what did he mean by that? Hopeless.

Eventually I forced myself to get on with some writing and after a few minutes got into the groove quite nicely. I decided to do some character studies. My hero was tall and rugged and didn't suffer fools gladly. Not that I've ever met anyone who did by the way. He was calm and competent and he would be a well-respected ~~doctor, teacher, university professor~~ builder.

Yes of course! He would be a builder with a suede tool belt and extra long FatMax ruler for measuring things and he'd say things like: '*Well I've not seen it done like that but it's your money. Now where shall I erect these poles?*'

He'd have big steel-toe-capped boots and a van filled with manly stuff. Drills and boxes full of screws and rawlplugs and the pockets of his jeans would bulge with bunches of Allen keys. *Woof woof!*

He'd build shelves that were level and talk about ordering some *two be four* whatever that was. He'd talk knowledgeably to my heroine about damp courses and manholes and ask about her inspection chamber. I carried on into the afternoon and then realised with a snort that I had written fifteen hundred words of innuendo and a couple of filthy double entendres. It was a pity the *Carry On* films were no longer in production.

I didn't think this would win me the Booker prize after all.

I sat and thought about this for a few minutes.

Could love be light-hearted? Could the attraction, romance thing be mixed with giggling at the wrong moment? Perhaps it could. Maybe the falling in love, getting together with the hero and first-date sex could be amalgamated with falling out of bed and laughter? I felt a prickle of excitement and went to find some salt and vinegar crisps before washing them down with a large glass of wine.

Chapter Nineteen

Two days later I had worked out a plot that I thought would work. I made some more notes.

My heroine, an English teacher provisionally called Sophie, was to fall in love with ~~Brett Jack~~ Sam who would be the tall, thoughtful, sexy builder with a massive tool bag and smears of plaster across his chest. They would meet when he was working in the school constructing a shelving unit for the children's books in Sophie's classroom. They would share many a lingering glance over the *two be four* and she would be so impressed with him that she'd ask him to come and do her ~~bathroom.~~ No, too personal and it would involve too much reference to pipes and plumbing. So he would work on her conservatory where she liked to sit and read and mark her pupils' books.

Perhaps there would be a leak and he would come and fix it. How long would that take? Not long. Okay he would come and replaster a wall in her sitting room before he laid some wooden flooring. This would mean he had to be there every day for at least a couple of weeks surely? It would have to be in the school holidays though, which meant she probably wouldn't be marking her pupils' work. Perhaps she would be doing lesson plans? Plenty of time for her dull deputy headmaster Donald – who also had designs on her – to realise he had stiff competition. In every sense of the word. Which would mean he would try to bully the heroine by threatening her job. Sexual harassment! Yes that would be fab. Well not actually fab obvs, but it would be a good plot mover and a great reason for Sam to confront him and protect Sophie from Don's increasingly unwelcome advances.

I could almost picture it; Donald would be making an unwieldy lunge for Sophie in the kitchen as she spiralised some courgettes and Sam would find them locked in an unsightly embrace.

Let her go, you swine, and get out or I'll be forced to use this wire brush.

And then there would be some suggestive malarkey involving a concrete vibrator or some boning rods. I wasn't sure what these things were. I looked them up on the ScrewFix website, but they sounded distinctly possible. Then at some point someone was going to have to fall into something. A patch of cement or headfirst into a bucket of paint. And all the time there would be this marvellous undercurrent of sexual chemistry and repressed urges until eventually, with his carpenter's pencil still tucked behind his ear, he would make passionate love to her over a Black and Decker workbench. No that didn't sound too comfortable. Perhaps on a pile of dustsheets while the kettle boiled suggestively on a

Primus stove behind them, ready for their post-coital builders tea.

Excellent.

I started work, only pausing to make coffee and eat my new snack love-interest, some maple pecan bars that were so hard they had to be healthy. The wrapper had a picture of a happy, glossy-haired couple laughing like maniacs in front of a backdrop of maple leaves and waterfalls. Perhaps they would have sex once they had cleaned the nuts out of their teeth?

I pressed on with my character studies all day, creating a character in Sophie who was cheerful, accident-prone and just out of a relationship with a sports teacher called Paul. Reading back through my notes I realised Paul was little more than a character assassination of Benedict with his quinoa salads, ionically balanced water bottle, bicycle and kale addiction. Perhaps libelling a barrister wasn't the best thing to do so I toned things down a bit for fear of legal reprisals and made him a history teacher instead. And took out the bit about the kale.

I emerged from my fantasy world to find it was Friday and I hadn't thought about Joe more than once an hour, which was something. I had filled pages of my new notebook with notes, thoughts and random jottings. I'd even roughed out a scene involving a digger and a cement mixer. I seemed to have strayed out of plotting a romance and into revenge accidents when ~~Benedict~~ Paul was accidentally covered in mud, smacked in the face with a floorboard and fell backwards into a water-filled trench.

I went out to the kitchen and pulled the kettle onto the Aga hotplate. The evening meal was going to be the remains of a stew I had made the day before. I seemed to be in the habit of eating the same thing for two or three days in a row. I made some coffee and was about to go rummaging in the biscuit tin when I heard the front door open and someone come crashing through with a shout of 'Mind the paintwork for God's sake! That's Farrow and Ball!'

Oh God. What the ...?

'Sally!'

'Hello, here we are! Did you get my message?' Sally said cheerfully, dumping a large canvas holdall on the floor and nudging her daughter's leopard-print Trunki forward with one foot.

'What message?'

'I sent you a text two days ago. To say Enid had a half-day and we would be down for the weekend. No? Oh well the phone reception here is a bit patchy I guess. Never mind, we're here now. Nightmare journey. I mean Night. Mare. Enid, stop opening the cupboards and take your case upstairs.'

Enid was basically Margaret Thatcher in a six-year-old body. She gave her mother a sour look.

'I'm *starving*,' she said with feeling.

'You might be hungry, Enid sweetie, but you're not starving. We know the difference. And you had the lovely sandwiches that Daddy made, didn't you.'

'They were crappy.'

'No they weren't, they were lovely. And we don't say that word,' Sally said.

'Well you say it all the time when you're reading those books you get sent.'

Sally laughed rather manically and shepherded her daughter out and upstairs with the promise of *a lovely tea in no time*. I thought this was unlikely unless Enid's idea of a lovely tea was two-day-old lamb stew or, failing that, random biscuits and a glass of Merlot.

'I do sometimes wonder what I'm doing having a house so far from London,' Sally said, coming back into the kitchen and slumping onto one of the kitchen stools. 'Henry says it's about time we sold this place and then we could buy somewhere more exciting. Somewhere with the vague possibility of sunshine more than three days a year. I'd forgotten what a bloody long way it is to Devon and the roads here are just awful, aren't they?'

'Well they can be bad, especially on a Friday afternoon,' I said. 'Actually you have made really good time. Now would you like a glass of wine?'

'Is the Pope a Catholic?'

I poured her a generous glass full and passed it over. She took a hearty slurp and sighed with pleasure.

'Henry not with you?' I said.

'No, he had some football thing to go to tomorrow. Knows a chap who knows a chap who has a director's box somewhere. Could be Wycombe Wanderers? I wasn't going to be responsible for ferrying him there and collecting him afterwards beerified and whisky-frisky. Anyway, Enid has yet another day off school on Monday so I thought we might as well come down here. Get some country air into her London child's lungs for a change. How is the book coming along?'

'I'm plotting and doing some other stuff. Newly single teacher meets builder, scuzzy deputy headmaster gets his comeuppance.'

'Jolly good, look we passed that pub on the way here that always looks rather nice although I'm ashamed to say I've not been in for years. Shall we go there for an early tea? I don't think I can bear to do anything domestic this evening and to be fair Henry's idea of a lovely sandwich is probably not Enid's.'

'The Cat and Convict? Well it's very good.'

Sally laughed. 'That's the one – is there a convict?'

'No but there is a cat.'

'Then Enid will love it.' She looked at her watch. 'Five thirty. Do you think it's open?'

We got to the pub ten minutes later.

*

'Yere she is, the famous author!' Pete shouted across the bar as we came in. He was looking rounder and more red-faced than ever and was polishing a beer glass with his favourite tea towel. 'And she's brought a friend for me, like as not!'

Sally looked around rather flustered while Enid, like the six-year-old she was, ran to stroke the pub cat who was curled up like an ammonite on its favourite chair by the fire.

After a great deal of debating and argument Enid agreed that sausage and mash was not gross and Sally and I decided to take advantage of the Friday Curry Night offering although we both declined the pint of Cat's Piss that went with it.

'So you'm brought a chum to meet us?' Pete said, lingering by our table with a wistful expression. 'That's nice. We like a bit o' glamour.'

Sally frowned for a moment until she realised Pete was being serious and then she relaxed in the warmth of his admiration.

'From London, are you?' he said, applying his trusty tea towel to the horse brasses hanging beside the fireplace. 'We don't see you too often; you're the lady who owns Barracane? We'd like to see you a bit more, pretty duck like you.'

'I come down as often as I can,' she said, bridling with pleasure at the compliment.

Sally's older than I am, and you would think she was a bit more resistant to such clumsy flattery. Apparently not.

'And who's this dear little maid?' he said, nodding at Enid so his chins wobbled.

'Enid Mary Gardener,' Enid said. She pointed at a glass case that was snarling over the mantelpiece. 'Is that a real fox?'

'Well 'un was once,' Pete said.

'Fantastic Mr Fox is my favourite,' Enid said. 'I saw a run-over fox once.'

'Well yon fox isn't fantastic. And down here we don't mind foxes being run over so much. They is something else beginning with an F if truth be told. And I wouldn't be surprised if your Joe's in later,' Pete continued, 'regular curry lover, he is.'

Pete went to put another hefty log on the fire and tell Enid that the cat's name was Puss, a fact she obviously found unimpressive by the look on her face.

'Something beginning with F. Is his name Fluffy Fox?' Enid asked him. He gave a guffawing laugh in reply.

'Now are you ladies sure you ain't a wanting the pint of Cat's Finest that comes with the meal? Is very good?'

'Well better not, I'm driving,' Sally said.

Pete looked at his watch. 'It's gorn six, me duck, they'll have all clocked off, by now. I'll warrant most of 'em will be in yere later and arter all, you don't have far to go.'

'Still, better not,' Sally said.

Disappointed Pete returned to his side of the bar and Sally turned to me.

'*Your Joe?* Who's your Joe may I ask?'

'He is in fact your nearest neighbour, so I'm surprised you haven't met him already,' I replied a bit stiffly.

'I generally come to Barracane to be quiet and recover, not get involved with local yokels,' Sally said.

'Joe Field is far from a yokel,' I said.

'Touched a nerve there have I?' Sally said triumphantly.

'What have you been up to? Is that why you keep pinging back here?'

'He's just a friend. Enid, be careful, not too close to the fire.'

Enid gave me one of her best haughty looks and carried on stroking Puss. She looked at the stuffed fox again.

'Is it called Furry Fox?' Enid said.

'No, I doubt it,' Sally said.

Our food arrived a few minutes later and Enid was persuaded to come and sit between us.

We chatted easily enough about London and books Sally had been sent and passed on some gossip about the aristocratic twins she was now representing. Apparently their ghost writer was having a nervous breakdown already because he couldn't get any sense out of either of them.

'Why do you bother?' I said, between mouthfuls of delicious Lamb Dhansak.

'It will be a bestseller, you wait and see,' Sally said, reaching over to try and cut up her daughter's sausages.

There followed a brisk exchange between mother and daughter as to whether any 'stinky food' had been transferred onto Enid's dinner.

'So, come on then tell me *all*,' Sally said.

'All what?'

'Very funny. About *your Joe*. Is he nice? Is he five foot four with a farmer's tan?' she murmured so that Enid couldn't hear.

'What's a farmer's tan?' Enid said. 'And is it *Fat* Fox?'

'No. Just eat up, there's a good girl,' Sally said.

'No, not exactly,' I said in answer to Sally's question.

'So?'

I looked up as the door to the car park banged shut, and rapidly swallowed my mouthful before I choked. Joe was standing by the coat rack, unwinding his scarf and stuffing his gloves into his pockets. Pete scurried along behind the bar as fast as his bulk would allow and caught Joe's attention and pointed in my direction. I ducked my face into my glass of wine and tried to convince myself I wasn't blushing.

Sally nudged me with a knee. 'Go on. Tell me about him.'

'Who?' Enid said, swinging her legs.

'Little pigs have big ears,' Sally said. 'Finish your lovely sausages, Enid, they look yummy.'

'Can I have ice cream?' she said, peering dubiously at her plate.

'Maybe.'

'Do they know what ice cream is here?' she said with all the superiority of the lifelong London dweller.

'Of course they do,' Sally said, 'don't be silly.'

'Hello, Louisa.'

Joe was standing just behind Sally's chair and she screwed round in her seat to look at him. She then turned back to look at me with eyes like billiard balls.

'Hello, Joe. Joe, this is my agent Sally Gardener and this is her daughter, Enid,' I said.

Joe came round to shake hands.

'Do join us,' Sally said, patting the chair next to her.

'Oh, better not, I wouldn't want to interrupt you, and I need a word with a couple of people in the bar,' Joe said.

'That's a shame,' Sally said. 'Lulu was just about to tell us all about you.'

'Have you got a farmer's tan?' Enid piped up.

'Don't talk with your mouth full,' Sally said briskly.

We chatted for a few more minutes and then Joe went through to the public bar. Sally waited a diplomatic moment and then turned back to me.

I widened my eyes, trying to appear innocent. 'What?'

Sally wasn't fooled for a second. 'Don't you *what* me, Lulu Darling. That is my neighbour? Are you serious?'

'Yes, and ...?'

'And have you?' Sally said, with a sideways jerk of her head towards Enid.

'Have I what?' I said.

'You know perfectly well.'

'No,' I said.

It didn't work.

'*You have* haven't you!' Sally said, her knife and fork clattering onto her plate.

'Sally!'

'And there was me worrying about you stuck down here on your own! Little did I know! You lucky cow!'

'Mummy, you said it was rude to call people a cow,' Enid said. 'Can I have some ice cream now?'

'Please,' Sally said absently, still looking at me with an inscrutable expression.

'Please can I have some ice cream now?'

'You haven't finished your dinner,' Sally said.

'I'm full up of dinner but I'm not full up of ice cream,' Enid said quite reasonably, 'and is it Foxy Fox? I hope so because I can't think of anything else beginning with F.'

Sally gave me a meaningful look. 'Foxy is about right I think. I'll be asking you about this later on, Miss Darling.'

'Yes, I thought you might,' I said.

Chapter Twenty

The following morning Enid hauled herself up onto one of the kitchen stools to watch me making breakfast. Nothing too taxing; we had agreed on scrambled eggs because Enid didn't believe me when I told her how yellow Devon eggs were.

'Why are they that colour?' she said, poking at the sunny mound on her toast. 'Is it safe to eat?'

'Of course, and it's that colour because the hens are so happy,' I said.

'How do you know?'

'I know everything that's important,' I said.

'What's worse to meet on the stairs, a zombie or a werewolf?'

'I don't know, because that's not important.'

This seemed to placate her and she took a big bite of toast.

'Mummy is still asleep,' she said at last, 'and she was snoring.'

'Well it's tiring driving all this way,' I said. 'It's nice for her to have a lie-in.'

'What are we doing today?'

I felt a stab of panic. Who knew? I had no idea how to entertain a six-year-old.

'Did Mummy say anything?'

Enid shrugged. 'She said we could go to the museum or the shops and I said I didn't want to do either. We're always going to the museum in London.'

'Well what would you like to do?' I said.

Enid thought about it. 'I'd like to watch TV. Am I allowed?

That didn't sound too difficult to me. What a strange thing to ask. Perhaps she was routinely kept away from the evils of the haunted fish tank as my father used to call it.

After she'd finished we went into the sitting room and I turned the TV on. As it was Saturday morning there was something on that was sufficiently hyper, noisy and colourful and Enid slipped slowly down the arm of the sofa and into the seat, transfixed. On the screen there was a young man in a red shirt and yellow trousers shouting, trying to make a long pink balloon into a dachshund and failing abysmally. I left her to it.

In the kitchen I cleared up a bit and made a pot of coffee. Sally had serious addictions to both nicotine and caffeine so I guessed it wouldn't be long before one or both drove her downstairs. I poured myself a mugful and put Enid's toast crusts out onto the windowsill where a succession of small birds swooped down to peck. Then I started to think about Joe again. And my latest plot. Last night I had batted away most of Sally's questions because Enid had got her second wind and stayed up later than was usual, then been in a clingy mood, wanting her mother to go up the 'scary stairs' with her and read her a story before she finally went to sleep.

I drank my coffee and ate some toast and peanut butter, trying to forget exactly how calorific it was. I seemed to have the willpower of an amoeba these days. I was thinking of buying some bigger, or at least stretchier, trousers online to spare myself the shame of having to try them on in an actual shop. I had a lovely selection of clothes and could, if I was honest, now only get into about a third of them. And when it came to shoes, the heels I was used to wearing every day no longer seemed feasible. I consoled myself with the thought that I hardly needed to wear designer clothes or stilettos down here; this was more warm jumpers and wellington boot country. I sat chewing and feeling like a barrage balloon. Then I thought about something else before I got depressed.

'Where's Enid?' It was Sally, wrapped in a towelling dressing gown, blinking against the light.

'Watching TV,' I said, 'something to do with Balloon Modelling and a great deal of Shouting.'

'Oh great, she'll be hyped up on adverts and questionable language for the rest of the day,' Sally said, slumping onto a kitchen stool and flapping a hand for some coffee. 'I'm absolutely sure she has some homework to do, so that will be a joyful way to spend an hour or two later on. Why do we pay these exorbitant fees when she's home more than she's at school and every week there seems to be another request for money? Trips out, new uniform, new stationery, not to mention after school club activities, which all cost a bloody fortune. I mean what the hell are they doing there? Polishing uncut diamonds or renovating Old Masters? When I was her age I was playing in the sand pit and reading comics. Now they need an iPad, a laptop, exotic holidays and designer trainers. And the birthday parties? Oh my God don't go there. Last time Enid was invited to one the mother sent out suggestions for acceptable presents. It was like a wedding list.'

'Good grief, what did you do?' I said, horrified.

Sally patted at her pockets and pulled out her cigarettes. She lit one up and inhaled with a sigh of pleasure.

'Can you open the window a touch or Enid the Moral Conscience will be shouting at me. I ignored it of course. Why would I buy Enid's classmate a cashmere ballet wrap, pink, size three when I haven't bought one for Enid? I just sent some theoretically educational craft toy with billions of tiny beads and a tube of glue. It was, I'm afraid to admit, the most irritating thing I could find. Chloe's mother will hate me forever and with any luck we won't be invited back next year.'

'Sounds a nightmare.'

'You're lucky you didn't have kids,' Sally said, blowing her cigarette smoke towards the window, 'very sensible indeed.'

That sentence suddenly sounded awfully final. I mean I wasn't forty yet; plenty of women – Sally included – had their first pregnancy at my time of life. Celebrities were always popping out kids with foolish names whilst in their forties.

I tried to think of one while Sally hunted in the cupboards for an ashtray.

Weren't colours popular names these days? What about Mauve or Turquoise? Turquoise Darling. A place of conception like Kensington or Knightsbridge might work? But what if your baby was accidentally conceived in Bere Regis or Hemel Hempstead?

What about favourite food names? Pickle Darling. Avocado? *Wagon Wheel*?

I realised Sally was talking to me.

'Sorry, what did you say?'

'I said have you sold your flat yet? And what are you planning to do today?'

I pulled myself together. 'No I haven't sold the flat although the agent was quite positive now I've got rid of Benedict. What day is it? Saturday? I should go to Stokeley to stock up. Any requests? You could come with me if you like?'

Sally pulled a face. 'I won't, thanks all the same. I'll try and prise Enid away from the TV and get her to find her homework book. Get the *fun* part of the weekend out of the way. Then perhaps we could play a board game later or watch a nice film. As long as it's not *Frozen*. I only have to see the DVD cover to want to punch someone. Did I thank you for giving her that? And hopefully we can get her to bed at a reasonable time today so that I can grill you for information about what you have been up to with my neighbour.'

'There's no need to be so territorial; you'd never set eyes on the man before last night.'

'Well don't think I've forgotten, that's all I'm saying.'

Sally went to see what Enid was doing and came back and pulled out another cigarette.

'She's watching a young chap dressed as a clown falling into a paddling pool full of custard. So while we have a minute, tell me how you got hot and steamy with Joe Field.'

'You're making something out of nothing, Sally.'

'Really? Why do I not believe you? In that case you can tell me about it. I mean, it's not as though you're pregnant or engaged is it? Go on and don't leave out any details.'

'He mended a puncture when Jassy and I were here and then when I came back he invited me to dinner. And while I was there his daughter was ill, and it was meningitis.'

'Is she okay?'

'Yes she's fine. We got an ambulance and when he got back in the morning, well, you know.'

'And?'

'You really are nosy, Sally. I don't ask you intrusive questions about your sex life do I?'

'You can if you want, it wouldn't take long. I'm living the dream vicariously. Was he ... shall we say *rewarding*?'

'That's much too personal and you are a rude cow to ask me.'

'I'll take that as a yes. How absolutely marvellous.'

I went to get my purse and shrugged on a coat. 'I'm off to

get some food before you ask any more embarrassing questions.'

'You won't get away with that. I'm going to get you pissed later and find out all the sordid details,' Sally said with a knowing gleam.

I unplugged my mobile from the charger. 'So have you got any special requests? Not dairy intolerant? Gluten intolerant?'

Sally thought about it. 'Just intolerant.'

*

I did my shopping, stopping in the café for coffee and some speedy Wi-Fi, then drove home past Lower Tor Farm at my usual slow pace but there wasn't any sign of Joe. Up on the side of the hill in the far distance I could see some sheep bunched together as though they were being rounded up or herded or something. Then I saw someone driving a quad bike – perhaps that was Joe? It was too far away to tell.

I wondered what particular aspect of sheep business he was up to: catching or branding or something? Could you brand a sheep? Wouldn't the wool catch fire?

At last I got back to Barracane House, parked behind Sally's VW and started unloading the shopping into the kitchen. Enid immediately joined me and began 'helping'. Her idea of helping was to pull things out of the bag and drop them on the floor saying 'boring' until she came upon some Tunnock's Tea Cakes and started investigating them with a damp finger.

'Are these marshmallow?' she said rather suspiciously.

'Yes, they are. If you don't like them leave them alone.'

'Enid, what did we say about eating between meals?' Sally said. 'We agreed we wouldn't do that, didn't we?'

'You said you were going to give up smoking as a New Year's revolution,' Enid fired back.

Sally took the cakes from her.

'There are birds on the windowsill,' Enid said, and ran across, delighted.

'They are still eating your toast crusts from breakfast,' I said.

'Oh!' Enid pulled up a chair next to the sink and stood on it to see the birds more closely.

She wobbled rather alarmingly and I went over to put one arm round her to steady her.

'What are they?'

'The brown ones are sparrows and the ones with the long tails are tits.'

Enid giggled, one hand over her mouth. 'You said tits!'

I laughed with her. It felt rather nice actually. She was a skinny little thing, her hair falling out of its scrunchie into her eyes. I pulled her hair back and tied it up properly. Her hair was silky soft and smelled of flowers. Would Jassy have a child like this? A little girl who liked princesses and unicorns and had a bedroom with a white bed, sequinned party dresses and an obsession with pale pink? Or would she have a boy with the same floppy hair as Ralphie? A child who would be dressed in cricket sweaters before he could walk.

Enid held out both arms to me and I lifted her down from the chair. She felt as light and bony as a kitten.

Sally looked over. 'Enid, go and write your name as neatly as you can, three times, and Lulu and I will make a delicious lunch.'

'I'd like an avocado and bacon panini,' Enid said over her shoulder.

'What? She's six!' I said.

'Oh well we all know *I want* doesn't get,' Sally muttered. 'How about cheese toasties?'

'I can make some soup if you like.'

'Can you. I'm impressed!'

*

We spent the next half an hour chopping up vegetables, a task Sally seemed to enjoy at first, but then she got bored and went to smoke in the open kitchen doorway.

'So when do you expect to see Joe Field again?' she said, dangling the subject temptingly in front of me.

'No idea,' I said trying to sound casual.

'You could invite him over.'

'Yes I suppose I could.'

'Or *I* could! What's his phone number?'

'I have no idea and if I did I wouldn't tell you.'

Sally rolled her eyes at me. 'Spoilsport. I've had to put up with all the Benedict shit before now, and Charlie before him. I told you he was shifty at the time if I remember. Not to mention Luke. I don't see why I shouldn't be involved in this romance too.'

'It's not a romance.'

'If you say so. What's happening to that soup now?'

'Leave it for a bit and then I'll blend it.'

'I don't think I have a blender.'

'Yes you have, look. Sally – why have you got a kitchen full of equipment if you never use it?'

'I don't cook, I just heat things up but I can't resist buying kitchen gadgets. I've spent hundreds in a fantastic cook shop I know.'

*

After lunch I went to catch up with some plot ideas while Sally tried to persuade her daughter to go for a walk to the end of the lane.

'But there's nothing *there*,' Enid said as her mother wrestled her into her coat, 'just *nothing*.'

'There are fields, and sheep and birds and nice clean air,' Sally said with a touch too much enthusiasm.

'Can't we stay in and watch *Frozen*?'

'Absolutely not.'

There was then a spirited discussion about what it would

take to allow the *Frozen* DVD out of Sally's case. They eventually agreed on homework done and an hour's nature ramble.

They set off with a great deal of noise and fuss from Enid about wellingtons being lame. I escaped into the sitting room with my laptop and listened to the fading sound of mother and daughter arguing as they went up the lane.

With a sigh of relief I addressed the problem of keeping my nubile heroine out of the sweaty clutches of her deputy headmaster. In my imagination he was slowly changing from being a tall, balding redhead, into Benedict's friend Percy. I thought for a few moments about the many times Percy had been sexist, humourless and creepy and wondered how Benedict was getting on in his search for a new flat. Or perhaps he had settled for sleeping under the swivelling eyes of Percy's axolotls.

There was a brisk knock at the front door. Followed by a long ring on the doorbell. With a sigh I got up. Surely Sally had thought to take a key? And that definitely wasn't an hour.

I opened the door.

'Hello, sweetheart, you won. I couldn't stay away any longer.'

I watched, mouth gaping with shock as Benedict walked past me lugging a leather holdall that suggested he anticipated a longer visit than just an hour or two.

He turned, dropped his bag and came to give me a hug.

'There she is! My little Lulabelle, I realised you wouldn't be the one to bend so I've admitted defeat.' He dropped to one knee in front of me. 'I'm here to beg your forgiveness. Let's give it another go. We'll put all the unpleasantness and the silly squabbles behind us and make some plans for a holiday. Put the kettle on, what do you say?'

Chapter Twenty-One

I was speechless. I stood with my mouth open as Benedict wandered around the sitting room, unwinding his plaid scarf from its complicated metrosexual knot and rolling it around his wrist.

'This is a nice place, if you like that sort of thing, I suppose,' he said. He poked about in the bookcases, which of course were full of immaculate hardback books of every genre. He pulled out one on Rameses the Third, flicked a few pages and put it back the wrong way round.

'So are you having a nice rest? Away from all the hustle of Town?'

I turned the book round the right way and found my voice at last. 'I'm not resting, I'm working actually.'

He laughed and stood, hands in pockets, looking out of the window; master of all he surveyed. It was very irritating.

'Nice view,' he said, 'lots of grass. I suppose it's peaceful isn't it? Nothing too taxing. I suppose that's what the problem was: you were overtired, you needed a rest.' He turned round and looked me up and down. 'You're looking well anyway, sort of different. Have you done something to your hair? It makes your face look fuller.'

'This is you trying to butter me up is it? Telling me I've put on weight.'

He looked shocked. 'I didn't say that. Don't be so touchy, Lulabelle.' He came over and stood in front of me. 'It suits you. The country lady look. All you need is a string of pearls and a hacking jacket; very hip.' He reached into his bag and pulled out a tissue-wrapped parcel. 'I've bought you that cashmere cardigan you wanted, remember? I knew you wanted it and I just didn't get around to buying it. Right size, right colour.'

'That's very kind—'

'You see I do listen sometimes.'

'Benedict, the cardigan is lovely, but the last time I saw you I was changing the locks. What part of that didn't you understand? And how the hell did you know where I was?'

He laughed. 'I followed the app on my phone. Find My Friends. Remember? You didn't really mean it, I know you. I've been doing a lot of thinking, Lulu, since our little falling out and I've realised you were right.'

This stopped me in my tracks. *You were right* was not a phrase I had ever expected to hear from Benedict, even if I'd just won the Nobel Prize for Chemistry.

He accepted my silence and carried on. 'I took you for granted, I was silly old Benedict and I'm sorry. I know I've been a bit preoccupied with work and this blasted Fennimore versus Blacklow case. If you knew what a load of shit I've been putting up with from Julian in the last few days, you'd – well, look, that doesn't matter. What matters is I've been a mean old thing to my little Lulu and I'm sorry if I made you cross.'

At least he didn't say '*sowwy*' this time.

'If,' I said, '*If?* I've chucked you out and changed the locks. I've put the flat up for sale and come down here with the sole intention of getting away from you!'

He enfolded me in a bear hug. 'Now then, darling girl, that's nonsense. Things just got a bit out of hand didn't they? I know it was my fault. I've thought a lot about it and I can see I was untidy, didn't help you enough. I should have done more and appreciated you more too. I'm willing to put everything behind us. Clean slate. I'll never be so thoughtless again, I promise. I'll do more to help, and I'll get Eddie to work out a proper spreadsheet for us.'

'Who the hell is Eddie?' I said, trying to disentangle myself.

'Eddie. Eddie with the limp. Eddie Cavendish; he works in the finance department and he owes me a favour. He could work out a spreadsheet for us to use to allocate monthly outgoings and then we could share the load. I know it might seem as though I've been taking advantage even though I have been paying the electricity bill for the last six months. And that's not to be sniffed at, I can tell you. All those showers, and the washing machine—'

'You have showers and dirty washing too you know!'

'—and lights left on all the time.'

'I was always turning lights *off* as a matter of fact, Benedict! And to be honest I'm not sure I want Eddie with the limp to be party to our monthly expenditure. Next thing you know he'll be querying some receipts and asking if I really need to go to Whole Foods quite so often and couldn't I go to Tesco instead.'

'No, all right then, scrub that out, you might have a point.' He took my hand and kissed it, looking at me with sad eyes. 'But I mean it, Lu, I've been thinking about all the happy times we've had together. Remember when we went to Venice for the weekend, and we just wandered round the little streets hand in hand? And when we went to Edinburgh for Hogmanay? We tried all those different whiskies and I bought a kilt. And that fabulous bedroom with all the tartan overload; remember that? We had such fun. And that trip to the Lake District when it rained all the time and we just stayed in bed and had room service. We've got a lot of lovely memories, Lu. It could be like that again, I know it could.'

'Well yes—' I said feeling rather sad.

Benedict seized his moment. 'I had a brilliant idea while I was driving all these thousands of miles to find you.'

'A brilliant idea?'

'Absolutely brilliant.'

'I find that hard to believe.'

'It's such a brilliant idea that I can't wait to tell you what it is. I was going to wait until later but—'

He stood looking at me for a second, his eyes alight with excitement. He grinned and held his arms out towards me.

'Let's get married.'

'*What?*'

'Let's get married. I know that's what you always wanted. I know it would make you happy.'

'*Getting married?* Getting married *to you* would make me happy?' I parroted foolishly.

'Yes I know it would. And that's why I'm asking,' he said, pleased with himself. 'I know it's a bit out of the blue but it's the obvious answer isn't it?'

I was dumbfounded. I think he took my silence for girlish delight.

'Milo and Ruth got married at Two Temple Place, do you remember? It was beyond fantastic. We could do the same. Don't you think? It would be such fun.'

I looked at him open-mouthed; he chuckled.

'I mean it Lu, I love you. Let's get married.'

I was stunned. I really hadn't expected this. I tried to think calmly and not say, *If you were the last man on earth* ...

'I can see it's a bit of a shock. I'll give you time to think about it, sweetheart. Now, where are we sleeping?'

He disappeared upstairs and a fair amount of grumbling and arguing heralded Sally's and Enid's return from their country ramble. Enid stood on the middle of the kitchen doormat, struggling to kick off her wellingtons while pulling off her pink gloves and dropping them on the floor.

'I'm never going there again,' Enid said in a loud whine. 'You said it would be fun and it wasn't.'

'There's always lots of mud and poo in the country,' Sally said. 'It's no one's fault, it's because lots of animals live here.'

'Well someone should clear up after them and then people wouldn't stand in it would they?' Enid said. 'It's disgusting.'

Sally gave me a resigned look. 'Sheep poo one, Enid nil. Good God, Benedict, what the hell are you doing here?'

'Hello, Sally my love,' Benedict said, coming down the stairs to double air kiss her cold face. 'You don't mind do you? I just wanted the chance to make up with my girl.'

I held up a protesting hand. 'I'm not your girl, Benedict, remember? I am your ex-girl. I am your ex-woman actually, cardigan or no cardigan. You are the one with trousers that are up and down like a dog at a window.'

Benedict laughed and came to put his arm around my shoulders but I moved smartly away from him and he tripped a bit and with a muffled oath stood in the glob of sheep poo that Enid had left on the doormat.

*

'Why is he here? What are you doing FFS?' Sally hissed at me when Benedict had gone grumbling into the utility room with an old newspaper and some disinfectant to sort his soiled brogues out.

'Me? It's not me,' I said, outraged. 'I didn't invite him here. I don't want him here.'

'Well you didn't expect to hide from him for the rest of your life did you?'

'Chance would be a fine thing, with my frigging phone telling him my every movement. Right, I'm blocking him.' I fumbled for my mobile.

'I didn't think he would make a beeline for you quite that quickly. Perhaps he really does want to make up?'

'So he says. He was remembering all the happy times, all the trips we'd taken.'

'And are you reconsidering?' Sally said, eyebrows raised.

I thought about it. It was true we did have some happy memories but I knew they weren't enough.

'Look I want him to leave me alone to get this book finished and I'm sure you want that too, bearing in mind all the complaining you've been doing about Enid's school expenses.'

'Sorry, sorry I can see you're upset. Look let's have a glass of wine or a gin or something – settle the nerves? I've got some lovely Cabernet Sauvignon you'd like. Unless you've found it? I hid four bottles in the broom cupboard behind the red bucket.'

'Sally, it's half past four!'

'This is a fucking emergency.'

Enid appeared in the kitchen doorway, her mouth turned down in a classic arc of disapproval.

'You swear too much, Mummy, and you smoke too much and you drink too much.'

'Be grateful I don't like locking small girls in the coal cellar as well,' Sally muttered.

'We don't have a coal cellar,' Enid responded in a sing-song voice, reaching up towards the biscuit tin.

Sally moved it further away. 'Well be grateful for that too.'

Enid waved a DVD at her. 'Can I watch *Frozen* now?'

'Oh for ...' Sally went into the sitting room with Enid at her heels and returned alone a moment later.

She glared at me. 'Bloody *Frozen*. You cow.'

She went out into the scullery and returned with a bottle of wine, which she sloshed into two glasses, handing one to me with an apologetic smile.

'Sorry,' she said, 'by the way, where is he?'

'He went upstairs,' I said, taking a slurp of my wine.

'Perhaps he's lying on the bed now wearing only his socks and an impish smirk, hoping you'll get your kit off for a joyful reunion?'

I pulled a face. 'He must have the hide of a rhinoceros if he thinks that.'

Sally lit up another cigarette and went to stand in the open doorway. 'So how is the book coming along?'

'Well I'm doing my best but it would be better without imagining Benedict upstairs posing like an Italian gigolo and expecting a quick shag.'

Sally pursed her lips and thought about it. 'Maybe a slow shag?'

'I don't want any sort of shag remember?' I said exasperated.

'Oh yes.'

Well perhaps that wasn't entirely true. It was a question of with whom.

Chapter Twenty-Two

We spent a tense hour in the kitchen with Benedict pretending that nothing was wrong, me suggesting he should go back to London, Sally getting pissed and Enid coming in asking why we were being so *weird.* By six o'clock I couldn't stand it any longer and went out to the car. I didn't know where I thought I was going but I ended up sitting in the car park of the Cat and Convict watching a young couple dressed in regulation white shirt, black trouser/skirt combo snogging behind the dustbins and smoking until someone wearing chef's whites came out from the kitchen and shouted at them.

It was a lovely early summer evening. The sun was going down behind the distant hills, which sent out rays of pale golden light, and a flock of birds flew overhead in a neat V formation, making for the coast or possibly a landfill site.

A muddy car pulled in beside mine and I was aware of the driver looking over at me. I flicked a glance. It was a little blonde, vaguely familiar, and beside her was a chap with a baseball cap and a vacant expression. They got out and the blonde tapped on my window.

'Hello,' she said.

I struggled to remember her.

'Ellie,' she said, 'we met here a few weeks ago. You were having a meal with Joe.'

Ah yes, his childhood friend, the Young Farmers Club, the one who tried to muscle in on our conversation. Something about a pony for Ivy.

'Hello,' I said with what I hoped was a friendly smile, 'how are you?'

'Great.' She looked over at her companion who was now standing in the doorway to the pub rolling up a cigarette. 'I didn't think you'd still be here.'

'Oh, why not?'

'Well, you know.' She smirked.

No.

I suddenly wanted to really annoy her; yes I know it was unbelievably childish.

'Oh I've been back loads of times. I'm here for a long stay at the moment, finishing my next book.'

'Oh, yes the soppy chick lit stuff.' Ellie pulled a face.

I ignored her. 'And Joe has been so welcoming. And Isobel and Will. They've been really friendly. I went over there for dinner the other night.'

'Really? Well I suppose they are nice people.'

She stood looking steadily at me, obviously weighing up what to say, probably debating with herself whether I was worth her time or not.

'Joe's okay then?' she said.

'Yes he's great, fine.'

There was another pregnant pause. Over in the doorway her companion cleared his throat, reminding her that he was still there. Ellie ignored him.

'Joe's always polite to people. It doesn't mean anything,' she said.

I put on an innocent expression and shrugged my shoulders. This annoyed her more than anything, as I had guessed it would.

'You're wasting your time,' she blurted out.

'Sorry?'

'Joe. You're wasting your time with him. He's never got over Clare – Ivy's mother. I don't think he ever will. But if he does, you won't be the one to do it.'

We locked eyes for a long thoughtful moment. Clare. So at last I had a name.

'Clare? I said, trying to sound careless.

'Ivy's mother,' Ellie repeated.

This was my opportunity. 'What happened?'

Ellie gave a slight sneer at my ignorance. 'Joe hasn't told you? Clare died three days after Ivy was born. He never got over it. She had a heart attack.'

I gasped in horror at this disastrous news.

Not once had I imagined such a tragedy. I felt awful. I'd been assuming Ivy's mother had run off with someone like Alan the Australian sheep shearer. I'd imagined her a heartless flirt, twirling her hair between her fingers. Someone needy and insecure who had been left alone once too often while Joe went off onto the moors mending dry stone walls. Or perhaps he had been looking for a lamb under a snow-heavy hedge, his dogs at his heels, and got home to find her gone. Now I had the image of a beautiful young woman pale and still, a new baby in a cot at the foot of the bed, Joe bewildered, heartbroken, mourning his lost love.

Ellie straightened up. 'He'll never get over it,' she repeated. 'Never. A lot of people have tried with him.'

It's a long time since I've done this.

'You're wasting your time.' She turned and strode off across the car park to where her companion was puffing at his roll-up, watching her with weasel eyes.

Ellie swept past him into the pub and he ground his cigarette out under his heel before he followed her.

I sat for a moment trying to organise my thoughts. I was oddly unfamiliar with death. My parents were abroad most of the time but still hale and hearty and my grandparents had died before I was born. I still had my sister, my few relations, my friends. No one close to me had died that I could remember. How would it feel to be Ivy, growing up with no mother, just photographs and people's memories of her? Had Clare been funny, kind, sexy, loving?

Had there been other, pathetic women like me who had thrown themselves at Joe and into his bed hoping for more than one or two nights of passion? Had he felt anything for them other than the relief of occasional sex? Was I just the latest in a long line?

It's a long time since I've done this.

Perhaps that wasn't true at all. Maybe the county was littered with women he had lured into bed and then rejected?

I'd even told Jassy I loved him. Sally knew what I'd been up to. Damn, blast, and bugger.

I was in love with him. He made me feel something I'd never felt before. I'd thought there was something special between us. What possible grounds had there been for that? I thought back and tried to remember. Had there been a special lingering glance? A declaration of something? Not that I could recall. Was there a moment when he had touched me and made me feel as though I was different or exceptional?

Well there had been that time when he had turned the bedside light on and watched me. I shivered at the memory.

'Look at me. I want to see you.'

I put my face in my hands. Oh God, could I be more embarrassed?

Perhaps he had just needed to remind himself which one I was?

*

I think I'd had some stupid idea I would go into the pub, have a meal. That I would find a sanctuary there away from

Benedict and his idiocy. Marry him? Ridiculous, why would I marry *him*? I didn't love him. I knew now that I didn't. But I'd thought I loved him once, when our relationship was new and he had made a bit more of an effort. But then I'd thought I loved Joe.

Oh God.

There was no way now I was going to risk seeing Joe, or letting Ellie make me feel worse about myself than I did already. I needed to face up to this and sort it out. I wound my window up, started the car and drove back to Barracane House.

Sally was sitting on the sofa next to Enid and they were both watching *Frozen*. Enid was transfixed, her skinny knees drawn up to her chest, sucking the end of her hair, her lips moving in time to the soundtrack. I watched her for a few minutes and she was word perfect.

Sally looked up. 'You're back then. Any thoughts about what we can have for dinner. Enid's a bit hungry. I suppose we could go to the pub to eat?'

'No!' I said a bit too quickly. 'There's plenty of stuff here. I'll make something. Where's Benedict?'

'He came downstairs, took a glass of wine and said he was going to have a bath. I'm guessing you two are going to spend the rest of the weekend arguing? So pleasant for me and Enid.'

'Sorry but I didn't invite him. I didn't tell him I was here.'

I picked up my discarded wine glass and refilled it. I had no idea what I was going to make for dinner; I certainly didn't know what I was going to find that Enid would think acceptable.

'Enid likes fish finger sandwiches,' Sally said helpfully. 'There are dozens in the freezer. Actually so do I.'

'Me too,' I said with some relief.

I put a tray full into the hot oven of the Aga and made them into sandwiches. There was some brisk discussion about ketchup or mayonnaise as we all settled down in front of the TV to watch *Frozen* yet again, and then Benedict appeared. He had obviously been asleep; his hair was sticking up and his cheek was creased from the pillow.

'What are you eating?' he said. 'Fish finger sandwiches? Are you serious? I can't eat that! I've driven for hours to get here. I need some proper food.'

'No one asked you to come,' I said under my breath.

He stood rubbing sleep out of his eyes for a few minutes, waiting for me to offer him something else. I didn't.

'Right then,' he said crossly. 'Anyone coming with me to find something decent to eat?'

We turned back to the TV and ignored him. He jangled his car keys for a moment and then with an exasperated noise he went out, slamming the door behind him. Then he came back in and kissed the top of my head.

'Don't lock me out will you, darling?'

I went to bed at about ten and Benedict still wasn't back. I moved his suitcase off my bed and into the spare room and I locked my bedroom door behind me. Then I wedged a chair against the handle for good measure.

The pillows on my bed were creased from where he had laid his head on them so I turned them over.

He came back at around midnight, stamping up the stairs with all the disregard of the inconsiderate drunk, rattling on my door handle and mumbling through the keyhole at me.

Worried in case he woke Enid I got out of bed and unlocked the door.

'For heaven's sake keep the noise down! Go into the room over there,' I hissed.

'But I love you,' he said, leaning up against the doorjamb.

'Stop making such a racket,' I said. 'You'll wake everyone up.'

'I don't care,' he said, suddenly belligerent. 'I love you, I want to marry you. I told them all. I know you will say yes because you love me, don't you?'

I pushed him out and across the landing into the spare room where he collapsed onto the bed.

'You're an irresponsible fool to be driving,' I said angrily as I pulled his shoes off.

'Not,' he said. 'I told them. I explained. You're going to marry me and we'll live happily ever after in a house on Primrose Hill with a garden and a pergola and a child in a pram and a nanny.'

'No. You're drunk,' I said. 'Stay there and don't throw up on the floor or you'll be clearing it up in the morning.'

'You do love me, don't you?' he said. 'Lulabelle?'

I turned in the doorway and looked at him, my mind suddenly clear. 'No.'

He laughed rather wildly and slapped his hand down on the bed. 'Yes you do.'

Chapter Twenty-Three

The following morning – Sunday – I was up, showered, dressed and writing by quarter to seven. Something had happened to spark me up. I typed like a woman possessed and before I knew it I had written a particularly saucy scene where my heroine and the Muscular Builder had enjoyed an intimate encounter on a recently delivered mattress. I'd changed his sphere of activity with the wooden flooring to her bedroom as the sitting room seemed too pedestrian. Much refreshed, I set the kitchen table for breakfast and waited until there were signs of life from the others.

Sally was down first; still in her pyjamas and looking a bit the worse for wear.

'Benedict snores like a warthog. I could hear him through the wall. I woke up and thought there was a train going through the house.'

'He was always like that when he got drunk. I'd forgotten,' I said. 'Anyway, I used to wear earplugs. Coffee?'

Sally waved a mug at me. 'Of course. And then at half past three Enid came in and insisted there was a mouse in her room.'

'Was there?' I said, rather alarmed.

'Of course not. What self-respecting mouse would live here when they could be living in Stokeley?'

She took her coffee away and added milk and two sugars and then she opened the kitchen door and went to have a cigarette.

'I'll have to give these up soon,' she said. 'Enid the Moral Conscience is on my case. I swear when she's older she will be researching the evils of cigarette smoking on the internet so she can tell me all about the grisly death I am heading towards.'

'Benedict proposed,' I said.

'Proposed what?'

'Marriage.'

Sally started laughing and then she realised I was serious.

'What did you say?'

'No. I said no of course. He came stamping back at midnight, drunk and convinced I'd said yes.'

'You didn't did you?' Sally said, alarmed.

'No I didn't.'

'What an idiot he is. I've got to go back to London after breakfast by the way,' Sally said, attempting to blow smoke rings in the still air. 'Apparently there is some sodding birthday party she's been invited to that I didn't know anything about until I found the invitation screwed up on the bottom of her school bag. Some kid called Crispin or Caligula or something. I'll have to call into a service station en route to find a present, which means a neck pillow shaped like a dachshund or a *SpongeBob SquarePants* backpack. Neither of those things will be acceptable so Enid will be struck off their list too. By the time she leaves that school only the teachers will be talking to us.'

'Please make Benedict go too,' I said plaintively.

'I meant to ask, where's his car?'

'What?'

'His car isn't outside,' Sally said, pulling back the curtain to check. 'No, it's definitely not there.'

I rubbed my hands over my face. 'He came back late and definitely pissed. I expect he's crashed it into a ditch somewhere.'

'Let's hope no one else was involved.'

*

Benedict appeared an hour later, grey, rumpled and asking for coffee and paracetamol in a feeble tone that was supposed to arouse my pity. I pointed at the cafetière on the table and he trudged over to fill a mug.

'How can you bear to stay in this place when you could be back in London with me?' he said. 'Back with cafés and shops and the Gang. Everyone is asking where you are and what's the matter with you.'

'There's nothing the matter with me. I love it here. I'm down here for peace and quiet and no distractions so I can write, not for the shopping experience. I'll be glad when you clear off and I can get on with it. Though how you are going to get back to London is anyone's guess.'

He looked puzzled. 'What do you mean?'

'Where's your car?'

Benedict sat and sipped his coffee and thought. I could almost hear the neurones in his brain firing.

'Car,' he said.

'Car.'

He thought a bit more.

'You went out in your car and came back at midnight pissed,' I prompted.

Realisation dawned. 'Ah yes.'

'And?' I said, irritated.

'I got a lift back. A fat bloke behind the bar took my car keys off me and someone else drove me here.'

'How did he know where to bring you?'

'I told him I was staying with the author.' His face brightened a little. 'My fiancée. I think I may have invited him to the wedding. Still, I don't suppose he will come, surly bastard.'

'Benedict, we are not engaged.'

'And that's another reason why you need to come back to London, to organise the wedding.'

'We are not engaged, you fuckwit. Thank you for the offer but I am not going to marry you, Benedict, and that's final.'

'But where am I going to live?' he said sadly.

'Oh I see! I thought so. That's why you proposed? So you

could move back in to my flat? You are the pits, do you know that?'

He slumped across the table his head resting on his folded arms. 'Stop shouting, Lu, there's a love. My head is splitting.'

'Get that coffee down you. Get packed. As soon as you are sober we'll go and get your car.'

I went into the sitting room and found Enid there, glassy-eyed, watching *Frozen* again. From the thumping noises upstairs I guessed Sally was packing their bags. I went into the dining room and pretended to do a bit of editing.

With the promise of an early lunch at Enid's favourite fast food place, Sally got out of the house by eleven thirty and I waved them off with a sigh of relief. Just Benedict to get moving now.

I found him asleep on my bed.

'Benedict, get up, get dressed and get your stuff together.'

He looked at me and reached out an arm.

'Come and give me a cuddle? For old time's sake.'

'Get up, I'm taking you to get your car so you can go home.'

He sat up and swung his legs over the side of the bed, running a hand through his hair so it stuck up at all angles.

'I don't know what's the matter with you, Lulu; you never used to be like this. You used to be nice to me. Be nice to me?'

'I am being nice. I'm offering to take you to the pub so you can get your car and go home. Anyone else would make you walk there.'

I started putting his stuff back into the holdall and he watched me. Half an hour later we set off towards the Cat and Convict. Then we had to go back because Benedict had forgotten his phone charger.

A few minutes into our trip I saw a familiar Land Rover coming towards me. It was Joe. I could feel myself blushing and I prayed Benedict wouldn't notice. The width of the lane being what it was I pulled into a gateway to let Joe pass. Would he stop and talk to me? I wound my window down and tried to look casual. Just for a second he caught my eye and then he was gone, the Land Rover sweeping past me in a spray of mud.

'Bloody yokels,' Benedict shouted after him, 'no manners.'

I thought about it and was suddenly excited. Perhaps he was on his way to my house? Maybe when I got back he would be waiting for me? But where was Ivy? I hadn't seen her in the car.

We got to the pub car park and Benedict started patting his pockets. 'Have you got my keys?' he said.

'Of course I haven't. I thought you said someone had put them behind the bar?'

'Oh yes. Can you go and ask for me?'

'Why should I go? I'm not your mother, you go and ask!'

'Please, Lulu, and ask about my new jacket too. The blue one with the tartan lining. I can't find it. I'll never ask you to do anything else I promise. It's just that last night I might have ... you know?'

He pulled a pained expression.

'What, insulted someone? Thrown a punch?'

He shrugged and gave a tight smile.

'Oh God; you didn't?'

I went in. There were a few drinkers propping up the bar and Pete the barman was tipping spilled beer off the rubber mats into the sink. He looked up and saw me.

'Oh, you,' he said, rather grimly, 'come for your boyfriend's keys have you?'

'Sorry. And he's not my boyfriend.'

Pete ignored me and reached behind a giant bottle filled with small change for some charity or other and handed them over.

'Whoever he is we can't have that sort of thing in here,' he said, still not looking at me. His normally jolly and welcoming face was stern, the disapproval settling into the creases of his chin. 'Tell him he's banned. I'm as easy-going as the next man, anyone will tell you, but not that. I was surprised, I don't mind telling you. Not heard language like that since 1998.'

It was on the tip of my tongue to ask what had happened but I suddenly didn't have the energy; I didn't want to know.

'Sorry,' I said again, 'thanks.'

I took the keys and ran back to where Benedict was looking over his car for scratch marks or random damage.

'What did you do in there last night?'

He raised his eyebrows. 'Nothing. Just put a few people straight.'

'Heaven knows what that means. Here are your keys, I'll get your stuff from my car.'

*

I was back at Barracane House soon afterwards but there was no sign of Joe.

I felt a deep plunge of disappointment. Embarrassment or not, random sex or not, I wanted to see him. Perhaps all the cars parked outside the house over the weekend had put him off. Perhaps now everyone had gone he would pop by to see me? He liked popping by. He was well known for it.

I straightened up the house, collected the wet towels, stripped the beds and changed the sheets. Then I put a load of laundry on and hoovered up the crumbs from the kitchen floor. The sink was filled with soggy biscuits that Enid had optimistically thrown into what she thought was a waste disposal unit. It wasn't.

By the time I sat down with a cup of tea and a KitKat (the only snack left in the tin because Enid didn't like them) it was getting dark. I went upstairs and put my bedroom light on, like a beacon stretching out across the fields that Joe might see, might recognise as a signal.

What was I, fifteen?

I searched for something to watch on television and found a dreary documentary about one of our monarchs. Far from being a cheery old cove with an eye for the ladies, he would nowadays rightly be described as a sexual predator. I had a glass of wine and watched a natural history programme about some rare beetle in the Fenlands; riveting stuff.

Then I fell asleep, waking up at one thirty in the morning with a crick in my neck and half a glass of white wine seeping into the sofa cushions. It had not been what one might call a good day. And things were about to get worse.

Chapter Twenty-Four

I'm not a person who suffers from migraines but the following morning I thought that might be about to change. My head was fuzzy and heavy with a nasty little pain behind my eyes. Coffee seemed like a very bad idea so instead I had a glass of water and two aspirin. I made toast but couldn't eat it, it seemed too noisy for one thing and my jaws were tired, as though I had been clenching my teeth all night. Instead I sat at the kitchen table and put my head down on my arms. For a moment I considered going back to bed. I could almost imagine the relief as I sank down onto the pillows and pulled the duvet over myself. Then I heard someone driving up the lane. My eyes flew open and I waited.

Seconds later I heard a car door slam.

Then someone knocked on the front door.

Hardly daring to hope or breathe, I went to answer it.

Joe stood there, tall and broad and even more attractive than ever. I sighed with relief. It was as though the sun had come out and everything dark and tiresome that had happened in the last few days didn't matter any more.

People say that when you drown your life flashes before

your eyes. It was the same with that moment. Any number of random thoughts crossed my mind. He was here. I had put on some mascara. His wife had been called Clare. I was wearing a pale pink sweater. I'd erased all traces of Benedict. I'd changed the sheets on my bed.

I felt a smile spread across my face. 'Come in,' I said, holding the door a bit wider.

Joe didn't return my smile. 'I'm returning this,' he said and he held something out to me. It was Benedict's new blue coat. 'Your friend left it behind in the Cat last night.'

My friend.

I took it. It felt heavy and unpleasant, slightly slimy with the feel of new wax on the fabric.

'Thanks.'

'Right then.' He turned to go.

'Would you like something? A cup of tea? Coffee?'

Would you like to come upstairs for an hour or two? I was already thinking I might go back to bed. It would be much more fun if you came with me.

'No. I'm fine thanks,' he said.

His eyes were cold, polite, as though we were strangers. But we weren't strangers were we? We'd been more than that hadn't we?

'Is everything okay?' I said.

'Fine.'

I watched as he walked away towards the Land Rover, trying to think of something to say that would bring him back.

Benedict. This was all because of Benedict.

'I'm sorry,' I called.

Joe turned as he reached the car and opened the door.

For a long moment he hesitated and then he spoke. 'I don't like people lying to me. I don't like people who say one thing and do another. I don't like to see Pete's wife Betty being insulted and verbally abused like that and I don't like being made to look a fool particularly by someone like him. And Col has a heart condition. He's seventy-one for God's sake. He's not one for brawling.'

My mouth was dry with the shock. God, what had Benedict done?

'I don't understand.'

He got into the Land Rover and turned it round in the lane before he stopped next to me and wound the window down.

'You could have told me. You should have told me,' he said.

I couldn't speak; there was so much hostility in his eyes. Helplessly, I held out a hand to him.

Tell me what's wrong. I don't understand.

'You're getting married, and to that ill-mannered oaf of all people. The things he said ... That's what I don't understand. You could have told me. Before I—'

He shook his head, and drove away, the Land Rover bumping down the rutted lane.

I went back into the kitchen and sat down. My legs suddenly seemed too weak to support me. What the hell had Benedict said? What had he done?

I closed my eyes. I could still see Joe's expression – cold, offended. But just as quickly I remembered his face above mine again. Passionate, so masculine, his features softened by the lamplight.

Look at me. I want to see you. Look at me, Louisa. Look at me.

I don't know how long I sat there thinking. Going over what he had said, what I had said. He thought I was going to marry Benedict. But I wasn't. I really wasn't even considering the possibility. Not in my wildest, weakest moments. What was I going to do now?

I almost got into my car to drive after him, to explain. But that would make me look like a complete flake. Or I could ignore the whole thing, pretend nothing had changed? No, that was unacceptable. That was what Benedict had tried to do and it hadn't worked.

Or I could write Joe a letter. Phone him up? Morse code? Go and see his mother and get her to explain? Carrier pigeon? Semaphore? Of course none of *these* things were ridiculous.

Eventually I came back into the real world and decided I would spend the rest of the day calming down and working out a strategy. Then I would go and see him and talk to him sensibly and rationally about the misunderstanding. And then I would find out what Benedict had done or said and then I would probably cringe all over again.

I was startled out of my thoughts by hearing my mobile ring. It was the first time it had rung in ages, mainly due to the unpredictable phone reception. First of all I had to find the blasted thing. It must be in the kitchen because I could hear it jangling away somewhere. Then the ring tone cut out, which was annoying.

Ring again, I willed and fortunately it did – long enough for me to track it down under a pile of tea towels.

'I was beginning to think you must be dead,' was the cheerful greeting.

'Christy!' I said, recognising the gravelly tones and throat-clearing.

'This is the fifth time I've rung you today,' she said, sounding distinctly aggrieved.

'Sorry, I did tell you the reception was ...'

'Yes, well, I've got you now. Look I've had an asking price for the flat. Mr and Mrs Ramsey, did I mention them before? No? Well they tried to put in a spurious offer some weeks ago and I told them where to shove it. This morning they are back with the full price. Cash buyers wanting a second property for one of their kids. What do you say?'

'Wow,' I said.

Christy clicked her tongue in annoyance. 'Yes but "Wow" is not a satisfactory answer. I have them on the other line now, waiting for your response. Do you accept?'

'Of course!' I blurted out.

'Fine, full speed ahead then. I'll send something over to your solicitor immediately. They are in a tearing hurry as the little dear starts a new job at some ghastly high-end fashion place soon. Job; that's a laugh. I went past there the other day, five tatty-looking T-shirts in the window with random splashes of paint across them. Well I assume they were merchandise; they could have belonged to the builders for all I know. Now then, you'd better get yourself organised. I'll be in touch in the next day or two so stay where you are so your phone picks up my call. Though why you have to hide yourself down there in the back of beyond ...'

Christy rang off and I sat a bit shell-shocked. Yes I'd liked the concept of selling my flat but now it looked as though I had. The days of walking around the corner to join up with the Gang, of buying overpriced bread or vegetables from shops with artfully distressed floorboards, of drinking weird cocktails in dark bars, glamorous parties in after-hours museums – all these daily possibilities were coming to an end. How did I feel about this? Was I glad? Sad? Scared? Was I going to chicken out at the last minute and change my mind?

Even this week there had been an article in one of the Sunday papers advising against what I was planning to do. Don't go; you'll never afford to come back. As though London was the Promised Land and the gates were going to clang shut behind me forever.

I'm not someone who usually harbours unrealistic or sentimental thoughts about my parents but just at that moment I would have given a great deal to talk to them. I wondered where they were. The last I heard from them they were on the Pacific coast, thinking about going to see the Great Lakes.

I imagined them bowling along an empty Interstate highway through Wyoming in a massive Winnebago, my father singing along to Eagles classics and my mother shouting at him to shut the fuck up.

Actually I knew what my mother would say: *Go on, what's the worst that could happen?* My father would shrug and say: *Well I don't know sweetie, whatever makes you happy.*

Neither sentiment was particularly helpful.

I wiped away silly tears that were tingling my eyes and took a deep breath. I had a book to finish. I had my sister's pregnancy to think about too. I'd not been the slightest bit involved or offered any support up until now; I must do something about that. And on top of all this I was soon going to be effectively homeless. Okay, I wasn't actually going to be homeless, but I was in a way.

There was so much to think about, to worry about. In less than three months I was going to be forty. Forty, FFS! In November I was going to be an aunt. Auntie Lulu. Aunt Louisa. God that sounded old. Was I going to turn into a crumpled old spinster aunt, rambling on about men and politics and complaining about young people?

Right, calm down. This was the next bit of my life, but I'd got this far and it hadn't been that bad. Surely I could do this. If I finally got a grip.

That night I went to bed early, walking upstairs in the gathering darkness; knowing where the stairs ended, where the bedroom door was. I knew this house so well now, I could avoid falling down the small step into the bedroom, knew how the bathroom light above the sink worked. It was funny; I was comfortable with the occasional creak of old timbers, the way the east wind could yodel through the letterbox. It was almost like home. I didn't miss the noise of London or the crowds. I didn't actually miss Jassy that much although I was fascinated by the thought of her as a mother. I certainly didn't miss the traffic. Life in London had been punctuated by the constant worry about finding a parking space. I now lived in a place with grass growing down the middle of the lane leading to Barracane House. I could have parked ten cars in the overgrown wilderness that was the garden.

I stood at the dark window and looked across the valley, aware of the waning moon and the wink of stars between the clouds. Somewhere in the darkness were people and houses, curtains closed against the night. People were watching television, eating meals, drinking champagne, or Ovaltine. Out there were children going to bed and people going on night shifts. Somewhere there was a man with bright blue eyes who could change tyres and make a beef stew. A man who loved his daughter and nursed a broken heart. Joe.

I leaned my head on the cold windowpane. Suddenly I wanted him so much I couldn't think of anything else. I wanted to feel his arms around me, to rest my head on his chest and breathe him in. I knew he wasn't the solution to my problems but he was like a rock in the middle of the swirling river of my life. What a ridiculous thing to think about someone I hardly knew. Still, I had kissed him, met his mother, I'd had sex with him several times. Surely that counted for something? Perhaps I did know him in the biblical sense.

All that *so and so knew someone and begat someone else.*

I had known Joe Field. I liked him. I loved him.

Tomorrow I was going to do something about this. Tomorrow I was going to sort this out.

Chapter Twenty-Five

I was up early the following morning having slept as badly as it was possible to do without actually staying awake all night. I showered, pulled on a checked shirt and some jeans and looked at myself with a critical eye. Did I look as though I was capable of persuading Joe that I was worth taking seriously, that I was the woman who would make a difference to him in the same way he had done to me? Did I even look vaguely okay? I went to check.

I looked terrible. Pale and weary with purple shadows under my eyes.

Massively alluring. Not.

I tried to rectify the damage to my face with some artfully applied cosmetics. Hmm, now I looked like a tired woman with blusher on. None of my clothes seemed to go together or even fit me properly any more. I shambled downstairs and made some toast and peanut butter and sat at the kitchen table munching. I'd hatched a plan in the middle of the night that had seemed to make sense but now I couldn't remember much about it except it seemed like a desperate attempt to humiliate myself.

Then I had a revelation.

I was overthinking this. I couldn't defend whatever Benedict had done, and why should I? He was after all *nothing to do with me.* All I could do was explain the facts to Joe and hope for the best. If nothing else, at least we could remain on friendly terms. Maybe. It would be nice to see Ivy again too, and see if she had taken her two kittens in yet. And then there was Isobel who was a lovely woman. She and Will could almost be my surrogate parents, although I'm sure the idea would have surprised them.

I couldn't be held responsible for Benedict or Jassy or anyone. Only for myself.

I felt as though a great weight had lifted from my shoulders. All the bollocks that Jassy kept banging on about – our so-called *brand.* The need to appear at various charity events wearing complementary outfits. As the elder sister it had been decided I would stand on the right, Jassy on the left like some sort of double act. A literary Morecambe and Wise or Ant and Dec. I doubted we would be doing that again any time soon.

Last time we had been to our joint book launch Jassy had been ill and wandered the room with a glass of champagne and a temperature of over a hundred when surely, she would have been better off in bed. I've got to be there, she'd said, her eyes a bit glassy, our *brand* ...

Sally had worked it so our books had to come out together so we shared a book launch at a glitzy venue in London. I'd work one side of the room and Jassy the other and then halfway through we would get the nod from our publicists and change over. What a load of nonsense. Why on earth did we agree to do it? Jassy was a far better writer than I was. She would be more than capable of having a book launch on her own. She'd probably like being the centre of attention instead of having all the double act fuss.

When I went to see Joe I'd be calm, polite and pleasant. I could bake a cake for Ivy. No, perhaps that was taking things a bit too far. Especially remembering my last effort.

I needed time to think. Perhaps I would go for a walk. Like country people did. Of course!

I'd seen them parking their cars in the special council car parks halfway up Dartmoor. They wrapped up warmly in tweedy things and hats and proper gloves and pulled on woolly socks and boots and strode out, arms swinging. Some seemed to have ski poles too, although I didn't quite understand that. And they had maps on strings around their necks. Well at least I had the map, although I wasn't sure where I'd put it. And they had compasses and GPS tracking devices and backpacks filled with thermos flasks and Kendal Mint Cake. I didn't have any of those things. It seemed a lot of trouble and expense to go to, just to walk two miles.

Okay, forget the walk. Did I have any excuse to drop in on Joe? No.

But I would go over to Lower Tor Farm in a purely neighbourly fashion to ask about his sheep and Ivy and I would take the car, so if it all went terribly wrong I could escape quickly.

*

I knew that it was still term time and that every afternoon the school bus dropped Ivy at the end of her drive. So I really should time my visit for late morning or early afternoon. And perhaps I should organise a suitable excuse in case I needed to leave within a few minutes. A library book that needed changing perhaps, or an appointment at the dentist or hairdresser. Hairdresser; that was a joke. I had taken to pinning my fringe back with one of Enid's unicorn-decorated hair slides I'd found in the bathroom.

The nearer I got to the lane leading to Lower Tor Farm the more nervous I became.

Hi, I just thought I'd drop in, sort out that little misunderstanding. You seem to be under the impression I'm engaged to Benedict? Well obviously nothing could be further from the truth. He says he's in love with me but in fact …

Hi, I just thought I'd drop in. Benedict? Yes we were an item, I mean we lived together and I guess there was a possibility that he thought … I might have considered it at one point but then he got a bit …

Hi, now, about Benedict. I changed the locks you see and he was sleeping next to Percy's axolotls … He kept dropping hints last year, a week before Valentine's Day about a special thing he was going to buy and I thought he meant an engagement ring and then he came back with a bike.

No, that sounded pathetic.

Hi, I just thought I'd pop in on my way to the shops. Can I get you something for the weekend?

Nooo!

Hi. I just thought I'd drop in, see how you are. Benedict is slightly off his head at the moment. I mean any man who thought they were in love with me would have to be crazy wouldn't he …

No.

When I got to Lower Tor Farm it looked as though there was no one home. I parked the car and got out, listening to the utter quiet of the place with pleasure. Above me the sky was clean and cloudless, the sun warm on my shoulders.

Suddenly there was a cacophony of woofing and the two sheepdogs came cannoning out of a barn towards me, tails thrashing. They circled me happily, as though they were hoping to herd me back toward the house, and then they ran back to the barn yelping their excitement.

Joe came around the side of the house a few seconds later, dressed in a well-worn blue shirt, jeans and wellingtons.

He hesitated just for a moment when he saw me.

'Afternoon,' he said.

'Hello.'

I didn't know what to do next. I just stood with my hands hanging, probably looking rather foolish. He stopped a few feet in front of me.

I screwed up my courage. 'I need to talk to you.'

'Go on then.'

He wasn't making this easy. Well why should he?

'I don't know what Benedict did the other night in the Cat or what he said, but he had no right to behave badly.'

'He was very drunk,' Joe said.

'Yes, judging by the state he was in when he got back he must have been.'

There was another uncomfortable silence, which Joe made no effort to fill.

'I'm so sorry,' I said.

'Well maybe I am too,' he said.

'You're sorry?' I wasn't expecting this at all. 'For what?'

'I had no business holding you responsible for your fiancé's behaviour. I was just a bit shocked, you know? Surprised.' He gave a tight smile, obviously ill at ease.

Suddenly I didn't want to mess about. I just wanted to be honest with him.

'I'm sorry. He's not my fiancé,' I blurted out. 'I don't mean I'm sorry he's not my fiancé. I don't know what Benedict has been doing or what he said but he's not my fiancé.'

Joe ran one hand over his hair trying to flatten the curls that had been ruffled by a sudden breeze.

He sighed. 'It's none of my business, Louisa. I have to say he didn't seem the sort you would go for but what would I know?'

'You do know. I didn't know. I mean I know now. He's not.

I mean when I change the locks and put my flat up for sale it's usually enough to get through to someone you don't want them living there. But Benedict refused to get the message. And I don't think it was me he was besotted with, just the location of my flat.'

'And where was that?'

'Notting Hill.'

'That was Clare's favourite film.'

Clare. He'd mentioned her at last.

'I'm sorry. I heard she – you know – you lost her.'

He looked at his watch and then took a deep breath. 'I didn't lose her, she died, Louisa. I can say it now, although it did take some time to get to grips with it.'

'I'm sure.'

'Look, I have a busy couple of hours ahead before Ivy gets home.'

I was practically walking away before he got to the end of the sentence.

'Wait, I think we need to meet up for a proper chat. There are a few things I want to say to you. Things we need to clear up.'

I spun round so fast I nearly fell over. 'I'd love to,' I said.

'Not the Cat though. I know a place the other side of Stokeley.'

'Fantastic!'

'Maybe Saturday evening would be okay? Ivy has a sleep-over birthday party that night so I won't have to get back early.'

'Any night. I mean, any evening, suits me,' I said, my brain racing ahead, wondering what bra I would choose to wear.

I looked up at him, which was quite difficult when we were standing so close to each other. His six feet four next to my five foot two.

'Saturday then?' he said.

'Saturday,' I said rather breathlessly.

I really was going to have to work on my playing hard to get routine.

'I'll collect you about six thirty?'

'Absolutely. So—' I hesitated again '—are we good? I mean are we okay?'

He looked very serious. 'I'll see you on Saturday. Now I must get on.'

I got into my car and drove back to Barracane House, my head spinning. It was the same sort of feeling I'd had when I'd been in the fifth form and Greg Knox, known as Knox the Fox, had invited me to his birthday bash. Okay, nothing happened and he had been discovered behind the greenhouse fumbling with Jackie Green's bra, but the anticipation was similar. God I was in real trouble.

Chapter Twenty-Six

Just as I pulled into the lane, my phone rang. It was Jassy.

'I've still got morning sickness,' she said, not messing about with any pleasantries. 'I'm pregnant with something the size of a grape and I feel like death. This is going to go on for months, do you realise this? For *months.* I have so much to do and no one to help me apart from Maudie and she's worse than useless. She's been back to the hairdresser again and she's beginning to look as though she's set the ends of her hair on fire. It looks terrible. The ends are practically bleached white.'

There was a clatter on the other end of the phone and Jassy shouting *hang on* and then there was silence apart from the sound of running feet and a door slamming somewhere. A few minutes later she was back sounding rather sorry for herself.

'I've been sick again,' she said.

'Poor thing, it will pass though won't it?'

'Fuck knows.'

'Careful, the baby is probably listening. You don't want its first word to be embarrassing do you?'

'I couldn't give a sh ... shampoo.'

'What does the doctor say?'

'I keep getting palmed off with some woman who talks about "Baby" and "Daddy" and isn't interested in me other than as a receptacle of Nature's Little Miracle. I keep wanting to tell her Nature's Little Miracle is being a frigging pain in the arse at the moment and smack the smile off her face.'

I laughed. 'I still can't believe you're going to be a mother.'

'Nor can I. Well, apart from the fact that I can't smoke, drink alcohol or eat pâté. Or soft cheese. Or rare meat. Or the sixty-three trillion other things I used to enjoy. I've gone off coffee, fish and tomatoes and I can't brush my teeth without retching. I really thought you would be a bit more involved. I mean, I'm your only sister. Surely ...'

Jassy went on in this vein for some time while I parked the car and let myself into the house. Of course she was right. I was being worse than useless and I felt a spasm of guilt.

'Look, I'm sorry.'

'Yes that's all very well.'

'It's Devon, Jassy, not Outer Mongolia.'

'It might as well be! Do you know your flat is sold subject to contract? I looked on Rightmove. And you haven't even bothered to tell me.'

'It only happened the other day. I'm sorry.'

'So how is the book coming along? The one that made you go off in a tearing hurry?'

'*Choose Yes*?'

'Well?'

'It turned into *Choose No.* I gave up with it. I thought I'd told you. I'm working on something else.'

Jassy clicked her tongue at me. 'I've given Sally my latest. It's now called *The Girl with the Gun* and she loves it. She was asking about what you were doing with *Choose Yes*. I mean how are we to do another joint book launch if there's only one book?'

'*Choose Yes* got a resounding No from her too. So I'm writing something else. You might have to have a book launch of your own this time.'

'What?'

'Think about it, Jassy, you could have all the limelight, all the press coverage, all the flowers and the fuss.'

There was a deafening silence while the thought of this sank in.

'Well, I suppose.'

'It would be fabulous. A big do, lots of champagne, chocolates, pictures of your book cover on some cupcakes. You'd be brilliant.'

'I suppose so. You mean you wouldn't mind?'

'Not at all. You've done these things loads of times; you're brilliant at it. Anyway, I'm the one who is struggling. You are the one who isn't. I'm not going to hold you up.'

Jassy dealt the killer blow. 'Even so, if you're not slaving over a hot typeface you could at least organise my baby shower.'

I felt a swoop of horror. 'God you're right, I'd forgotten.'

'Obviously,' Jassy said rather acidly.

'Isn't it a bit early to be thinking about that?'

'No it's not,' Jassy said firmly.

'So where do you want to go?'

'It's supposed to be a surprise.'

For a mad moment I considered asking if she would like to come to Barracane House. Jassy, Ralphie's sister Maudie, and the high maintenance bride-to-be Keira. Some champagne, alcohol-free obviously, cheese board – perhaps not soft cheese, one of my highly unusual soups? But then there were so many other friends who would want to be invited.

'And don't suggest Barracane House,' Jassy added quickly.

Of course she wouldn't want to come here again. What a stupid idea.

'And not a spa, I don't want to be in the birthing pool with burn marks on my back from a hot stone treatment. Remember Saskia when she got married? She looked as though she had ringworm or something. They had to Photoshop the marks out of the pictures.'

'No, of course we won't do that.'

My mind skittered from one possibility to the next.

Before I could suggest anything, Jassy was back.

'And I don't want to go abroad. Ralphie is going to Prague for a boy's weekend sometime soon. You just know someone is going to get left behind or end up in hospital.'

'Okay, something different then.'

'Obviously nothing that requires specialist equipment or safety nets. No mud, water, pottery painting, or stupid games. Diana had a baby shower recently where someone microwaved different chocolate bars in disposable nappies and you had to guess what type of chocolate it was. It was revolting and the only one anyone got right was the Bounty because of the coconut.'

'So what do you want to do?'

'I don't mind. I'm easy. Anything. It's up to you. Have you spoken to the others?'

'No, perhaps I should.'

'I don't see why it should be so difficult. You've got months to come up with something. I'd just prefer it to be before I get too huge and look like a hippo in the pictures. Or perhaps I should leave it until after the baby is born,' she added thoughtfully.

I grasped at the opportunity.

'If you did that we could all go to a luxury hotel in a gorgeous suite. Indoor pool, afternoon tea in a conservatory. Absolute relaxation interspersed with vats of Prosecco that you could drink,' I babbled, 'and we can tell you how marvellous you look and what a fabulous mother you are. We might even ask someone to take some carefully staged photos for the glossies. You know the sort of thing, you up to your neck in the Jacuzzi looking glamorous, surrounded by the rest of us with mud packs on, looking slightly crazy.'

'Well it's not very imaginative but yes that might do.'

'Phew, thank heavens for that.' It didn't sound too difficult.

'But it better be good or I'll really kick off,' Jassy muttered.

'Thank you, Mumzilla.'

'Something luxurious. And exclusive. Nothing tacky. No nasty sachets of instant coffee or little pots of UHT milk.'

'Okay, I've got the idea,' I said.

'Though I'll have to pump and dump first.'

'What?'

'Express some breast milk beforehand. Otherwise Sparkler will get her first hangover second hand. The woman at the clinic keeps going on about Sparkler "latching on" as if she's going to be a new girl at school trying to join the cool gang. And I want a free mini bar in my room. If I'm off alcohol for months I'll have some catching up to do. I'm not going anywhere where there is a five-quid pack of Pringles in the fridge or those revolting biscuits with a ten-year use-by date.'

'No, of course not.'

'Hang on, where would Sparkler fit in to all this?' Jassy said after a moment.

'We'd leave her with Ralphie for the weekend.'

'You're joking. I'll have to get a nanny. I can't leave Ralphie in charge of changing the loo roll. He's going to be a useless father. He said yesterday don't forget he's off to Australia at the end of November for The Ashes tour and could I make sure I have the baby before he goes. Bloody cheek.'

'I'm sure he will be fine when it happens. He'll step up and be besotted before you know it.'

'Well that's okay then. If you're sure. So then, what time do we expect you?'

'I … er … remind me?'

She sighed. 'This weekend. Keira's wedding dress fitting. Your bridesmaid's dress? You agreed on the date. You suggested it. You've *got* to be there. At midday on Saturday. Please don't tell me you've forgotten?'

'No, of course not. You mean *this* Saturday?'

'It was your idea, Lulu. Of course I mean this Saturday. I mean it's not as though you have anything better to do, is it? Not like you've planned a weekend of debauchery. Or have you?'

I laughed carelessly. 'Of course not.'

The very idea.

'Right then, I'll see you soon. And then you can tell me all about your ideas for my baby shower. Will you come up on Friday? I'll have the sofa bed ready for you if you can't use your flat.'

'It's not sold yet – don't worry, I'll stay there. I don't particularly want to listen to you and Ralphie frolicking all night in the next room.'

Jassy gave a hollow laugh. 'Trust me, there is no question of *any* sort of frolicking. I've told him that sort of thing is strictly off limits. Unless he's prepared to hold the bucket by the side of the bed while I throw up. Talking of which … I'm going to have to go …'

'So like the home life of our own dear Queen.'

Seconds after I'd rung off I remembered with a clang that I had just arranged a date with Joe on Saturday. It was vital I was there. He wanted to talk to me. Thoughts skittered around my head for a few minutes wondering if it was possible to do both. Obviously it wasn't. There would undoubtedly be a gathering of the Gang that evening when I would be expected to discuss Jassy's baby shower, a weekend of fun and games. Well, fun. Well a weekend anyway.

The possibility of getting back to Devon by six thirty on Saturday evening was nil. I'd have to change it with Joe. He would think I was a right flake, which possibly I was. Jassy was quite right: this weekend had been set aside for Keira's wedding dress fitting months ago. You didn't change appointments with *Evanka Mila* unless there had been a nuclear war or at least a death in the family.

*

Of course Joe wasn't at home when I called in to rearrange our date. Why was nothing ever easy? But the chap I had met on my first visit was there. It looked like he had just returned from somewhere muddy.

'Joe's not yere,' he said.

He still had the same tweed cap and today had accessorised it with a washed-out blue boiler suit, some battered old rigger boots and the same incomprehensible accent. This must be

Frank. No, Frank was the terrier. This must be his farm manager Jim. Or it might be Ken.

'Any idea when he will be back?' I asked.

He pushed out his lower lip thoughtfully. 'Gorn up tarp field,' he said.

Top field. 'Where's that?' I asked, knowing the answer already.

'Backalong.'

By dint of his pointing and waving up towards the hills behind the house I gathered Joe was somewhere up there.

'Jest a step, maid,' he said, 'no more 'un a step. Thee'll be there'un back in no time.'

'Fine,' I said cheerfully, locking the car and zipping up my coat. It looked like a nice sort of day, it didn't look like rain and it wasn't far according to Jim/Ken.

I was glad I'd had the foresight to put my boots in the car and I pulled them on before confidently stepping out towards the hill.

I was surprised to discover that despite having gym membership I was far from fit. (Yes I do realise I have to actually go there.) It might have been *jest a step* for Jim or Ken but it was like an army assault course for me. I followed the muddy path, found a stile and hopped over into the first field. I had been told to expect to go through three on my journey. A field to me meant something the size of a pony paddock. These were massive, vast swathes of scrubby grassland, interspersed with dry stone walls, hedges blasted by the wind to strange angles and the occasional optimistic tree. There were rock outcrops, grassy tussocks, the remnants of cobbled paths, and metal gates held closed with loops of orange twine.

By the time I got to field number two I had unfastened my coat and put my scarf into my pocket. I could feel I was red-faced and I had to stop several times to catch my breath. A few minutes later I saw another stile in the distance and I made my way towards it, puffing with every step like a consumptive.

I was nearly there. In fact, I could see someone who resembled Joe on the other side of the field. It looked as though he was mending something. I stopped and wheezed a bit before I clambered over. Everything was going to plan. We could have a nice chat about the farm and the sheep and stuff. I'd explain everything and he would understand.

I stood up as I crossed the stile and saw he was waving at me. I waved back at him, exultant. But then somehow I lost my balance, caught the buckle on the side of one boot on a loop of wire sticking out of the hedge and began to topple over.

No. This couldn't be happening.

I described a slow parabola down into deep tyre tracks filled with water and landed with a loud, despairing scream. Instantly the water filled my boots, seeped up my sleeves and soaked my jeans, enveloping me in a cold, wet, muddy bath. I lay there wondering which bit of me hurt the most. Had I broken anything?

I hesitated. I could scramble up and start trying to pretend nothing had happened or I could just lie there howling.

I tried to get up – I certainly didn't scramble, because I didn't have the energy and I'd landed on my boobs, which had probably been the nearest thing I had to a soft landing. I put my hands over them sadly and whimpered a bit. Then I grabbed hold of the stile plank, which promptly collapsed, pitching me face first back into the mud.

I got onto my hands and knees and grabbed at the stile again earning myself a few splinters in the process. This time the wood held, and I dragged myself up, inch by painful inch, spitting and swearing, mud streaming down my coat and into my boots. I stood there, arms stretched out like a scarecrow, feeling utterly ridiculous. I had no idea what to do next. I would have to walk back through the fields to my car, my feet squelching at every step.

I needed to get home, take off my clothes and have a hot bath. But could I get into my car like this? Would I need to strip in Lower Tor farmyard first? Would Ken/Jim still be there? I could just imagine him averting his gaze under his tweed cap and shuffling off, filled with confusion at the ways of townies.

I heard the noise of an engine coming towards me. I looked up. My heart soared and then plummeted. It was Joe on a quad bike, making his bumpy way across the field towards me. One sheepdog was running full pelt behind him, and when he drew nearer I saw the other one was balanced on the back of the quad bike, tongue lolling, front paws on Joe's shoulders.

'What are you doing? Are you all right? Have you hurt yourself?' Joe said as he reached me. He got off the quad and came towards me, his wellingtons sinking into the quagmire. He reached out to help me onto more solid ground at the edge of the field.

I took hold of his hand and squelched after him, almost losing one of my boots in the process.

I could see mud on the side of my nose but my hands were even filthier so I couldn't wipe it off. Joe reached into his pocket and pulled out a large blue cotton handkerchief. He held me under the chin and gently wiped my face.

'What on earth are you doing up here?' he said.

I realised I was screwing up my face exactly as I had when I was a child and my mother gave my face a spit wash. His hands were shaking. Then I looked up and realised he was chuckling.

'Nice place for a picnic, I thought. Actually, I was looking for you,' I said.

'Me? Why? Couldn't you wait until Saturday?'

'I've got to talk to you.'

He licked the corner of the handkerchief and dabbed at my cheek with it.

I stood, still dripping, until he was satisfied with his handiwork. I was plastered with mud from head to toe, my feet were cold in my water-filled boots and my new jeans were probably ruined.

I don't think I had ever felt so stupid.

He shook his head. 'Oh, Louisa—'

Suddenly there was the sound of a horse snorting or whiffling or whatever it is horses do and it pranced into view – with its rider obviously – stopping in front of us.

The rider laughed long and loud, so much so that the horse threw its head up and started trampling around. The woman on board pulled at the horse's bit.

'What the hell are you doing?' she called.

Oh great. Of course it was Ellie. She was immaculate in proper riding gear, hard hat, jodhpurs, a yellow polo-neck sweater, a waxed jacket and a superior expression. Her horse was somehow equally grand with just an artistic trace of mud on its hooves. It was steaming gently and puffing out big snorty breaths of vapour.

'Oh hi,' Joe said, and he smiled up at her.

She stared down at him with a dazzling beam. She looked as though she had been riding all her life. Straight back, heels down, thighs like whipcord. There were some back issues of *Horse and Hound* lying around in Barracane House and I'd leafed through them, so I knew.

'I was just taking Dickie out for a hack,' she said. 'Glorious day, isn't it? We've had a fantastic ride out. I thought I saw you mending the gate, Joe. And I see you've met up with an old friend.'

Old friend?

'Yes that bit of the fence is pretty rotten. I think I'll need to replace it,' Joe said.

He rubbed the horse's nose and it whiffled a bit more at him.

'Well give me a shout if you need a hand,' Ellie said, patting Dickie's neck with a resounding smack. 'Remember when we had to rebuild that wall? It was rather fun wasn't it?' She darted me a look. 'Life in the country is like that I'm afraid, always something needing to be done. And if you're trying to get into the swing of things, you don't need to get *quite* so close to the mud.'

I gave her a cheerless grin and peeled off my gloves, which was perhaps a mistake as now I had to hold on to them and they felt like a pair of lifeless slugs in my hand.

And who calls a horse Dickie, FFS?

Joe turned his attention back to me and his smile faded.

'You're a sight. I think you'd better get home, don't you?'

Ellie pulled her horse's head away from me and it curved and tittuped around so its hooves dug out great muddy divots and flicked them at me almost as though it was doing it on purpose.

'I'd give you a lift but I don't think poor Dickie would take the weight,' Ellie said sadly.

Cow.

'Don't worry, I'll sort it,' Joe said.

I stood, hands dangling like a sulking toddler.

'Well good luck. Joe, I'll pop in with the details of the Show later, or perhaps we could meet up for a drink? I'll be in the Cat on Saturday, I could pass them over then?'

'Well ...' he said.

Bugger.

Ellie favoured me with a smug smile and watched me plodding behind Joe towards the quad bike.

Much to the sheepdog's annoyance Joe turfed him off and pulled me onto the quad bike behind him, ignoring my protests that I would make everything filthy. Slowly he took me back down the hill to Lower Tor Farm. The ride was bumpy and I winced and whimpered at every jolt. At last we reached the farmyard where mercifully Ken/Jim had gone and wasn't there to see my humiliation.

'Have you got any other clothes in the car?' he said as I clambered down.

At that moment there was a shout from the lane and Ivy appeared, carrying her bag over one shoulder. She must have just been deposited there by the school bus.

'It's Lulu! It's Lulu! Have you come to see me?' she called.

'How are you, Ivy, good day at school?' I said, trying to appear relaxed.

She pulled a face. 'Okay. Why are you all covered in mud?'

'I fell over. In a big muddy puddle,' I said.

She giggled, holding her sides. 'You look like a big swamp monster! You're so funny.'

'I don't feel very funny, I feel a bit silly,' I said.

'Come and see the kittens! They only arrived yesterday. I told Daddy you wanted to see them. They are so sweet. I've called the tabby one Silkie and the tabby and white one Mittens because she looks as though she has gloves on.'

'I'd love to but I can't come in looking like this,' I said, edging toward my car and wondering if there was something in the boot I could sit on to protect my beautiful cream leather seats.

Undeterred, Ivy grabbed my hand, hustled me to the back door and brought the kittens out to show me. They were really delightful, looking around with big eyes, their noses twitching at the fresh wind. Or possibly at the smell emanating from me.

Eventually Ivy took the kittens back into the house and I made my way to the car. Joe came with me, offering an old feed sack as a protective covering for my car seat.

'Take care,' he said, his mouth twitching, 'I'm sure you'll get the mud out by Saturday.'

'That's why I'm here. I can't do Saturday. I forgot I have to go back to London on Friday. I've got a long-standing date with a bridesmaid's dress. I really can't get out of it. It's a fitting for a friend's wedding dress too. It's a bit of an occasion. I'm sorry.'

He shrugged. 'It's fine.'

'Oh. Is it?' I said, disappointed that he didn't seem to mind. Perhaps he would meet up with Ellie instead and give her the benefit of his night off.

We stood and looked at each other. I wanted so much to kiss him. Or perhaps for him to kiss me. Did he feel the same way? Apparently not.

He stood very still for a moment. 'I've been thinking about it all. You said that man is not your fiancé; he seemed to think something very different.'

'It has been sorted, believe me. I've made it very clear. To him I mean.' I suddenly felt rather stupid and uncomfortable.

'But you seem to be—'

There was a shout from the house.

'Daddy! Come quick! Silkie's run up the curtains and I don't think she can get down!'

'I'd better go. I'll see you,' Joe said.

I drove away, feeling perfectly disgusting in my muddy jeans and wet coat and sick with my failure. And of all the people to witness my clumsiness, Ellie the perfect country girl with the posh horse and the ringing laugh and the un-muddy trousers had seen me. Ellie with the glossy hair and the years of shared history with Joe. Ellie who knew how farms worked, who would undoubtedly make a splendid farmer's wife once she got rid of the spotty oik with the baseball cap. My heart plummeted as far as it could go.

A horrible thought struck me; if Joe believed at any level that I had been intimately involved with Benedict recently, what would he think of me leaping into bed with *him*? I bet he thought I was a right tart. I didn't need to look in the mud-smeared rear-view mirror to know I was flushed with embarrassment.

Chapter Twenty-Seven

Now normally I'm great at shopping. Normally I enjoy it. That day I didn't.

Keira the blushing bride had arranged for us to meet up at the shop, I mean the *atelier* Evanka Mila. Birgitte – a fussy over-tanned woman who sported a manicure that I would have thought prevented her sewing anything – was going to do the final fittings.

First we had to get through security, which meant standing in the outer hallway until a massive man with a neck as thick as Keira's waist decided if he would let us in or not. Then we had to be escorted up the staircase to the room where Birgitte was waiting with her two habitually silent assistants.

Maudie and I watched from our brocade chairs, while Jassy – who wasn't a bridesmaid but didn't want to miss anything – poked around in the cabinet of tiaras and feathered head-dresses. Then she sat down heavily as though she was carrying a suitcase and put both hands on her small bump. I'm beginning to think this is what pregnant women do so no one thinks they are just tubby. I looked at her for a few minutes, marvelling at what was going on inside her. Would it be a boy or a girl? Guy or Sparkler? How did it feel? More importantly, what would the birth be like?

Jassy had already expressed a wish to have a tranquil, candle-lit birthing pool with soft music playing and a bottle of Cristal champagne on ice waiting for her once the whole thing was over. I wondered if this was likely. Not that I've thought about it too closely, not when it pertains to me anyway. The whole thing sounds too ghastly for words but, still, at the end of it Jassy and Ralphie would have a son or a daughter. Despite myself I felt a teeny pang of curiosity. It might even have been envy.

Jassy saw me watching her.

'*What?*' she said crossly.

'Nothing; pregnancy hasn't improved your temper has it?' I replied.

She huffed and stroked her bump again. 'See how cheerful you'd be if you were throwing up every morning, had heartburn most of the day, and needed to wee every five minutes.'

Back in the real world Keira was quickly hauled into her dress, a delicious ankle-length confection of pale coffee-coloured silk with enough embroidery, beading and lace to satisfy a Romanov tsarina. We all got a bit tearful when we saw her. She really did look glorious. Keira climbed up onto the carpeted podium so we could all admire her.

'What do you think?' she said, knowing what we would say.

'Oh my God, you look like an absolute dream,' Maudie

said rather breathlessly. 'I hope I look that good in my dress.'

'Fergus is a lucky boy, he won't know what's hit him when he sees you,' Jassy chimed in.

'Fabulous,' I said, 'just wonderful.'

'Really? Are you sure?' Keira said, twisting and turning to get the best view of herself in the mirrors. 'I mean it's not too Disney Princess is it?'

'You look wonderful,' I said, 'you know you do.'

Keira gave a pleased smile. 'I do rather, don't I?'

Birgitte twitched at Keira's skirts and muttered at her assistants who brought her a velvet pincushion shaped like a dachshund. She used a couple to adjust some infinitesimal thing she didn't like.

'So this will be ready for you one week before the wedding. Don't lose weight. And whatever you do don't gain weight – that is all I am asking,' Birgitte said sternly.

We all laughed at the very idea. As if. I think Keira has been a size six all of her adult life. She eats like a horse and never seems to gain an inch. It's very impressive. And annoying.

Maudie darted eagerly into the other dressing room and I was led away to my doom. I knew exactly what was going to happen, I'd even started having nightmares about it.

A few minutes later from the other side of the curtain I heard Keira twittering and exclaiming about how amazing it all was.

'You look incredible. No, you do, Maudie. Oh God, I love that dress. So slinky and gorgeous. Don't you hate those shapeless things most bridesmaids wear? Your waist looks so tiny, Maudie!'

'I love, love, love it,' Maudie sighed back. 'We look so fabulous. Hurry up, Lulu.'

There was a great deal in the same vein for a few minutes. I heard her outside, twirling and probably admiring her non-existent bottom in the unforgiving mirrors while Jassy heaved herself up out of her chair to try on veils and satin shoes.

I stood in my strictest underwear and looked at my dress, hanging optimistically in front of me. It was beautiful, the palest dusty-pink silk and organza, knee-length and swirled into a tight bodice and skirt. This was a dress that would take no prisoners. It looked down at me, a slight smirk on its face. You're never going to do this, it seemed to say. You have sacrificed me for several packs of chocolate digestives, some Wagon Wheels and that pie and chips you snarfed up. *Remember?*

Irritated by my tardiness, Birgitte flung back the curtain and joined me in the chamber of despair.

'Now let's see,' she said, taking the dress off its padded hanger and holding it out encouragingly for me to step into, 'I'm not sure ...'

No, I wasn't sure either.

Between us we managed to get the dress over my new writer's arse and Birgitte wittered and fussed for a few minutes.

'What has happened?' she muttered. 'I'm not sure this is ... surely ...'

She tugged the sides together and little by little the zip did up. I wondered if I was going to be able to breathe and if I did, would I suddenly burst forth?

'I'm sure ... this is the right dress.' Shamingly she even went to check the label on the hanger.

'Come on!' Jassy called. 'What's the problem?'

Eventually there was nothing for it, I had to come out and show them.

'You look ...' Keira started brightly before she'd had a chance to see me. Her tone dropped. 'Really ... curvy.'

As far as the Gang are concerned 'curvy' is code for something worse. Much worse.

Jassy frowned. 'It's a bit tight,' she said. 'Are you sure that's the right one?'

'Quite sure,' Birgitte said defensively.

'Oh.'

The room went horribly quiet for a few seconds while everyone stared. I felt tears fill my eyes.

'Well there must be something wrong. You must have used someone else's measurements,' Jassy said crossly. The other two started nodding and tutting.

I shot her a grateful look. She was shifting the blame from me and my sloppy eating habits on to the hapless shoulders of some seamstress somewhere. I could almost imagine the poor woman, hunched over her sewing machine in an attic, snivelling while Birgitte whacked her with a fabric offcut.

Birgitte hesitated for a second and then rose to the occasion magnificently.

'I can only apologise, I am mortified at my mistake,' she said, fluttering her hands in dismay.

The mood in the room lifted in a second and the other two started twirling and chattering again.

'What a shame, Lulu darling, I'd be crushed if it was me,' Keira said.

Oh yes, Keira with her bird-like wrists and tiny arms, who had probably never in her adult life found a garment that was tight or too small.

*

Shortly after that we decamped to a wine bar to celebrate, or in my case get over the humiliation.

I sat nursing a glass of champagne, vowing never again to look at a chip or a biscuit and above all wishing I was back in Devon.

'It will be fine,' Jassy whispered, 'you heard her, she can get those alterations done in no time.'

'Thanks,' I said humbly.

'Silly woman, I bet this sort of thing happens a lot.'

'Yes I expect so.'

'You looked really nice though,' Maudie said, rubbing my arm. 'The colour really suits you. Sweet.'

Oh God.

I saw Keira and Maudie exchange a little, swivelling look. It didn't matter how much this was excused or brushed under the carpet, it would be all round the Gang before sunset. There was a certain aspect to the friendships that delighted in this sort of thing. Schadenfreude. It wasn't very nice really.

*

Keira decided the four of us would all go out and meet a few more of her friends that evening and have supper together. I felt so bad about my dress that I couldn't really refuse, although all I wanted to do was go to sleep. Just as I was trying to think of a suitable excuse my mobile rattled with the arrival of a text from Jassy.

'Where are you? We're waiting for you!'

I got up, collected my handbag and went down to hail a taxi. When I got to Vino Verity (another new wine bar that last time I looked was a cake shop) the other three were already sitting at a table, in almost complete darkness. Why do they do this? Do they not want people to be able to read the menus and order?

Looking at the general décor it was obvious someone had spent a lot of money on mirrored tables, green velvet chairs and retro advertising signs for things like Pernod and something called Moxie. The one behind our table was for Noilly Prat, which I've always thought sounded a bit rude. And next to that one proclaimed: *Gin Drinkers are Sassy, Classy and*

Smart Assy. I was unsure whether that was a recommendation or not.

Maudie and Keira were already slugging down Prosecco like there was no tomorrow while Jassy scowled at her fizzy water and lime.

'How's the new book going?' Keira said after a few minutes of desultory chat about the weather and an on-going political scandal concerning a cabinet minister and his cleaning lady.

'Okay,' I said accepting a glass of fizz, 'I've dumped the one I was working on and started again.'

'Oooh brave,' Maudie said, 'and Jassy says you've sold your flat?'

'Just about. I'm supposed to be exchanging soon, and completing soon after that.'

I realised one disadvantage of the mirrored tables was they allowed a view up everyone's noses. I sat back a bit.

'I think you're insane,' Jassy said crossly. She put her drink back onto the table and rested both hands on her bump again.

'Yes I know you do, but it's too late now. I've made up my mind,' I said.

'But why? You have everything you could possibly want here,' Jassy said. 'Where are you going to live?'

'I'll find somewhere,' I said. *And that's far from the truth.*

'Someone I work with told me they are converting an old warehouse by the river into apartments,' Maudie suggested, 'near the Thames Barrier. They look fabulous. They're going to have air con and Jacuzzi baths.'

'And every road jammed with people wanting to get to the O2,' I muttered.

At this point a snake-hipped waiter with a white cloth tied around his waist slithered up with a tray full of calories.

'We ordered before you got here,' Jassy said unnecessarily, 'the sharing bowls are supposed to be really good. The others are late; they're always late. They can order when they get here. I'm not supposed to let my blood sugar drop.'

Knowing my sister I'd bet her blood sugar hasn't dropped significantly since 1986.

I sat watching as the waiter unloaded two portions of cheesy fries, battered calamari rings, some deep-fried Brie segments and breaded mushrooms. I'd be lucky if I got out without splitting my trousers.

'Bermondsey then? That's supposed to be the next big thing,' Keira said, returning to the subject of my impending homelessness after a few minutes. 'You ought to ask Patsy when she gets here. She'll know.'

Patsy was the self-appointed property expert in the Gang as she had a fiancé who worked for some high-end agency in Mayfair selling car parking spaces and dilapidated mews cottages to Russian oligarchs. She had recently taken an internship with *Vogue* and had spent her entire life within spitting distance of Harvey Nicks, so I thought I'd ignore this gem.

Keira then leapt up and wandered around looking for mayonnaise and ketchup and then came back to hoover up half of the calamari with gusto. I watched her as she sat in her tiny child-sized jeans and T-shirt. Perhaps she had tape-worms?

I nibbled at a breaded mushroom while Keira inhaled most of the cheesy fries and showed us photos on her phone of the flowers and the table settings. I felt a sudden plunge of depression; it was too much. So was sitting surrounded by twig women, listening to the sly little digs about me as the message got round the table about my dress not fitting. They'd pretended to be horrified but let's be honest they were thrilled. They were those sorts of friends. The discussion started to take off before it was halted rather dramatically when Jassy stepped in, calling them unkind and nasty-minded. She then embellished the apology Birgitte had given, clutched at her bump and effectively stopped everyone in their tracks.

*

I got back to my flat and slumped onto the sofa, absolutely whacked. I sat for a moment by the open window, listening to the rumble of the traffic out in the street. In all the time I'd lived in London I'd got used to it; now I wasn't. I wanted peace, tranquillity, the occasional hoot of an owl or the noise of sheep being moved from one field to another. Perhaps I was turning into a mad recluse? I would end up living in a croft in the Outer Hebrides wrapped in a tartan shawl, writing under an oil lamp with only an old dog for company. No, I couldn't do that, the internet would be even worse than in Devon.

Devon.

I sat and thought about it for a while and longed to be back there. Why did I feel this way? Was it Joe? Did I just want Joe? Was I confusing my desire to be back in Barracane House with my lustful urges towards Joe? Would I want to be there if he had been old and bad-tempered and toothless?

But he wasn't. He was kind, and thoughtful and bloody marvellous in bed. I really liked him. And he seemed to like me. He made me feel comfortable with myself, and happy. Really happy in a way no one ever had before.

I wondered if he had met up with Ellie and if he had, what they were doing.

Anyway as far my housing needs were concerned I knew exactly where I wanted to go; I just didn't dare actually say it out loud. Not even to myself. I wanted to go somewhere so out of everyone's comfort zone that I was surprised at myself. And I had a sudden yen to keep chickens. I could almost imagine myself going out to feed them kitchen scraps and handfuls of corn. Or whatever it was they ate. Chickens?? Perhaps I was having a midlife crisis?

Chapter Twenty-Eight

I lurked in my flat for the next few weeks while Scheherazade's parents bullied both sets of solicitors and tried to bulldoze the sale through.

Birgitte managed to do something miraculous with my bridesmaid's dress that didn't involve a length of elastic and two bulldog clips and the actual event was great fun.

Three days after Keira's wedding my solicitors did something to justify their outrageous fees and exchanged contracts. I assumed they would then all be booking onto the *Queen Mary 2* for a world cruise on the proceeds. Apparently Mr and Mrs Ramsey's daughter was keen to move straight in when she returned at the end of July from doing good works in Mozambique, so she could start her new job selling overpriced and badly made clothes to impressionable people.

Meanwhile Jassy was making the most of her pregnancy, thinking up new and unexpected food cravings to keep Ralphie on his toes. She started with processed cheese slices and moved swiftly on to éclairs from Patisserie Valerie, asparagus wrapped in Parma ham and then toothpaste straight from the tube. She seemed to spend most of the day in bed, typing and then deleting everything she'd written. She claimed to have something called 'baby brain'. Considering she was only four months pregnant I did worry about what state she would be in by the time the baby arrived in November.

Ralphie went off to India to do some more cricket coverage and while he was there managed to be photographed with a pneumatic redhead, which didn't improve Jassy's humour one bit.

And I thought about Joe.

I pushed on with my new plot about the teacher and the muscle-bound builder, adding some awful accidents for Dastardly Don the deputy head involving falling into a ditch, being splattered with creosote and knocked over by a roll of insulation. I would have to see if Mr Tumble was available if it was ever made into a film.

Then, at the beginning of August – my birthday month – I prepared to move out so that little Scheherazade could move in. I'd sorted out most of my stuff apart from the few odds and ends Benedict had left behind, which I sent round to his chambers. I didn't receive a reply. Perhaps he had got used to the axolotls or moved in with Tess or Milly or some other poor sap.

I'd agreed to sell Scheherazade most of the flat contents including the ginormous fridge freezer that she was unreasonably thrilled with. She was planning to fill it with 'bubbly and scrummy things' as she'd put it in her email. When I found out she was only twenty-two I felt curiously depressed.

Where had all that time gone then? Did I have anything to show for it apart from nineteen books, some beautiful designer clothes I couldn't fit into, an impressive shoe collection I never wore and a load of expensive furniture I didn't have room for? No significant other, no children, no firm grasp on the future either. Bugger.

And now I had to really start looking for somewhere to live. Christy Church lost interest in me once the sale of the flat was in hand. I suppose I could have gone back to her with my buyer's hat on but I knew I wouldn't.

*

Two weeks before my birthday I had a call out of the blue from Sally. She'd seemed to have lost interest in me too actually, now the Trust Fund Twins were splattered all over the gossip columns and magazines in various stages of undress.

One of them had snared a premier league footballer and was now writing a weekly column called *Waggy Tales!* for some redtop rag and then appeared in *OK!* in little more than a Chelsea scarf. The other was spending most of her time at Hurlingham watching her boyfriend thrash polo ponies round a field. She'd been photographed treading in the divots in a pair of Jimmy Choos and a skirt that showed her knickers. It was all very disheartening.

There always seemed to be a selfie of them somewhere in the media, pouting and gurning in the accepted way. I tried copying them once, pushing my mouth out into a trout pout and widening my eyes. I looked like someone had shoved a firework up my bottom.

'Lulu? Sorry to have been neglecting you. How's life?' Sally said after a preliminary bout of coughing that suggested she hadn't given up smoking yet.

'Oh you know, fine,' I said.

'You don't sound fine, you sound like you are in the Slough of Despond.'

Slough. Perhaps I would have to go and live in Slough?

'I'm moving out soon.'

'That's interesting...'

'Well, remember, I turfed Benedict out and put the flat on the market. I was told it would take no time at all but in fact ... well never mind. A child called Scheherazade is moving in so she can walk to work at some boutique.'

'Oh yes. Well lucky her!'

'Yes.'

'Where are you thinking of going?'

'I have absolutely no idea.'

There was a moment's silence while Sally cleared her throat a couple of times and made cigarette-lighting-up noises.

'Look. I'm going to come straight to the point. No good beating around the bush. I don't suppose you want to buy Barracane House do you?' she said very rapidly in a tone expecting the answer would be no.

I caught my breath, my thoughts wheeling. 'You're selling?'

'Well you seem so keen on the place. I told you ages ago I was thinking of selling. Enid was singularly unimpressed with her last visit, especially with the sheep poo incident and the lack of internet and Sky TV. Henry thinks we should buy somewhere in the Dordogne. I told him that's probably further than Devon but he—'

'Yes!' I yelped.

'Yes what? The Dordogne is further than Devon?'

'No. I mean yes, I would like to buy Barracane House.'

As I said it I felt a shiver of excitement, mixed with apprehension. I wanted this. I wanted to move to Devon. I felt right there. I was going to take a leap of faith.

Sally's tone brightened. 'Goodness me, I was afraid you would have had enough of rural life. How is the book coming along by the way?'

'Fantastic!' I said. Perhaps I was being a bit ingenuous on that point. All I could think of was putting this plan into action.

'Well that's good to hear. Look, are you really interested in buying Barracane? If you want to make me an offer for the contents too you would be doing me a favour. I quite fancy buying a *longère* near Roscoff. I can go around all the gorgeous little *brocante* places in France. All those quirky little markets where they sell Louis Quinze chaise longues and painted chairs for a song. You don't have to say yes, you know. Henry was going to go into Knight Frank tomorrow to sound them out. I expect they'll snap his hand off.'

I took a deep breath. This. This was the moment when I would take control and do something for me.

'I want to buy it. As soon as possible.'

'Well, okay then. I suppose we'd better get in touch with our solicitor. And as far as I'm concerned you can move in any time. After all I'll know where you're living.'

'That would be wonderful. Please do.'

'So when do you think this new book will be ready for me?'

'The sooner I get back down there the sooner I will finish,' I said.

Sally snorted. '*She said temptingly*. Leave it with me and I'll have a word with Henry. He will be pleased, and of course we save estate agents' fees. And Enid will be thrilled. She might even learn some French. She'll be able to invite her friends over to stay in France in a few years. If she's got any left by then of course. I'll be in touch.'

She rang off and I sat looking sightlessly out of the window. Not seeing the sullen grey clouds over London. Not hearing the muffled traffic noises down below in the street. At last, like the sudden release of floodwater from behind a dam, I allowed myself to think of Joe and everything that he represented to me. I imagined the cerulean skies of Devon above picture-book countryside and heard the wind breathing soft summer zephyrs across the garden of Barracane House.

It wouldn't be like that of course. I knew it wouldn't. I'm not completely daft.

*

Two weeks later I was sitting on the floor packing the last of my books and DVDs into plastic boxes. Folding my huge collection of scarves. Sorting out my clothes into piles marked yes, no, chuck. There seemed to be a lot in the last two piles. Perhaps I would have to rethink my wardrobe. I would need thick jumpers, moleskin trousers (not made out of real moles obvs) and fleece-lined coats. Tweed.

The flat looked smaller now. Sort of different and uninteresting. All of our history there had been expunged. I expected Scheherazade would soon sort that out with posters of Harry Styles or Kurt Cobain or whoever was in vogue at the moment. There were a few scuff marks where the sofa was pushed back against the wall and some ghostly squares where pictures had been taken down. Still Scheherazade was planning to have the whole place decorated before she actually moved in so it didn't really matter.

My removal company was going to arrive early the following day and intended to deliver to Barracane House that afternoon. Not that there was much to move now I'd unloaded most of the furniture on to my buyer.

It would also be my fortieth birthday. I'd already received flowers and presents from friends at a farewell dinner where Maudie cried as though she was never going to see me again. Jassy had presented me with a gorgeous cream handbag that would be the last word in impracticality for life in the country and Sally had given me a joke present of a book on chicken husbandry. Why wasn't it called chicken wifery?

I was about to start a new life in a new home in a new county. That had to be exciting and significant. I was suddenly bucked by an interesting thought. If I lived to be eighty it was quite possible I would spend the second half of my life in thorn-proof tweed, waxed jackets and boots. I would change my car for a four by four thing so I could negotiate the mud and see over hedges.

I hadn't read the book on chickens but I'd leafed through the pictures and it looked pretty straightforward. Chickens came in all sorts of shapes and sizes, some more attractive than others. Some even seemed to be wearing feather bobble hats and legwarmers. Once I was settled I would buy some chickens as a birthday present to myself and a cool chicken hutch or shed thing or whatever they were called. Brilliant. I could imagine myself picking warm, new-laid eggs out of their nests and wandering around with an enamel bowl of grain and scraps while the chickens scurried around my feet looking up at me.

The removal men arrived before seven o'clock, smart in matching yellow polo shirts, and they made short work of my belongings. They stored everything down the far end of their van, lassoing it to the walls with thick straps, and then they perched on the wall outside, smoking and drinking tea out of Thermos flasks. Half an hour later we were on the way.

The roads stretched ahead of us, busy with people coming into London while I was heading the other way. As we crossed under the M25 a final horrible chill of doubt shot through me. Was I doing the right thing? Was this a ghastly mistake? Was I just pinning all my hopes on a dream? And where did I stand with Joe? I hadn't seen or heard from him for a long time. What if he'd met someone else in the meantime, or Ellie had managed to persuade him she was the right one for him?

I shook my head. It was far too late now. I put on some very loud music to blast the negative thoughts out of my head; there's nothing quite like Steppenwolf and ZZ Top to get the blood racing.

Devon was playing ball for once. We crossed the county border sign and I gave a little cheer, raising my hands off the steering wheel. In front of us the day was simply glorious with a bright, cloudless sky and a brilliant sun dipping down towards the bulk of Dartmoor. There was a steady stream of caravans and campervans heading west too. Some with surf-boards strapped to the roof.

Most of my doubts allayed, I pressed on down narrower and narrower roads, the yellow bulk of the removal van trundling behind me, its wing mirrors dismissively sweeping the hedges to one side. In my rear-view mirror I could see the three men sitting in the front seats, one reading a paper, the other eating a huge roll and the third hunched over the steering wheel looking very gloomy indeed.

At last we pulled up at Barracane House, and I jangled the front door keys in my hand, excitement mounting. The van driver got down and looked around him with a confused expression.

'Reminds me of the old joke my dad used to tell about the Hullawi tribe.' I looked suitably blank so he filled in the punch line. 'Where the Hullawi. Get it?'

Ah.

Anyway, they took what they called the Treasure Chest into the house: a plastic box containing my kettle, teapot, milk and sugar and four mugs. They waited outside the back door, smoking roll-ups and complaining about their boss while I made the necessary refreshments and opened a packet of Hobnobs, which they fell on with enthusiasm.

Suitably revived they started whipping boxes and bags into the house and within an hour had finished. More tea, more biscuits, a brief consultation of a much-battered and torn book of road maps because their satnav wasn't working properly and they were off. They had another job the following day, this time moving a couple from Cornwall to London. The family were doing just about the exact opposite to me. I wondered why and how they would get on.

I cleared away the tea things and went out into the garden. The evening sky was tinted with exquisite shades of violet and apricot like expensive silk now the sun was setting and above me the vapour trails of two planes neatly crossed, making an optimistic kiss of welcome.

*

I didn't do much after that.

Sally had cleared out her things of course, which meant the beautifully stocked kitchen was now empty with none of her exciting gadgets or labelled Kilner jars in the pantry. I had a few bits of crockery and cutlery including the four mugs, a wooden block with some wicked-looking knives and the set of expensive saucepans I had bought two years ago and hardly used. I arranged these with great ceremony in the cupboards and stood back to admire them. Then I unpacked my food stores and put things into the fridge. It all looked a bit pathetic, not like the kitchen I had remembered. But then Sally had confessed to an unquenchable passion for cook shops even though she didn't use half the things she bought. I'd need to go shopping. Perhaps Exeter?

I messed about for half an hour, plumping up cushions and placing a tartan throw artistically over the back of the big chair by the fire. Then I went upstairs and turned all the lights on, wondering if Joe would see them. Yes, I know – childish.

I don't think I'd ever felt so happy.

Chapter Twenty-Nine

I spent the following morning getting the place looking as welcoming as I could. There was still no sign of Joe. What should I do? I was developing a gnawing hunger to see him again. What was he doing? Where was he? I should tell him I was here.

Then I went out to stock up my cupboards. Running out of milk no longer meant a quick stroll around the corner to buy some more; now it would mean a car trip into Stokeley. The glossy row of Sally's cookery books had also been taken away so along with my trolley full of groceries I bought a couple of recipe books with what looked like straightforward instructions in them. By the checkout were a lot of leaflets about local attractions and activities and one of them was offering chickens for sale, chicken huts and things for 'all your poultry needs'. Marvellous!

Apparently you could even board your hens when you went away on holiday at a place called *The Eggcelsior.* Not wanting to let the grass grow I phoned the number, spoke to an elderly lady and ordered six chickens and a henhouse that I was assured was the finest and securest they had.

'Will they try to escape?'

I received a wheezy chuckle in reply.

'No 'ems quite happy to stay in there, missus; it's them as wants to get in you has to watch fer.'

Ah, yes of course.

'I'll bring 'em over as soon as, or, maybe now I think about it I'll get Amos my old man to pop over.'

What was it with Devon people and their habit of 'popping'?

*

I got home about midday and as I was unpacking the shopping from my boot I heard the sound of hooves coming up the lane behind me and some excited yelping.

'Lulu! Lulu! It's you!'

I turned to see Ivy coming towards me, proudly perched on a pretty grey pony and bouncing up and down in her stirrups with delight. Next to her on a glossy brown horse was Ellie, who didn't look delighted at all. In fact, her expression brought to mind sucked lemons and smacked arses.

'Hi,' she said as they slowed to a halt beside me.

'What are you doing here?' Ivy said, giving her reins to Ellie and sliding down from her pony.

She came running across towards me, her legs spindly in jodhpurs, and hugged me round the waist.

'I'm so glad you're here. I asked Daddy millions of times if you were coming back and he said he didn't know but he didn't think so. He'll be so pleased when I tell him. I've been asking and asking to ride up here but Ellie always said it was too muddy and I'd have to spend ages picking stones out of Smoke's feet. Have you seen Smoke? I'm having a try-out on him to see if we get on.'

I put an arm around her shoulders. It was a nice feeling. She grinned up at me and I smiled. She really was a cute child.

Ellie gave me no such welcome but sat pulling irritably at Ivy's pony when it tried to start eating grass.

'Another holiday?' Ellie said from the lofty heights of her horse.

I felt a tiny moment of triumph. 'No actually. I'm here for good this time. I've bought Barracane House and this is my home now.'

Ivy gasped, her eyes round with excitement. 'Really?'

'How lovely,' Ellie said in a tone that said the complete opposite. 'You'll find it a bit of a change from London. A bit too much for someone like you, if you ask me.'

I wasn't asking her.

'No, I liked it so much I thought I'd stay,' I said. 'I'm happy here.'

Ellie muttered something and jerked at her horse's bridle so it tittuped around like a ballerina, snorting and huffing.

'Come on, Ivy, think of the horses; Smoke will be getting cold and if he's going to stand around eating grass it will be me who has to clean his bit,' Ellie said.

Ivy gave me another hug and darted back to the pony, hitching one foot into a stirrup and hopping around when the pony fidgeted.

'Stand, Smoke, stand,' Ellie growled.

Eventually Ivy was back on board and Ellie dug her heels into her horse and they went back down the lane, Ivy turning around to yell, 'You must come and see my kittens – they're so naughty!'

They disappeared at a brisk trot, Ivy waving all the way.

Well Joe would know I was here now.

*

Two days later and I still hadn't seen him. What was I imagining; that he would turn up to see me within minutes? He had work to do. He wasn't able to mess around like I did, straightening cushions and pretending to write.

That afternoon the chicken woman's old man Amos arrived, jaunty in a Man Utd bobble hat with a huge, silent companion who was introduced as his son Reub. They arrived in a filthy old van with the back doors lashed together with rope. Several lengths of wood and rolls of chicken wire were protruding from the back. I don't know why but I'd expected it to come ready made like a doll's house that would be lowered into my garden with a crane. As usual I hadn't thought it through.

After refusing my help and offers of tea, they set to on the corner of the garden. Hammering and shouting punctuated the rest of the morning as Amos berated Reub for being a 'danged fool'.

'What are you doin' you ... for heaven's sake boy! Call that straight? It's bent as nine roads to Cullompton! Give it 'ere.'

I kept out of the way.

At last there was a brisk rap on the back door, and Amos stood there red in the face, Reub skulking about behind him, putting a toolbox back into the van.

'Well there 'un is, missus,' he said, ''un's all ready. Come and see.'

I followed him round to the garden and there was my henhouse, bigger than I'd imagined with wire netting sides, on the floor and over the top. Amos pointed it out proudly.

'Stops old foxy from digging in, see. And the magpies gettin' in over the top.'

'Where are the chickens?'

Amos turned and shouted. 'Reub! Reub, you useless ... mother, give me strength!'

Reub shuffled up to us, carrying a wire crate containing six white and very bedraggled specimens of chicken-hood. The chickens looked as though they had all been in a particularly vicious brawl. None of them had a full complement of feathers and patches of pink and unpleasantly scaly skin shone through.

'Goodness me,' I said wondering how tactfully I could refuse them.

I had wanted some fat, sleek, picture-book hens. Stout Buff

Orpingtons perhaps or Cuckoo Marans with their bright orange eyes and smart white legs. I had imagined them clucking and preening, following me around the garden, or pecking in the lawn for insects, having dust baths in the flower beds, not cowering unattractively like survivors of some awful punch-up.

Amos must have sensed my reluctance. 'Well 'em may be not what you expected, but they'll soon fatten up and the feathers'll grow back good as new soon enough. It's a kindness you'll be doing as well. Battery rescue hens, them is. Poor things.'

'Yes, of course it would. Poor things,' I said at last, looking bleakly at one of the hens, which returned my gaze, looking equally sad.

'Then I'll leave you to it,' Amos said.

'Um, you couldn't help me get them in, could you?' I said, panicking slightly. 'I've never actually handled a chicken before. I mean, how do you catch them?'

He gave me a withering look. 'Look at them poor critters. They'm not exactly going to take much catching are they? Reub!'

Reub took the cage into the hen enclosure, tutting and grumbling all the way, and then he opened a hatch in the top and scooped out the scruffy hens and deposited them onto the ground where they stood, blinking and clucking for a few minutes.

Amos closed the henhouse door and rubbed his hands down the front of his coat.

'There,' he said, pleased. 'Water in there and grain in the feeder – don't chuck it all over the shop or you'll get rats.'

'What else?' I said, following Amos to his van.

He looked puzzled, his mouth turned down thoughtfully.

'Nothing, far as I know. They'm not pets, you know. They don't expect bedtime stories,' he said, and chuckled at his own wit.

'And when can I let them out? I mean, into the garden?'

'Leave 'em be for a fortnight, then they should be all right,' he said, a little more kindly.

'Thank you. How much do I owe you?'

Amos looked thoughtful and leaned on the side of the van.

'Well now, I don't know. You've paid for us to put up the hen run. What do you think they'm worth?' he asked.

'I've no idea,' I said, desperately trying to remember how much a chicken cost in Waitrose.

'Me neither!' Amos said and he got into the van and drove off without a backwards glance.

The chickens were beginning to cautiously move out from their initial defensive huddle, and then one, bolder than the rest, found the grain feeder.

'Happy birthday to me,' I said.

I watched them for a few minutes but I had the feeling I was putting them off so I left them to it and went to have a proper look around the garden. My garden! I'd wanted a garden and here it was. It was very neglected, that much was obvious, but there were a couple of trees in one corner. From the evidence on the ground they were apple. Maybe I could make pies, if I got to the fruit before the wasps did.

There was a scrubby and weed-riddled lawn stretching around to the back of the house and a massive compost heap overflowing from a wooden enclosure in one corner. Perhaps there had once been a vegetable patch or other stuff? I couldn't think what. But there was a huge bramble hedge full of ripening blackberries. Remembering how expensive such things were in London I felt quite excited. My delusions of myself as a countrywoman bottling fruit and making jam were boosted for a moment until I remembered I didn't have a clue how to do either. But I could find out. It couldn't be rocket science.

I went across to the other side of the lawn, which was thick and spongy with some sort of grassy stuff, almost knee high. Head back I revelled in the warmth of the sun on my face, thrilled at the blueness of the sky, feeling for the first time in years absolutely content. I briefly imagined how horrified Benedict would be at the prospect of rescuing this garden. Or even sitting in it. And then I fell in the pond.

I swear I didn't even know it was there. In fact, it was so well camouflaged with green stuff and plants that I'd missed it entirely. Until I trod confidently over the edge and pitched full length into it.

The weeds and whatever the plants were parted helpfully so I could see the murky depths and for a moment I panicked, lost one of my shoes and floundered around splashing and yelping. The thought flashed across my brain: would this be reported in the local press as suicide?

Well-known author Lulu Darling drowned herself yesterday, the day after her fortieth birthday. Friends said Ms Darling had been acting strangely in recent months and possibly showing signs of depression. Her sister Jasmine was too upset to speak to us, but her agent Sally Gardener commented, 'She still owes me a book. I'm fucking furious.'

I suddenly found a foothold on something solid and tried to stand up, whilst shouting, 'I'm not bloody depressed!'

'I'm glad to hear it,' said a voice behind me. And then he started laughing. 'What on earth are you doing now?'

I turned, wiping weeds from my face.

'Oh hello, Joe,' I said relatively calmly under the circumstances, 'could you give me a hand out of here?'

'You're mad,' he said, still laughing. He stretched out a hand towards me and in a few minutes, with an inelegant slurping noise, the mud at the bottom of the pond released me after claiming my other shoe.

'Quite possibly,' I said, trying to maintain some dignity while squeezing water out of my hair, 'and if not I soon will be. They'll have to take me away to a place of safety.'

Joe pulled out a handkerchief and I wiped my face with it.

'Now then,' I said, 'can I offer you a cup of coffee or tea?'

'No, I think you should get into the shower before you get chilled,' he said, his mouth tightening as he tried to stop laughing.

'I think you're right. Was there anything particular ...?'

'I was on my way to the top field and thought I'd drop in. Ivy told me she'd seen you back again. She's very excited.'

'Is she?' This made me feel very happy. 'She's a lovely little girl.'

He grinned. 'She's great. You must come over and see her again soon.'

'I'd love to.'

'I see you have some hens?' he said.

'They've just arrived. Rescue hens,' I added quickly to explain their appearance.

'Ivy will be thrilled. She's been asking for hens for her next birthday present.'

By now I had squelched my way to the back door and was pulling my wet socks off. My jeans, never exactly loose, were shrinking onto my legs and covered in some sort of slime. My hair was plastered to my head and felt very unpleasant. I had the awful feeling I smelled pretty vile too.

Joe helped me off with my cardigan, which clung to my arms and needed a significant amount of tugging on his part. I held out my hand to take it away from him, thought briefly of hanging it up and then thought better of it and dropped it on the ground. What was the point? It was probably ruined.

'Every time I see you I'm busy making a fool of myself. Food splatters, mud, gorilla slippers, now this. God, what's the *matter* with me?' I said, my shoulders slumping despondently.

Joe stuck his hands in his pockets and looked at me for a second, his expression unreadable.

'Is it true? You've bought this place? Ivy told me you had. I wanted to check she had it right.'

I took a deep breath. Seeing him again I knew I'd made the right decision. I was so filled with happiness I felt I might burst.

'It's true. I've bought Barracane House. I've sold the flat in London and made the move.'

I wondered what he was thinking.

Please don't let me be stupid enough to ask.

He nodded. 'Go and get cleaned up and I'll be seeing you soon. Now I know where you are for a change.'

I waited until I heard his Land Rover rumble off down the lane and then darted upstairs, towards a hot shower. Peeling off sodden clothes is no fun at all, particularly when they are rather whiffy, covered in random bits of weed and green slime and even a couple of things that wriggled. I didn't look too closely but found a bin liner and dumped everything in for the time being. I'd worry about them later. Or maybe not at all. I had other things to think about.

Chapter Thirty

The following day for the first time at Barracane House I received some post. A *welcome to your new home* card from Sally, paperwork from the local council, things to do with electricity and water supplies, documents from my solicitor to sign and a handful of flyers. Included in the bundle was one for a new country store some ten miles away. Fired up with my new involvement with chickens I drove there straight after breakfast. Perhaps I would buy them some special grain that would restore their feathers in double quick time. Or some toys. Were there such things? I mean it wasn't as though they were puppies or hamsters. What would a chicken find amusing?

The country store was filled with huge bags of dog chow, horse things, vicious-looking tools and a great many articles I didn't recognise. It was very exciting. I made my way to the poultry section and browsed with what I hoped was an intelligent expression. There were all sorts of things. Several different sorts of grain and grit, Smart coloured rings for their legs, shining grain scoops, cages, feeders that dispensed grain when the chicken stood on a pressure pad, even some nail clippers. Was I expected to clip their nails? Hmm, I'd have to work up to that. The only sort of chicken entertainment was a peck block made of compressed grains and seeds that hung up on a rope like a giant Weetabix. Guaranteed to beat boredom. Did chickens get bored? I suppose it was possible.

I spent more on the chicken accoutrements than I usually did in Waitrose and lugged my trolley back towards the car, which was so monumentally unsuited to the job that I vowed my next task would be to swap it for a Land Rover.

I pushed the trolley back and noticed another stand full of leaflets. I saw with great excitement that there was a village fete coming up. And there were competitions! Fruit, vegetables, miniature gardens, bric-a-brac, and cakes! Best Victoria sponge!

I read through the details with mounting determination. Plain sponge cake, eight-inch diameter sandwiched together with buttercream and jam. First prize a five-pound voucher to spend in Beth's Bakery, courtesy of Mrs B Ford. I didn't know anything about miniature gardens or how to grow four carrots identical or otherwise, but I could do this! I would take part and cement my place in the local community as a skilled baker.

Having given the chickens their new amusement and scooped out their grit with a sparkling new metal scoop, I read a bit more of the hen book.

All the chickens in the book were really fat and feathery and glamorous, while mine were still plodding about looking a bit battered. Still the book assured me they would pick up in a few weeks. I got to the bit about putting Vaseline on their combs in the winter to avoid frostbite and then I gave up.

My phone rang.

'I've been meaning to come and see you,' Isobel said, her voice strong and jolly down the phone. 'The girls were asking if you would come and talk to us about writing again. There's something Connie was going on about: reading like a writer. Or was it writing like a reader? Anyway, what do you say?'

'Of course I would.'

'Lovely! So what have you been doing? How are the hens? I heard from Amos that you'd got some.'

Ah, the country drums had been beating.

'Yes they're rescue hens. They've just arrived.'

'Excellent! That's a great thing to do. How are they?'

'Looking a bit bedraggled, no eggs yet.'

'Oh give them time, you'd be looking a bit bedraggled if you'd spent the last year in a cage no bigger than you are. Utter bastards. I mean the battery farmers not the hens! And Ivy tells me you've bought Barracane! How marvellous!'

'I'm going to make a cake for the village fete,' I said when she paused to draw breath and I could get a word in edgeways.

'The village fete? Cake? You've got no chance. Betty at the Cat and Convict always wins. Come along on Thursday next week. I'll tell the girls, they'll be so pleased.'

'Isobel, while I have you on the line, I wondered if you and Will would like to come over for a drink?' I screwed my face up and crossed my fingers. Which meant I almost dropped the phone. 'The weather's been so glorious, it's a shame to waste it.'

'Hang on ...' There was a moment's silence while Isobel presumably checked her diary. She was back a few seconds later. 'What day is it today? Friday? Tonight?'

'Wonderful.'

'I'll have to bring Ivy – is that okay? I know she's been badgering Joe to go and see you. It's curry night at the Cat so I usually have her. Would you mind?'

I breathed a sigh of relief. 'Absolutely not! I don't mean *don't* bring her. I mean do bring her. I really wouldn't mind if you brought her.'

Isobel chuckled. 'I get the picture. Look we'll come over about five. Or is that too early? I was planning a picnic sort of tea in the garden anyway.'

'Great! That would be great! I love picnics.'

She rang off and I went to sort out the picnic table and chairs I had bought the other day but hadn't actually taken out of the cardboard.

Three broken nails and a squashed finger later I was ready.

Picnic.

I could do this. I really did love picnics. Something Benedict and I had always disagreed on unless it was out of the back of a friend's Range Rover at Glyndebourne. That particular evening was an event that bore no relation to what I thought of as a picnic. Crystal flutes, Pol Roger champagne, smoked salmon blinis and some revoltingly sweet cupcakes. Not a sausage roll, Hula Hoop or gala pie in sight. That life was behind me now. This was where I started again, where I got things right.

I put out some sandwiches and crisps and hulled a punnet of strawberries. I had been thinking of turning them into jam but had lost my nerve at the last minute.

What should I wear this evening?

I didn't seem to have any jeans that fitted without having to undo the button if I sat down. I hadn't yet got round to buying any moleskin trousers; thinking about it I hadn't actually seen any for sale and let's be honest they did sound rather hot. Perhaps I'd imagined them? I had some smart navy chinos and a couple of new sweaters that were okay. I dried my hair, made a bit of an effort with my make-up and went downstairs.

I sat in the window seat, watching the lane. I thought about Joe hungrily and wondered when I would next see him. When I did, would he be polite, passionate, matter-of-fact? Would we talk for a few minutes over a glass of wine and then pounce on each other? After all there had been a fair amount of pouncing in the past. I thought about Joe's broad chest, how I had smoothed my hands over him, and I shivered.

By the time I heard the car coming up the lane I was quite dithery.

I went into the kitchen so it didn't look as though I was lurking and when I heard the doorbell ring I counted to three before going to answer it.

'Lulu! These are for you!'

It was Ivy, standing on my doormat with a bunch of flowers wrapped in brown paper that she thrust towards me.

'Well thank you,' I said, recovering myself quite well.

'Welcome to Barracane House. These are from our garden. Daddy said you'd like them. I told him you were back and he said we should give you a present.'

She followed me into the kitchen where I found an empty jug, filled it with water and stuck the flowers in, pretending to arrange them.

'Where is Grandma?' I asked as casually as I could.

'She's getting the picnic from the car with Grandad,' Ivy said. 'Daddy's putting some deckchairs out in the garden. He says you've got chickens. Can we go and see them?'

Daddy?

Ivy took my hand and pulled me outside. I rather liked the feel of her hand in mine, tugging me towards the henhouse. She stood entranced looking at my motley crew who were huddled in a corner, gently crooning.

'They're beautiful,' she sighed. 'I love chickens. I'd like some of my own. I like watching them. Don't you think they're gorgeous?'

'Gorgeous,' I agreed and I didn't mean the chickens. I'd just caught sight of Joe and my heart was doing little excited jumps.

Joe was on what passed for my lawn, spreading a tartan rug over the bouncy grass and unfolding two blue striped deckchairs. Next to him was an impressive-looking wicker hamper fastened with leather straps. He looked up and grinned as we walked towards him, still hand in hand.

Isobel and Will came round the side of the house carrying a large red cool box between them and bickering about whether it was shady enough for Ivy and had she remembered to put on insect repellent.

'You said you liked a picnic,' Joe said, 'so I thought this was as good a chance as any.'

'I thought ... curry night?' I said.

He grinned at me, unfastened the cool box and pulled out a bottle.

'This is much more fun. Hope you like champagne?'

'Yes, I do. A lot!' I said.

'That's good. Your grass needs mowing, I could come over and do it if you like? I don't want you falling in again.'

His eyes locked with mine for a moment and I felt a wonderful surge of happiness shoot through me. This then turned into an unexpected surge of desire. This was very inappropriate considering I was still holding his daughter's hand and his mother was next to me unfolding her picnic table and worrying about wasps.

'Sit down,' Ivy said. 'We have sandwiches and cake too. I helped Grandma. They're not very tidy but they taste okay. Tomato, which are my favourite, and egg mayonnaise, which are my second favourite.'

'Marvellous,' I said. 'I'll make sure I remember that.'

'And I like strawberry cheesecake. Can you make that?'

'I never have but I could try,' I said.

'Can I help when you do?' Ivy said taking a bite of her sandwich.

'Of course.' I seemed to have a massive and untameable grin on my face that nothing was going to wipe off any time soon.

Joe held out a hand to me and I took it. He pulled me to sit down next to him on my new chairs while Isobel and Will parked themselves in the deckchairs. He uncorked the champagne and the cork shot off into the long grass accompanied by a squeal of excitement from Ivy. He handed me a glass.

'How long are you here for this time?' he said.

'I'm here forever,' I replied.

He smiled at me. 'Forever?'

'Forever.'

'Then welcome to Devon, Louisa, Ivy will be so pleased.' He stopped and gave a funny little smile that made my heart turn over. Then he leaned towards me and kissed my cheek very gently. 'And so am I. I hope you'll be very happy here.'

We chinked glasses.

'I will,' I said, and it somehow seemed prophetic.

Acknowledgements

This is my fourth book and its production has been made possible with the help of many people who have my thanks and gratitude.

To all the incredibly enthusiastic team at Avon Books UK especially Katie Loughnane, and editors Louise Buckley and Helena Newton. Also Becky Glibbery for my lovely book cover.

To my Twitter friends the LL's who are always there with reassurance and humour.

Jane Ayres
Christina Banach
Susanna Bavin
Catherine Boardman
Kaz Coles
Kirsten Hesketh
Chris Manby
Vanessa Thornton-Rigg

To my Facebook friends in the Savvy Authors Snug, a marvellous group started by Tracy Buchanan. Thank you for your ideas, support and enthusiasm.

Thank you to all the readers, reviewers and bloggers who have been so generous with their time.

And finally to Arthur, Henry and Mabel. You're the best and I love you.

If you enjoyed *The Mini-Break*, why not try another breezy, feel-good read and take to the high seas with Maddie Please...

Available now in ebook and paperback!

Even when you think you've lost everything, hope and romance can be just around the corner ...

Available now in ebook and paperback!

It's time for Billie Summers to have an adventure, but it might not be exactly what she expected...

Available now in ebook and paperback!